"The mystery continues, in plain sight."
Ross Coulthart

Other books by this author

Genesis Makers
Evolution
Evolution 2
Emissary
Emissary 2 The Sixth Extinction
Intercepting Aragon

NON HUMAN

by

Scott K Bywater

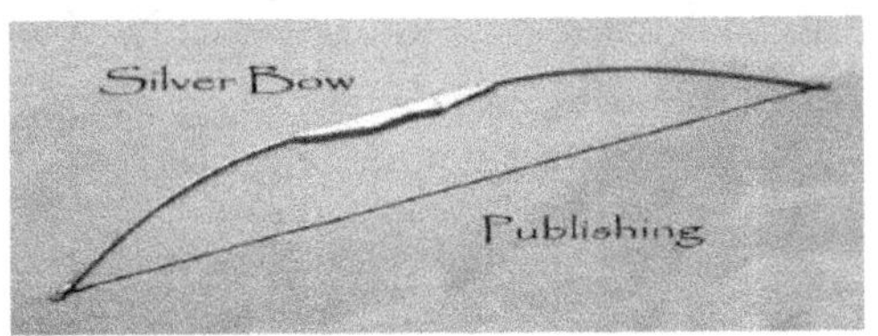

720 Sixth Street, Unit # 5
New Westminster, BC V3L 3C5
CANADA

Title: Non human
Author: Scott K. Bywater
Cover Art: by Joshua Nicholas Bywater
Layout and Design: Candice James
Editing: Candice James

ISBN 9781774033647(softcover)
ISBN 9781774033654(e-book)
© 20251 Silver Bow Publishing

Library and Archives Canada Cataloguing in Publication Title: Non human / by Scott K Bywater. Names: Bywater, Scott K., 1962- author. Identifiers: Canadiana (print) 20250220296 | Canadiana (ebook) 20250220369 | ISBN 9781774033647 (softcover) | ISBN 9781774033654 (Kindle) Subjects: LCGFT: Science fiction. Classification: LCC PR9619.4.B99 N66 2025 | DDC 823/.92—dc23

To Mary, Josh and Alysha –
thank you for helping me through a trying period of life.

To Ian from BHS –
more of a friend than a carer.

And to Ross Coulthart –
who taught me that UFOs and non-humans are real.
They buzz Earth in their craft, like bees to a daffodil.

Contents

1.Taken / 9
2. Pianif / 32
3. Non-human Tech / 57
4. Earth / 95
5. Krissy / 107
6. Intel / 137
7. Response / 157
8. Future / 173
9. Agents / 178
10. Outcome / 186
11, More Agents / 189
12. Disclosure / 196
13. Exposed / 203
14. Non-human / 207

Author Profile / 210

1

Taken

"If you wish to make an apple pie from scratch, you must first invent the universe." — Carl Sagan

Jack walked slowly down the wooden steps, and trudged noisily onto the gravel driveway and stopped, gazing at his mum's teary eyes and drawn face. Krissy presented Jack with a perfect *how dare you leave me alone*, face. She hadn't given her blessing to the trip, but dad clearly needed it, he simply *had* to go. It was only two days, anyway.

'Goodbye mum,' Jack whispered a bit tentatively. 'Everything will be fine. You'll see.' Her face twisted, and she bit her lips to control the sobs. She hated the idea of being left alone in the house.

'B-Bye love' Krissy said dismally, knowing she was powerless to stop them. 'Your dad has just recovered, so, remember that. He hasn't got your energy, or much at all really.' She held a tissue to her nose. Her stomach was gurgling, and her brain spinning, to the point where she struggled to walk and talk. Or even stand up. Krissy had given up trying to change their minds. They were fixated on going.

'*Oh Christ*,' she moaned hauntingly, on the verge of panic. With no-one to talk to, she would have plenty to worry about. It would only be two days, but it would feel a *lot* longer. She gulped hard, and knew it'd feel like a *fucking* century. Being apart from her husband and son was finely tuned torture. And Jacky should recognise it as such. He should know better.

'Mum,' Jack said pensively, 'dad'll be fine. He needs this trip. He deserves it. Dad's in remission. And you know he loves the outback and old mines, *especially Yuma*.' Jack smiled nervously at his glowering mother. She was deeply worried about her husband, and reckoned separation, especially now, was wrong. Krissy had been his primary carer for several years, and only now, with him in remission, could things hopefully get back close to normal.

And *now*, they both decide to go on a freaking holiday. She knew *why*, but still, couldn't avoid the feeling her husband and son were being selfish. *He needs me*, she whined to herself. She trusted Jacky, but his father and her husband, was a different kettle of fish entirely. She knew him to be impatient and unpredictable, not character-traits that were a good fit for going on a trip without her. Especially, now, when he was so delicate.

'He wants this, mum.' Jack said nervously, smiling and biting his lips. On the inside, Jack had reservations too, but his dad really needed the outing. He deserved it. And he was finally well enough to enjoy it.

Jack walked back on the gravel of the driveway, and then he embraced his mum. By squeezing her, Jack forced out a heartrending sob, which made his mum lose all control. Krissy started crying in earnest. She wanted them to stay, and no amount of soothing words or justification, would change that. They were just whispers in a windstorm to Krissy. She looked at her husband, with her eyes full of tears. Krissy had been to hell and back with him. And now he up and leaves.

She'd done everything for him. Cooked, cleaned, washed, repaired, prepared meds, transferred, driven and toileted. Her work, it seemed, never, ever ended. Krissy had no time for herself at all or their relationship. Whomever came up with the "For better or worse" line, had a lot to answer for. Actually, Krissy did it out of love and devotion. And then they received the incredibly unexpected news of John's remission from late-stage cancer. The entire family was floored.

Without this turn of health events, John would've been dead in weeks. But, instead, the cancer was stopped in its tracks. The entire Stevens bloodline was jubilant. Then, Jack and his dad decided to go on a trip to Yuma. Krissy was gobsmacked.

'*Oh Jesus Jacky…*be careful with him,' she sobbed. 'He's all I've got. *I know,* he wants to go. But he's just got better.' His mum looked at him with bulging, tear-filled eyes. She was desperate and beside herself with grief. She was scared and terrified of something going catastrophically wrong. Krissy had talked herself into an apocalypse occurring if they left. She wanted to be with him, to make sure he was looked after properly.

Jack, on the other hand knew his dad needed space. He needed to get the hell out of his own house. It had become a prison in recent months. The poor guy felt incarcerated, and Jack could see it in his dull eyes, paleness and lack of energy.

When his dad spoke about returning to the Arizona hills, his eyes lit up, and his face broke into a huge smile. Jack couldn't deny him – but he knew it was going to be hard on his mum. She lived for her family, and to be separated was razor-blade agony.

Krissy trusted her son implicitly, but there was no care like a wife's, she thought. They'd been married for 44 years, and had never, *ever,* been away from each other. So, it was really hard to cut the cord after he'd just gone into remission from a potentially fatal disease. John was as weak as a kitten. In no condition to be going anywhere. She shook her head, and squeezed her eyes shut, to block out the nightmare that was unfolding around her. He wasn't ready to go anywhere, without his wife to look after him.

Krissy opened her eyes fully, and stood to her full height, because she'd promised Jacky, she'd be brave. *Put her big-girl pants on*, she'd told herself. But now, with them about to leave, she wasn't sure she could do it. Krissy looked lovingly at both of them, and her chin started to wobble. It was so hard to see them go. Her bowels felt loose, and she felt sick. John might be in remission, but to her, he looked to be at death's door.

Krissy placed a thumb on the front of the windshield in front of her husband, who sat quietly nervous in the front seat of the car. He returned the thumb, placing his, firmly on hers, and smiled weakly. He was as upset as she was, but he knew he had to stand on his own two feet. His doctor had just delivered the miraculous news. He was in remission – *not cured*, but the next best thing.

Now, he had to prove it to himself. Going on a short holiday with his son, was a great start. This would be the beginning of the rest of his life, he thought with a new confidence.

John was full of beans to be sitting in the car with his son and thrilled with the mere thought of Yuma beckoning. He hadn't been there for years, and didn't, in a *blue-Moon,* think he'd ever return. Now that he was in remission, he intended to live as normal a life as he could. Krissy would prefer he stayed home, but this was too much of an opportunity. In any event, it was only a paltry *two* days. Hardly even a trip, certainly not a holiday.

Jacky had *invited* his dad, but to leave Krissy was painful...harrowing really for John. She couldn't come, because she wasn't the type for dust, sweat and hard labour. She thought about it long and hard but finally had to admit she'd be a third wheel, and so she declined. Staying home would be horrendous, but going to Yuma would be worse.

It didn't seem right. But John knew, he had to prove it to himself, and the world, that he could actually do it. Remission from Stage Four was extremely rare and spectacular, but independence and freedom, were rarer still. Now that he was in remission, he wanted everything back.

***

They took their time driving, because there was a lot of scenery to take in, and it was truly gorgeous. The outback of Arizona was just stunning. Mesquite, sagebrush, dry riverbeds, yellow dust and sparsely vegetated desert hills were everywhere they looked. They spent the best part of an hour exploring the general area in their car. They both loved the outback.

Jack watched his dad inhale the landscape, as if he'd never seen it before. John was mesmerised, looking beyond the window, almost purring at the scenery. He thought he'd never witness it in person again. Jack grinned hugely. His dad hadn't smiled and meant it, for months. They continued down an old road to the west of the mine, to a location where the mine buildings began.

They followed the old road north of the mine, to the east. The dirt road they were on, connected up with an east-west running road that led to Picture Rocks Wash. Then they headed west and finally, came to the mine area. Jack saw the old broken headframe and the dumps, where they'd do most of their collecting. His dad had that excited gleam in his eye – "let me at it." Although, he'd been there before, this time was different. It meant more.

Both of them attacked the mine dumps and the upper levels of the accessible shafts. John was ecstatic just to be here, among the rocks and dust.

***

Jack had done hours of hitting and breaking, with the rockhammer and sledge, and had aching shoulders that penetrated all the way down his right arm. Jack was exhausted. He felt done for the day. He gazed at his dad, who was having the time of his life, lost in a cloud of orange Yuma dust.

Hours of sweating, and sunburn, thumping rocks and being swathed in dust, was enough. They looked at each other and silently agreed they'd both had their fill for the day. Their backpacks were heavy with specimens; they'd pried from the molybdenum rich rocks of Yuma.

John Stevens was his name, and Jack, was his son. It was a super June day, hot as hell, and no clouds, but now it was closing on dusk, and getting a bit brisk. John could feel the late-afternoon crispness in the air as he swung his hammer for the last time, with Jacky in the corner of his eye.

'That's it, Jacky,' he said wearily, after whacking a rock and looking closely at the broken pieces. He was searching for crystals of deep red wulfenite, something the mine was famous for producing. John was obsessed by anything mineralogical, *especially* wulfenite. Jack was ho- hum about it. He came on his dad's ventures solely for his love of the outback, and his love for his dad. In this case, it was to celebrate his dad's stunning reprieve from an early death.

The trip to Yuma was a testament to his father. His dad had been through a lot of pain, and deep uncertainty about his very mortality. He didn't even know if his life was going to persist. He fought a very determined disease that Mankind had no real answer to.

Jack felt waves of horror - his dad had endured a true hell. Now that he was in remission, he could take a breath and finally think longer-term. Jack was floored by the self-control it had taken. If it was him, he reckoned, he'd be a hysterical mess, just worrying about himself, with no regard to others.

The vagueness around simply living, would have been too much for him. Every time he had a chemo session, Jack would wonder if this was his last. Even the oncologist had no idea if his dad would live the week out..

It was a toss of the coin as to whether his dad lived or died. Sometimes, Jack felt like grabbing the doc by the throat and squeezing him until he said something definitive. Asking questions was just wasted oxygen. Eventually, after pitched battles, he gave Jack's dad six months to live – as long as he continued scheduled chemo sessions. Which was slowing it down, apparently. *Great.* Thanks a lot. Would it hurt to throw in a bit of positivity. This guy was doing his dad's mind-set, no good at all. Yes, he had a serious disease, and it was advanced, but please stop the perennial gloom and doom. Throw in the occasional joke or one-liner...anything light-hearted. These oncologists were a breed of their own, Jack reckoned. Death was a close relative.

Jack was pissed off with the nature of life generally, and realised his anger shouldn't be directed toward the doc. It wasn't his fault that chemo was the best Mankind could offer.

But despite his illness, his dad continued to put family first, and himself, last. He maintained all his relationships and always had time for his mum and his son. John was a better man than he was, Jack reckoned. He loved his dad dearly, and was so proud of him, to do all that, and be loving, even though he was dying.

John and Krissy had been married forever. They still pawed over each other. When many of his friends were moving out of the family home, Jack resisted it, despite his age. He loved his mum and dad dearly, and didn't want to be separated.

***

Jack was dirty, hot and exhausted, and didn't need to be told twice. He collected the crowbar, and the heavy rope and strapped on his dusty backpack. The car was about five hundred metres away. They were staying at the Best Western in Tucson, which was very basic, but clean. Jack looked forward to a long hot shower, to wash the orange Yuma dust away.

Jack gawked at his dad and saw that he was in the same boat. His dad's blue overalls were orange with dust. Jack did a double take at his dad, because the first look was strange. His dad was standing rigid, pointing his head up, and staring at the sky, as though his neck was fused in that position.

'Dad...w-what are you doing? Jack asked cynically, thinking he was playing some sort of game. There was no response, like his dad couldn't hear him. John's eyes were wide and focussed upward, seemingly gripped by something above. His dad didn't move a muscle – he looked frozen in place, like a popsicle or a storefront mannequin.

Jack turned fully and looked straight up, to see what his dad was gawking at. He was instantly blinded by bright white lights that shot above his head. The bright thing was zigging and zagging all over the sky. Jack was dazzled and knew what it was straight away. It definitely wasn't anything humans put up there. He could tell by the crazy way it moved. It was nothing like a plane or a helicopter, and no drone could move like that.

The object also had no aerodynamic surfaces at all, yet it sailed through the air like a helium balloon. It made sharp turns, seemingly untroubled by either gravity or inertia. It was now descending directly toward his dad. No doubt, the thing was a craft, perfectly saucer-shaped, and oddly, it made no noise at all.

And by the direction of its movement, it had a fondness for his father. The damn thing started high in the air but was now heading straight for his dad like an arrow.

All Jack could see was his mum's image front and centre, and his promise, that he'd look after dad, no matter what. His blood started thumping through his body...*what to do?*' He started panicking. His mum would kill him if anything happened to his dad. But it was out of his hands. An intense feeling of foreboding and hopelessness hit him like a Mack truck. He knew he and his dad were totally at the whim of this anomalous thing in the air.

Jack's legs were weak with panic. He looked down the mine dump and saw his dad staring vacantly at the thing above him, frozen in place. John was baring his teeth and had a corded neck, he seemed like he was trying to move, but couldn't.

'Dad...*run! Dad move, for fuck's sakes.*' Jack screamed at the top of his voice from higher on the mine dump.

Jack tried to resist panic, but his dad just stood there, seemingly waiting for his penance to be meted out. The image of his mum came at Jack again like a rifle shot, and he tried to stifle the sob he felt clawing up his throat. He knew she would be furious. This was *her* husband. *Just* in remission. But it was all out of his control. There wasn't a damned thing he could do about it. Jack also knew what reaction he'd get to that. It was the risk of going on a trip at all – Murphy's stupid law. Krissy was huge on Murphy, and she'd warned him about it, *over and over and over,* before going. It was the risk of stepping foot outside the house.

Jack had laughed at the concept. Why would anything go wrong? Again, her distraught image flashed in front of his eyes, like an angry news flash. He could hear her fuming voice, warning him *not to go,* with a pointing finger in his face.

Her warning was echoing in the air around him. Her voice was full of threat and emotion. She had been cautioning them, and Jack just brushed her off, like an annoying ant at a picnic.

'Bit late now, mum,' Jack said morbidly. 'S-Sorry.' He sobbed regretfully, trailing off to a hellish silence. Jack knew there wasn't a damn thing he could do to help his dad in this situation. All he could do was hope his dad found the power to move. To get away.

The craft was about 20 feet above his dad's head. The craft was just hovering there, silently, reflecting the burning Sun like a mirror. On the ground, his dad was frozen underneath it, all he could move were his arms, which were pointing at it. Jack watched him. 'Yeah dad, we can see the damn thing.'

On top of the mine dump, Jack watched on in horror. His own legs were strangely heavy, seemingly buried in the ground. In a moment of sudden panic, he realised he could only move a few inches at a time, by pushing against a potent force, that wanted him to stay stock still.

This thing in the air above his dad was amazing. It looked like it was polished, and made from stainless steel, having not a single mark on it. It was a classic saucer shape and had a long black antenna on its underside, that was mirrored on its topside. It just floated there, silently, with no aero-dynamic surfaces, no tail, and no noisy engines. Jack was floored, and realised in a rush, that this thing was floating there, *using anti-gravity*.

Jack inched closer, through sheer will, *pushing*, against the atmosphere, that had seemingly congealed around him. At slightly above his eye-level was the craft, and below him on the lower dump was his dad, who was held in place by the same invisible but potent force, that effectively, froze Jack.

'*Run dad, get out of there.*' Jack screamed, close to fall-down panic. He pointed with his hand and flourished hard toward the car. To his horror, his dad seemed to totally ignore him or maybe couldn't hear him. His eyes were fixed upwards. Incredibly, he was still looking at it.

Jack gave up trying to do anything because his own moving was so ridiculously difficult. If it was the same for his dad, he had no hope. The air around him looked normal, but something invisible was at play, trying to hold him still. The object seemed to change in shape. Currently, it was silver and triangular, with powerful lights on its underside, at each point of the triangle. Centre, top left and right, and bottom left and right. And they seemingly all focussed on his dad.

This thing was anything but stealthy, in fact, it was lit up like a *fucking* Christmas tree. Surely, others could see it or had seen it. Then, Jack remembered how isolated they were out here. No-one was within cooee. That was part of the appeal, but now, it worked fiercely against them. Jack was horrified because it was just them, for miles of sandy, rocky desert.

The craft they could see was huge, a disc, the size of a football field. Pulsing, almost breathing...going in and out of focus when Jack looked at it. When it went out of focus, it became fuzzy and then, soon after, came into crisp focus.

Video...he needed video ... or no one would believe him. He imagined the skeptical reaction from his mates. *Back-pocket,* he knew. Jack realised he brought his phone with him, but moving anything was now next to impossible.

Jack slowly inched his arms toward the back pocket of his Jeans. Puffing heavily, he eventually got great close-up video and shots of it. It was still hovering above his dad, about 10 metres off the ground. And maybe 20 metres from Jack. His dad was still not responding, and didn't seem to have moved, since it descended toward him. He was clearly trying to move, but couldn't, effort-lines showed on his forehead. Jack was bewildered and tried again, hollering, and trying to keep panic out of his voice.

'*Dad...can you hear me? You need to try to move.*' No response at all, and certainly, no movement. Jack doubted his dad could hear him. The poor sod was stuck, trance-like beneath the UAP, and was allowed almost no movement. He was enmeshed in something he couldn't fight through, that was also soundproof, apparently.

Jack was overwhelmed by yet another image of his mum. She was sitting on the couch and crying violently. How did he extricate his dad from this insane situation? His mum would expect him to help, and he wanted to, but his dad was totally the victim of something beyond his control. He had zero options. Jack grudgingly conceded that it was beyond his power, to help his dad.

Jack was burning hot, frustrated and mortified - he knew the awful things that had happened to local cattle. For them, it was an event worse than death. Removal of their organs, probably while they were still alive. The worst fate imaginable. Jack was having chest and abdominal pains thinking about it. Even though he struggled to move he kept trying and could feel the sweat running down the small of his back toward the ground. Jack was terrified for his dad, and wondered *why* this was happening to them?

He watched in disbelief, as the UAP suddenly dispatched a thick purple beam toward the ground, which totally concealed his dad. For all intents and purposes, he was now alone in the Arizona desert. Just him and the disc. What horrors were inside the vehicle, hadn't dawned on him yet?

Everything about his dad, when he did see him, was an unearthly violet colour - clothes and skin. Everything about him shone with a brilliant purple gloss. The beam came from the middle of the base of the craft. It now fully covered his dad, to the point of invisibility.

Jack slowly inched a shaky hand to his forehead, and was ready to scream for help, which he knew out here would be useless. So, he held onto it. He knew they were isolated and alone in the desert. There were a few feral rabbits, lizards and snakes, but that was it.

Jack felt like a two-legged stool as he stood in one spot and did nothing. Running and saving his dad was front of mind, but impossible. He could barely move. Below the waist, he was virtually frozen in place. His legs were heavy, like he wore thick concrete boots. He tried to lift his leg with his arm, but to no avail. Jack was stuck, lock, stock and barrel.

John was totally invisible inside the purple beam, probably still as rigid as a rock. Jack himself was petrified with the direction this was going in. He'd seen enough Youtube videos about radioactive craft and malevolent aliens, to literally scare his hair white. And now incredibly, they were *here*.

The light abruptly changed. The craft started issuing a beam of lime green light, which rapidly overtook the purple light, and illuminated his dad, who incredibly started moving upward in it. He was like a salmon, swimming against the current. Jack saw his dad's head pushed back as though he were in a strong wind. This green light somehow had potent attractive qualities, as he watched as the distance between his dad and the craft decrease.

Jack's eyes swelled to the size of billiard balls, and his heart started pounding even faster, as his dad was spirited further upward. Jack watched him pushed, or pulled, higher, and higher realising his destiny was *in* that craft. He was being *taken*. What in God's name would he say to his mum? Jack nearly fainted from abject horror. *Fuck me,* what to do? He was ready to explode. Jack had to help him, but he himself, was stuck fast like an insect on adhesive tape. Jack started trembling and shaking all over and having hot flushes that left him sweating and weak.

Jack was left with *nothing*, no movement and no idea. He started crying like a baby, knowing it didn't help him, but also knowing he had zero control over what was happening out there. He would swap places with his dad in a finger-snap, but he couldn't do that either. Tears of futility ran down his cheeks like rivers. The despair and helplessness were killing him. He was close to his dad but couldn't do a thing to help him. His dad was on his own.

The light from the craft hit Jack too, and he was even more immobile, having no control over his body at all. The green light was pulling and grabbing at him, with the qualities of viscosity, like stiff honey. The green light was like nothing on Earth. It was less like light, and more like a police hook grabbing at him.

Jack watched on in horror as his dad was taken further upward toward the craft, by the light. He could hear himself scream, even though he made no conscious decision to do so, as he watched his dad reach the craft, which was now spinning above him.

Jack focussed on his father, as he was spirited into the craft proper. What on Earth was his dad confronting? Jack's eyes bulged and his mouth fell open. The incredible and the *unimaginable,* he supposed. Jack looked upward as all his arm and leg hair stood to attention. He reckoned he was staring at the same fate as his dad.

Jack was floored, and felt like crying again, and swatting at the air. It was crazy. *It's bonkers,* he screamed to himself petulantly, as he stared at its anomalous dimensions. He was mentally numb, and could think of nothing. The best he could do, was hope that whoever flew this Godforsaken machine was friendly and a pacifist. What a forlorn hope that was, Jack thought morbidly.

Jack felt like he was enveloped in ten layers of tight, clear wrap and had his legs entombed deeply in the Earth. The mine dump and the rocks were now some distance below him, and he felt upward movement in the thick, greasy light. Although he was essentially paralysed, his heart was thumping in his mouth, as he looked around and then closed his eyes and let it be. He was soon unconscious.

Both were asleep, and now inside the craft. What had started as a joyous trip to the countryside, had taken a dark turn indeed. Jack and his dad were in the wrong place at the wrong time. Now, castaways from the planet.

***

Jack and John were both on stretchers, complete with soft white pillows and clean, white linen. Jack was now awake, and aware of his terrifyingly bright surroundings. Light around them was pure white and blinding, so *bright*, everything around them was hidden or fuzzy.

Jack knew where he was but found it hard to believe. It carried a whimsical, fairy-like, and panic-inducing feeling. Jack's eyes were like saucers. He timidly took in the horrific non-human surroundings, that he could see through the blinding light. They'd gone from very Earthly business to *this*. Again, the feeling was impossibility, grading to almost being comical. Jack was too scared to look, expecting the worst. His dad's eyes were tightly closed, and he clearly wasn't opening them for anyone or anything. His eyes were screwed shut to keep everything out.

The room they were in appeared to be a perfect circle, with twelve sleek, moulded chairs near the outside, around them in a perfect circle. Near each rectangular window was one of the chairs. In the centre of the craft were three normal-looking seats in front of a small black device that looked like an AM/FM radio.

Jack smelt the vague aroma of something unidentifiable, maybe cloves or nutmeg wafting on the air, that was easily breathed. Immediately behind the black device, were four odd looking tan cubes, looking like those in a kid's play pen. They knew they were on a non-human spacecraft, *a fucking* flying saucer, so *anything* was possible, they both assumed. Human norms were out the window.

Near them, were two humanoids - hideous beings, clearly reptilian in nature. They were tall, thin and muscular, maybe seven feet tall, like ugly, towering basketball players. But playing for no team they'd ever seen. Both had green, gnarly skin and long, deeply split tongues that seemed to be continually protruding. Their eyes blinked sideways and were large and black, with small orange pupils. These reptilian creatures had three fingers and a rather pendulous thumb. They had no hair anywhere, and long, deep heads. All in all, they looked monstrous and something you wouldn't want to meet at any time of day. Even though they were oxygen breathers, they were very different from humans.

John gawked at one of the creatures and felt the queasy. Then his neck started to swell uncomfortably, and quivered. It was an unfortunate reaction to fear, that hailed from his childhood. John looked around in wide-eyed horror, and felt the iciness hit him like a sledge-hammer. His brain screamed at him. *They shouldn't be here.*

This was John's first major outing, post-recovery. Jack hoped to *fuck* this didn't lead to a relapse. All of them, Krissy included, had been warned that when it came to John, to treat stress like a poison. It was supposed to be a blissful mineral collecting trip into the spectacular desert. Instead, it was a terrifying, panic-inducing catastrophe.

There was no obvious tail on the creatures that surrounded them, but their similarity to an evolved, bipedal dinosaur was undeniable. The lead being was passing a small object over his father, a scanner of some sort, presumably. The upright lizard nearest him seemed to be about to do the same thing to Jack. It held a small, black object in its paw, and it prepared to do the same.

Jack widened his stare and noticed how big the craft was. It seemed bigger on the inside than the outside, but he wasn't completely sure. Maybe it's like the Tardis, he thought jokingly. More likely, he was suffering from stress and anxiety, and things just weren't what they seemed.

The lizard nearest him seemed to be smiling. Jack was horrified by how forced and uneven it looked. It was like the crooked smile of an evil character in a movie. It strode toward him and Jack moved back until he was hard up against his dad's gurney.

John was just opening his eyes, and looking up with an effort. What he saw, made him scream bloody murder. He ripped his wide eyes to Jack, and yelled, '*No, no, no!*' Then John squashed his own face into the softness of the pillow and kept muttering profanity and refused to lift it, despite Jack's attempts. Whatever was around him, he found too disgusting to look at.

****

Amazingly and suddenly, Jack could hear words, English words, and by the stunned reaction of his father, who was sitting up now, he could hear them too. His dad was as all wide eyed and raised eyebrows, staring at his son, wondering what in God's name was happening. Jack looked around feverishly, and saw the pilot, perched behind his seat, gaping at them fixedly, and seeming to concentrate. *It must be him*, Jack decided. There were words between his ears, language forming direct in his brain. And what's more, he could understand it. It was *his* language...*English*.

They were injecting words and phrases directly into both of them. And, *incredibly*, it told him. 'My name is Pietr, and we mean you no harm, do not worry.'

Fuck me, Jack thought, stunned and flabbergasted. These creatures were amazing. Easy for him to say, was Jack's second thought. Plucked off an abandoned mine-site, and now laying prone in an alien spaceship. "*Do not worry.*"

'Yeah, right. Worry, is all were doing.' Jack said, probably to no-one, he thought. He assumed spoken words meant nothing to them.

Jack was lying there, alongside his father – exposed, terrified and sweating profusely. Heart pounding. Waiting for these non-humans to invasively attack their human bodies. Jack remembered the dead cattle, and the missing organs, and was horrified, wondering, if that agony was in store for them? The anguished, crying face of his mum came hard again. He took his dad directly against her will, and against her advice. Even though his dad wanted to go, it was *him*, that pushed. *Him*. He was the responsible party. Jack was up to the brim with recriminations and his eyes filled with tears.

Jack desperately needed to know their fate. The main creature said *not to worry*. He didn't believe him. Jack was on the verge of panic, wanting to grab his dad, and run...*but run to where?* He glanced at his dad, whose eyes were now closed again. Jack knew the buck stopped with him. He had to be the leader. He *had* to look after his dad.

Jack looked nervously at Pietr who was a bit taller than the other creatures. He hoped like hell his spoken words meant something. Jack assumed they had our internet, and satellite's that collected our EMAR, so hopefully, his spoken words wouldn't be in vain.

Here goes, he thought, crossing his fingers. '-Why are we here? Jack asked fearfully, looking directly at Pietr and shuddering. 'Do you intend to cause us Harm?' He asked him again. He held his breath, and his eyes started to water. Jack simply didn't believe them. His hometown biases were hitting hard, and he knew it. How could something looking like that, be trusted? Jack conceded anxiously that his home was Earth, and down there, lizards skated around in the garden. Seeing one brought on the "icks." It was no different here.

Jack realised that a lot of education was needed. These creatures might be "lizards," but they weren't close to our garden variety. Because these creatures had amazingly made it light years to Earth. Their tech put humans to shame. *Smart-shaming* was alive and well, a human thing, Jack conceded.

Jack worried about his dad, whose eyes were still closed and was deeply concerned about the creatures' intentions. They were *taken* for a reason, Jack knew. Jack inched closer to his dad, and wondered how he could possibly thwart them? They were all tall and built like NFL footballers. And *God knows* what weapons they packed. Jack reckoned his chances were close to 0% of overpowering them. He had to acknowledge that they were both totally at their whim. Jack looked at his dad, with his eyes closed, and suppressed a sob that was snowballing in his throat, a pressure that was trying to find a way out. What to do, Jack wondered panic-stricken?

The tall creature walked closer to them and looked as though he was about to fill them with speech again. Did he even understand the spoken word? Jack was deeply torn.

'As I said before, no harm will come to you. We have been told to garner two examples of intelligence from your planet. To facilitate contact with our Ruling Council. Then, we will return you to your planet, with some intel, that will assist you. We have previously procured your internet from the Mars Telecommunications satellite, so we know what knowledge humanity needs. There are large holes in your understanding of physics, and the Universe.'

Jack shook his head incredulously and closed his eyes. He felt like replying but didn't. John grimaced, although his eyes were still closed. It sounded like it might be a rather extended venture, but at least they intended to return us to Earth, John thought, relieved. But dark fingers of horror soon overwhelmed him. They wanted us to travel to a different *fucking* planet! How long would that take?

They were due home in two days, and were supposed to text Krissy regularly, and ring once a day. Looks like we're going to bomb out on all of those, he thought to himself glumly. Jack felt the sobs claw further up his throat.

It was too much to absorb, so Jack gawked around and tried to put his mind in neutral. Despite his disbelief and horror at being here, Jack's curiosity was aroused, given Pietr's comforting words, that seemed to make sense. They were to be taken to meet their Ruling Council. His dad seemed safe for the moment. The question of honesty, he knew, invoked xeno-psychology, a subject no human had the remotest handle on. Their mind-set could be anything. Maybe misleading or flat-out lying.

Whatever happened, they would be super-late getting home. That was a given.

'Pietr...er, what are they?' Jack asked curiously. He was pointing toward the four boxes that sat in the middle of the floor like they'd been thrown there. He couldn't help himself. Now that he was satisfied that their trip was for benign purposes, his deep desire for knowledge kicked in. He wanted to know what made this incredible machine fly. The boxes he referred to, looked like a collection of kids play blocks, scattered on the floor of the great machine.

'The first box sends a heavy fluid around the ship at the speed of light.' Pietr toned. 'The second box retrieves energy from the quantum field around us and powers the ship, including propulsion. The third and fourth box, he toned, are gravity amplifiers and gravity disruptors. So, you see, we have no use for engines and propellants. We can manipulate space and travel a lot faster than light.'

Having given up those little pearls, Pietr sat down in front of a device that looked uncomfortably like a black digital radio. 'This is how we interface with the vessel,' Pietr said. 'We also do it with our minds.' He said. The knobs had symbols next to them. They resembled hieroglyphs, or maybe ancient Arabic. To the human mind, they looked more like chicken scratchings interspersed with picture-words.

There was a screen next to the black device, which was full of what looked like chaotic light rays. Pietr said it showed likely future events, but to Jack and his dad it meant absolutely *nothing*. Jack looked at his dad, who was straining to see through one of the windows. He called to him, and they shared a brittle smile. Outside, were the gorgeous desert hills of Arizona from about 1,000 metres in the air. Jack could see his shining car, right in the corner of a window.

John had been through so many painful and annoying medical events. He'd had several rounds of chemo and radiotherapy, been imaged by simple X-ray, CT, and MRI, and been stuck with hundreds of needles. For John, hospital had been home for weeks. Jack was stunned by the man's personal fortitude.

Jack knew their experience would make anyone look a little off. But there was something distressingly familiar and unsettling about his dad's appearance that he didn't like. It reminded Jack of the old days. And they weren't good days. In fact, they were nothing short of horrific.

****

'Time to leave the planet.' Pietr toned to everyone, nodding firmly at the other creatures. 'We have everything we need.' Pietr toned directly to Jack and John. He looked at them aggressively, seemingly counting them, or making sure we were in the right place for space travel.

John looked out the side window and saw clouds below them...*already*. They'd ascended a long way, and he didn't even know it, or feel it. There was no sense of movement at all. He propped up on his elbow and turned to look at his son. They were gazing out the same window, and shared a small smile, as they headed for the darkness, which wasn't too far above them.

John wondered why they'd taken *them* in particular. Were we just in the wrong place at the wrong time? Or did they specifically target us, for some obscure reason. And as soon as we left the house, they pounced? He understood that he wouldn't ever know the answer unless he asked Pietr directly. And who knows if he'd tell him the truth?

Jack turned to his dad, and what he saw didn't fill him with optimism. His dad's lips were white and twitching, and both his hands were drawn into fists. His face was twisted with pain. John was clearly not doing well, and it wasn't just fear or foreboding. He was moaning and whimpering. Jack gulped heavily and glanced down at his dad's hands and was horrified to see them shaking involuntarily. *WTF*? Jack thought hysterically.

'Dad...are you okay? Jack whispered lovingly, trying to keep concern and urgency out of his voice. His dad didn't seem to be coping, which, given the circumstances, wasn't that surprising. But it was more than that. His eyes were closed, and he was rocking to and fro. His eyes flicked wide open, and he spoke croakily, clearly under the weather.

'What about your mum, Jacky? If we're late home...what'll she do?' His voice was a high-pitched cry of terror. His dad looked at him innocently, and sobbed uncontrollably, while still rocking. Jack could see, this was a huge problem - and there was no answer. They were surrounded by non-humans, who either didn't understand, or didn't give a damn. Their only concern was to get us to their Council. Nothing else was seemingly important.

Jack looked his dad straight in the eye, and saw the profound devotion and love, he had for his wife. He was deeply upset because she was at home, and waiting for them to turn up at the door. And there was nothing he could do to console her or help her.

He was powerless, and essentially hamstrung. These repulsive creatures literally held their futures in their paws. All he and Jack could do was hope that they did what they said they'd do. Being returned to Earth after their trip was finished.

The aspirations of Jack and his dad were void. The derision they felt from the lizards was palpable, although that may have been more human bias. His dad was distressed and deeply pained when he spoke of his wife. He didn't want to disappoint, or hurt her in any way, but that was exactly the likely result.

They said that we were to be returned to Earth, but just when would that be? Jack was worried about the travel time. According to them, we'd cover 12.5 light years in mere hours. He knew rapid travel played tricks with time. And this planet of their's lived in its own distinct time-frame. *So, God help us all*, Jack thought morosely. The date on Earth, when we finally get back, could be *anything*. He wouldn't tell his dad the bad news, but *everyone* we ever knew might be dead, when we finally get back. Jack's heart was pounding in his mouth. He imagined stepping off the non-human craft, to a world that had aged a thousand years without them. '*Fuck me*,' Jack whispered harshly to himself.

* * *

Jack could see as plain as day that their fate, was entirely in the paws of these non-humans. They clearly cared nought for their Earthly relationships.

John's care and love needed to be focussed on Jacky. He knew that. Getting home safely, and as quickly as possible, had to remain *their* priority. The throbbing he was feeling, and where it was emanating from, made him anxious and terrified.

Looking through a rectangular window, Jack saw the blackness of space, and the beautiful blue planet below them. No wonder non-humans wanted to visit it, Jack thought. Earth was gorgeous. Warm, oxygen-rich and 40% land. They were already in space, and orbiting the Earth, which was far below them. Jack didn't even feel it happening. When you take gravity out of the equation, getting to orbit is a stroll in the park.

They'd gone from the surface to space, in the snap of the fingers. And they felt *nothing*...no speed, or inertia at all. They weren't even strapped in, because we didn't need to be, apparently.

Jack reckoned they were camouflaged. Because sure as hell, they'd be easily spotted by the space hardware that orbited the planet. The ISS was just off the starboard as well. There were hundreds of NASA telescopes looking right now. We must be hidden from view. Or perhaps these particular non-humans just didn't give a stuff.

We were now adjacent to a huge red structure that was also in orbit. It presented as the yawning mouth of a gigantic whale. Jack's heart was back in his mouth, pounding violently, and sweat emerged on his forehead and back. He could see its girth through the side window, and it appeared they were heading straight for it, in orbit. Crashing into it, seemed unavoidable.

Jack gawked nervously at the creatures around him but no-one seemed agitated or panicked, which made him feel better. They all seemed calm and focussed, on what they needed to do. Some were relaxed and sitting in a chair. Their responsibilities were in the future, presumably. The fact that they were close to this object didn't raise a murmur. Jack assumed that non-humans would show at least some agitation, when confronted by danger.

It was interesting because the ISS wasn't far away. Gravity didn't affect the craft when they rose through the atmosphere. But now they were in a parking orbit, which was facilitated by gravity. So, anti-gravity was clearly something they could turn on and off at will.

The creatures took advantage of folded space. How they did it – he had no idea. It was a connection to somewhere else that had just been created. Jack wasn't overly surprised, after he was told by Pietr their trip would take a few hours. The craft had somehow created it.

The other side of the mouth must be their destination. Jack was floored, when he gazed at it, and took it in. Humanity had theorised about wormholes, but creating them was several bridges too far. This technology set them apart from humanity. They were reptiles, no doubt about it, but their tech was close to magic.

John stared straight ahead, and his eyes bulged, as Pietr got up awkwardly and walked to what they thought was the main pilot's chair. Jack was reminded that gravity somehow existed inside this craft, and it was oddly Earth-like. Pietr was joined by two others, who sat in the adjacent chairs. They were nearest the black radio, which Pietr gave focussed attention to. It had dials, levers, and buttons on it, with odd markings that resembled picture-hieroglyphics. These chicken scratchings were their own language, which presented to Americans as pseudo-Arabic.

Jack held his breath as they neared the mouth and noticed it had bright filaments of light hanging from its inside like chandeliers. They were on a collision course with it, but none of the lizards showed the slightest concern. It was clearly an expected outcome.

Jack and his dad saw the indifference plastered over their reptilian faces. They clearly felt little fear, with just vacancy in their eyes, as they gazed at the humans.

Why them, Jack and John wondered? Of all the humans on Earth...why choose them? Jack couldn't stop thinking about it. Were they simply in the wrong place at the wrong time? Or were they targeted? If they were targeted, *why* were they? Jack shook his head morosely, knowing he would never know the answer, unless he found the gumption to ask the question.

The mouth consumed them, and their craft with nary an effort. Wild colours and kaleidoscopic splashes and blobs replaced the Galaxy around them. It was a bumpy, jarring ride. Then after a short sleigh-ride, they were spat out, into orbit around a very different world indeed.

Exiting the mouth, Jack was now left to glory in the size and colour of the wormhole, that disappeared rapidly into the distance. It roiled and churned, and then vanished, winking out of existence like a spent magnesium flare. Then it was gone. Its life was fleeting, but it had delivered the craft from Earth to a new star system.

2

Pianif

"Somewhere, something incredible is waiting to be known." — Carl Sagan

Jack looked down, through the windows of the craft, to a strange looking, multicoloured planet. It seemed to be a similar size to Earth, and had beautiful blue oceans, but that's where any similarities ended. The hemisphere-spanning continent below them was gigantic, and took up most of what Jack was looking at. This planet was nothing like home.
The sky wasn't transparent, as it was on Earth. Here, it was a deep orangey-yellow with the same-coloured clouds – more like the color of a sandstorm, than an atmosphere. The continent they looked at was tinged with the colour of the atmosphere but was clearly darker than it was back home. In places, it was almost black, but other places were brown just like Earth. The atmosphere tinted everything with a rather unfortunate colour.
Pietr was fiddling with the knobs of the radio device. There was no steering wheel anywhere to be seen. They obviously navigated with the radio-thing and their mind. It all appeared very odd, but we hadn't crashed yet and seemed to be going in the right direction. No-one was running around panicking, which was a good sign. Jack was sure Pietr interfaced with the craft telepathically, he saw him hold the black device and really focus. But the nature of navigation wasn't top-of-mind for either of them.

Jack knew he was a worrier, he'd been told enough times, but his dad looked pale, gaunt and patently unwell. He was lying prone next to him and had his eyes closed. Jack knew he recently had Stage 4 brain cancer, and he'd had a huge and frightening shock, so he didn't expect him to be dancing on the stretcher. Still, he looked poorly. *Too poorly.* The cancer was currently inactive, even though he had it in several places in his body. It had responded positively, and rather unexpectantly, to the last round of chemo. The Doctors didn't say so, but Jack could see it in their eyes. They *expected* the cancer to return. His dad thankfully, didn't seem to pick that feeling up.

The Doctors told and emphasised to Krissy and Jack not to expose John to stress. Being abducted by non-humans definitely qualified as that. Deep, *deep* clinical stress.

His mum's desperate image shot to mind. Krissy spent her whole life looking after John, and in one foul swoop, it was all ripped away. Jack felt ashamed and culpable, even though he too had been kidnapped along with his dad. Just when his dad was well enough to walk by himself, without his mum, he was abducted by *fucking* aliens.

He wondered what he'd do if his dad relapsed. Jack clenched his jaw, and felt familiar dizziness, pretty sure that 9-1-1 wouldn't work where they were going. Jack felt like screaming and running. He had no answers. It was one hour at a time – that's all he could think of.

They fell toward an ocean - from orbit to wave level in a finger-snap and felt no momentum or inertia at all. Jack watched out of the myriad side windows, at the close blue ocean, and wondered where the hell they were? An exo-planet obviously – but which *fucking* one? There was a small, red star at about 3pm in the orangey-yellow afternoon sky. Just to hammer home that this was *not* Earth. In fact, this place was nothing like it. Small red stars were the most common stars in the Universe, so their location could be literally anywhere. Jack acknowledged that it could be a different Galaxy, a different Universe. '*Holy fuck,*' he croaked in awed disbelief.

Outside, through the windows of the craft, Jack could only see blue and green water and the occasional wave. During the time he took to look back at his dad, they had submerged. As to why, or how deep they were, he had no idea. But outside, was only water and the odd bubble. The water sort of looked like the ocean back on Earth, but up close, there was definitely a yellowish tinge to it.

Jack's heart had been pounding ever since he sighted the craft in the sky back on Earth. Looking at his dad didn't help any. He couldn't bounce ideas off him, because he remained fast asleep with a sheet over him, up to his neck. Jack was trapped by his own thoughts.

Krissy must have thought her husband and son were dead. Murdered at the grisly blood-stained hands of some outback maniac, who'd found them and then dispatched them, and buried them both in one of the abandoned mines that dot the Arizona hills. Their only remains, were the two soiled yellow backpacks, stuffed with wulfenite specimens. And Jack's Daihatsu, still parked near the old Yuma mine.

There would never be another sign of them, because, incredibly, Jack and his dad had been taken to another planet! Police searches, agency searches, private searches, *everything*, would find not a single clue.

All Jack could see was ocean water whizzing by the windows. There was no sign of anything alive. Jack had the strong feeling they were doing extraordinary velocity underwater, but he couldn't really tell. The water was fairly flashing by the window. Obviously, these vessels acted as submarines, as well as spacecraft. He wasn't surprised, because UAPs did the same thing, on Earth. Something to do with ionization allowed stunning velocities.

Still, Jack watched the craft eat up the water, and he was floored. *Underwater speed.* Sure, as hell, humanity couldn't do it. Our nuclear subs were limited to about twenty-five knots, he reckoned. This was the first time Jack had really contemplated the technical potential of this race of non-humans. So far, he was stunned. Their lizardness apart, the technology he'd witnessed, was amazing. Certainly, far in advance of humans. Jack couldn't help but picture all this tech, transferred to Earth.

Earth would eat it up like candy to a hungry child. But there were vested interests, and even legislation, that would make it difficult and even, *dangerous*. Especially if you dared to muck around with the planet's energy base. Oil and coal held an esteemed and protected position because they fed global governments like no other.

Jack stared at his dad, who again, was propped up on one arm, gawking out a window. Jack was now certain that his colour was off. And he was rubbing his hip with the other hand. While he did it, he was clenching his jaw and grinding his teeth, just like the *old days. Fuck, FUCK*, he thought glumly. It couldn't be, could it? It was the worst news for John, if true, but it was also lousy news for Jack. Because, somehow, *someway*, he'd have to deal with it. And they were in the worst place for it. His dad's physiology was all wrong if they sought help. It was a long way from help that suited a human.

Jack slowly contemplated the primeval creatures deeply, and was stunned. They flitted between planets, and had trans-medium craft that went into space, and also into the ocean. They made humanity look positively backward. UFOs on Earth could do it in the water, so why not here? He supposed Earth and humanity could learn a lot from this mob. But learning from lizards wouldn't be easy. Human arrogance and pride would get in the way.

Jack knew learning wasn't the purpose of this visit. We were brought here solely for their benefit. But just imagine...Jack speculated, looking at the craft, and glancing, perplexed at Pietr, who looked positively primeval. Jack didn't know what to think about the creatures. On the one hand was a technology literally to die for. On the other was a planet load of primeval reptiles. There was a huge dose of bias involved, Jack could see it vividly, like a Monet Impression.

This was the way of the Universe, and humans needed to accept it. There was a huge disconnect, which he needed to get over. Jack knew pre-conceptions were frequently wrong, and *dangerous.*

Despite their primitive appearance, this race had a vehicle that could move to orbit without rocket power and could treat the gravity-well with total disdain. *Goodbye rockets and propellant.* Jack wondered about oil. If they could access quantum power –

Zero-Point Energy, they'd have no use for it. Jack was hit by an iron block – he realised this race probably had it all. Climate-change was likely a problem for the ancients on this planet.

Jack smacked his hand on his forehead, and shook his head, grinning in awe. This race of lizards was probably the one's Arthur C Clarke was talking about. Super-advanced, to the point where their tech was like *magic*. Who'd have ever thought they'd be reptiles, Jack mused incredulously.

He gazed at the lizards in a new light. They looked like evolved crocodiles, but apparently, they were way more advanced than humans. Jack thought it was a huge quandary that initially, smacked him in the head. But in the next breath, he knew it was just the human mind-set. Which was full of bias and prejudice, with way too much emphasis on appearance. A tentacled octopus that might stiffen itself by inhaling atmosphere, might have a technology that makes humanity look like microbes. The Universe is so big, literally *anything is possible.* Jack knew that this expansive thinking on Earth, was very rare.

Looking like lizards, made them duller than humans, didn't it? Jack took a breath, and knew it was the meaning of the Universe. Every type of life gets a chance. "Looks," had *nothing* to do with it. Earth was one grain of sand on an enormous beach. He realised that prejudice had to be totally eliminated. Because once there's enough grains of sand, *anything can emerge*. And Jack and his dad were on one of those grains right now.

Jack glanced at his dad, and saw that he was still asleep, which was good, he needed it. But in the next breath, he was terrified – his dad had been asleep for a long time.

Jack got up and approached his dad's bed, looking closely at him, wondering if he should try and rouse him, or let him sleep more. Rousing him was purely for his own benefit, he knew. If he was just asleep, he needed as much as he could get.

Suddenly, he was overwhelmed with a voice in his own head. It was like the sound from a megaphone. He jumped, then staggered under its weight. It came from the nearest creature, who was in his face and looked ready to kill. The sound was coming from his own brain.

'*What are you doing*?' He was asked loudly and firmly. The words were deafening and static-filled, from the Caudate's antenna of his own mind.

After jumping, shrieking Jack sighed heavily. 'I'm, uh...checking on my dad...he's been asleep for a long time.'

'Okay...go ahead,' the Pianif toned. Jack looked at the creature more closely and he reared back, and nearly fainted. His monstrosity was very close. The bubbly green skin that smelt of cloves, was moist and only centimetres away. 'I am Dineptin,' he toned, looking squarely into Jack's eyes, 'and we are the Pianif,' he said. 'Again, we mean you no harm.'

Up close, Jack reckoned, they looked more like an insect. 'That is fine,' Jack nervously replied to the green, carbuncled creature. 'My father has been ill, and needs to be free of stress and anxiety, which is not what you are providing.' Jack's eyes were darting everywhere. Dineptin stood aside and allowed Jack to get closer to his dad. He inched around the creature and moved closer to his ailing dad.

His dad's eyes were still closed, and his face was twisted with pain. Disturbingly, he continued to massage his side as deeply as he could. Jack grabbed his dad's hand and helped him massage. John looked at him with tears in his eyes. The poor man was in agony. Jack could feel the sobs clawing their way up his own throat, but he needed to be strong.

'We have your internet from the Mars Satellite,' Dineptin toned, seeing Jack's discomfort, 'so, some of your languages are understood. There are numerous lessons available on your internet.' With that, he turned on a dime, and returned to the other side of the ship. Leaving them alone, once again.

Jack firstly made sure his dad was still breathing, which he was. Then he made sure his heart was beating correctly, which it also was. Eighty beats per minute. 'He's just dozing.' He said to himself. Jack hopped back on his own bed, and watched his dad, and the view through the window.

Jack hoped against hope that his dad would be okay. His colour suggested otherwise, but there was little he could do right now. He clenched his jaw to smother another sob. John looked terrible, like the old days as his dad continued breathing in shallow, quick gasps. Jack himself was hyperventilating, and close to all out panic. He hoped to God that his dad would be okay because he was powerless to help him here. They were two humans versus a planet full of Pianif. A genetically distinct, and different species. Medical help here was a pitiful hope.

Jack hoped and prayed that meeting their Ruling Council was in fact the Pianif's mission priority, the true reason we were brought here. Jack hoped like hell they were being honest when they said it. But he just didn't know. Their psychology and mindset were a guess at best. Hopefully, the Pianif mind-set was something like humans. Something familiar that could be grappled with.

John felt ill and helpless, being so far from the love of his life. Pietr, Dineptin, and the Pianif generally, had a lot to answer for, because they clearly didn't give a shit.

Now, of all things, they were on another *fucking planet*. Jacks sighed, shook his head disbelievingly and struggled to accept it. It sounded like a drug-induced fantasy. A bullshit story. Jack felt like crying but best, he focussed on his dad, who needed his help. His colour was now distinctly yellow, like an overripe banana.

Jack was no doctor, but he was sure his dad's colour change couldn't be good. It had to be a reflection of something inside him. He preferred not to speculate, but where and what? He'd talked himself into the worst.

Jack wanted to change his own mind-set and relax a bit. He could see where this was heading, and reckoned he'd need the headroom. So, he gazed away from his dad, and out of the side windows, and saw oceans give way to clean air and the orangey-yellow of the sky. They were out of the sea and into the sky. Off to see the Ruling Council, he assumed. Jack's heart skipped a beat, wondering what horrors that would involve.

Against his will, Jack glanced pensively back at his dad and noticed how tiny he looked in the non-human bed. He was alive, but had clearly lost a lot of weight.

Jack turned back to the middle windows of the craft and saw green ocean, then a dark rocky beach, then something red and narrow like a road, then small pyramids. Whatever he saw, looked familiar, but odd, all the same. He was comparing it to Earth, something he tried not to do. But couldn't help but do so.

Actually, it looked as he expected. *Completely different.*

They had landed on the ground, soft as a baby's kiss. The entire ride had been smooth, without the slightest perturbation. No seatbelts or harnesses were provided or needed. Inertia was nil. Jack could see a huge, colourful, pyramidal structure out of the front window of the craft.

'What the hell...?' Jack muttered to himself, preparing to get up. His dad was still prone on the bed, eyes wide open and frowning. He massaged the side of his stomach and looked at the structure immediately outside the window. The deeply unknown had Jack frozen-stiff and he could feel his heart beating like a drum. *Another planet*, he thought incredulously, feeling like everything was careening, not only out of control, but totally off the grid.

John's face had collapsed into a bitter mass of lines, twisted by fear and pain as he struggled up to the side of his makeshift bed, eventually sitting up. Jack saw dark circles under his eyes, rounded shoulders, trembling fingers and sweat pouring off him.

Jack felt useless knowing they were entirely reliant on a race that knew less than nothing about humans.

Tired, rundown, a yellowish hue, and always hot and sweating, and in pain. John was a mess. Jack himself had black circles under his blue eyes, and was struggling under the weight of his self-critical mindset.

How would these creatures react if his dad got really sick? What if he started with true end-of-life cancer pain – *what* would they do? What would he do? *Fuck me*, he thought dismally. There was no answer to that one.

***

It turned out they'd landed in the backyard of Pietr's own home, and as visitors from another planet, were about to inspect its pyramidal morphology.

John and Jack were led to exits in the craft that looked like silver tongues. These things didn't have stairs built into them and were soft, so *grip,* was anyone's guess. The exit looked more like a silver slippery-dip, and to make it worse, it looked a little wet. Jack grimaced at his dad and stepped forward. He wasn't confident of *not* falling on his arse.

It was steep and there was no sign of anything to make traction better. Jack looked at it, sighed heavily, and said, '*oh what the hell...*' and tried to walk down it, like Pietr, whose boots didn't look to be anything special. He desperately hoped he didn't make a fool of himself. He also realised that hundreds of Pianif had probably used it. So, away he went. And the stability of the surface was pretty damn good.

Having seen Jack negotiate it, John cautiously came down, followed by Dineptin, and the other creatures, who acted like they'd used it hundreds of times.

Jack turned his head and took everything in. Breathing was easy, but he almost choked on the first unimpeded glimpse of the surface of this planet. The sky was almost cloudless and was an opaque orangey-yellow. It was almost the opposite of the clear air on Earth. It was like he thought it might be on Venus, minus the heat and the pressure.

Turns out, that the atmosphere of this world contained sulphur-trioxide and argon in liberal amounts together with oxygen and nitrogen. They all summed to what they had here on Pianif, which supported a global civilization.

Jack gazed around in pure amazement. Everywhere he looked, there was something different to Earth. His eyebrows shot to the top of his head and stayed there, and he gaped in finely tuned wonder.

There was a small red sun about half the size of our Moon, at 3PM if it were back on Earth. Here – *who knew?* Pietr had long grass in his backyard that was screaming out for a cut – no problem there, but it was almost *black!*

It looked wrong, or fake. He had trees as well, but they too were dark grey and very different, with multiple trunks that sprung from one spot. Jack peered at the trees, and coupled with the colour of the grass, he agreed with his dad, that they all looked extremely off-centre, to a human at least. Textbook for a different planet, Jack reckoned flabbergasted.

He watched his dad lope unsteadily toward the back of the pyramid, flanked by several looming black creatures who were huge. Jack wondered what they'd do if his dad collapsed in a heap? What if he started seizing, having a heart-attack...or foaming at the mouth. He had to admit, he had zero confidence in them. And why should he, he thought? They looked like sportsmen, tall, with broad shoulders. Not intellectuals, certainly nothing approaching paramedics. Jack conceded again, that their future looked grim.

He assumed they had hospitals, and emergency services...but who would know? Would we be helped by that? Same answer. *Probably not,* kept ringing in his ears. Jack scratched his chin and felt like bolting. Would we be referred to their version of a vet? Their medical services would be designed for a Pianif, not a *human,* so any care would be very qualitative, and probably highly alternative.

Jack was getting himself worked up, not helped by seeing his dad careen from side to side, in front of him. His worries were getting real. His dad was getting visibly worse by the hour. Soon, He'd be in a coma. Jack knew it.

Pietr beckoned to both of them with his paws, to fall in line and walk along with them. There was clearly something inside this pyramid that he wanted them to see, as newcomers to their planet. His dad was almost inside, so Jack walked toward him, to help him get fully into this home. They'd decided that It was important, so no time to be difficult, Jack reckoned.

Pietr used a card to unlock the house. The entire structure made a distinct click. Still following the line, he saw them walk through the wall into the interior of the home, without hesitating. Jack followed and didn't hesitate, doing the same as everyone else.

They pushed through the gelatinous wall and ended up inside and standing in a bright, white room that was completely empty. On the floor was something that looked like garish golden carpet. The nature of the fibre was unknown, but there was no colour variation at all. It was bright gold from wall to wall, and the walls themselves were totally unadorned. The bright room did nothing for his dad's complexion and eyes. There was no getting around it, he looked like a tired, sick old man.

Seeing his dad like this, only led him to one, forlorn conclusion. He didn't want to admit it, but he couldn't paper over it. His dad was now bent over in pain, red hot, and the colour of a lemon ice block, just *like* the first time his cancer started showing. One look was enough, Jack thought. You didn't have to be a doctor to make a diagnosis.

Jack was distraught, shook his head morbidly, and couldn't think of a worse time to be sick.

His dad's colour, his anguished face, and his constant massaging of pain points were too much. He turned away, and let the sob out, and it consumed him. His shoulder blades shook with sobs he couldn't control. His dad saw how upset he was, and he hobbled up to Jack in his sweat-ridden shirt and held him tight, whispering in his ear.

'Jacky, for *Christ's* sake, you have to be the leader. Which means *you* need to get it together. My only hope is to get home,' he whispered. 'Me to a hospital, and us, to your mum. This mob want us to meet their rulers. That's fine, we agree to that, but *only* if we're taken to Earth first. It's a forlorn hope Jacky, but I can think of nothing else.' John took a raspy breath and turned around to gawk submissively at Pietr.

Jack was impressed with his dad's words. *Quid pro quo*, that's all they had. He was sure it wouldn't work. But they'd sure as hell try.

***

With a bit of walking, they were led to a completely closed room. Jack could now smell them. There were four big creatures, *Pianif*, in the room. It was a sweet, oniony smell...odd, and a little unpleasant, he thought indignantly. Jack scanned the room and thought it was rather dreary, which surprised him. Given the technology of the spacecraft, he expected to be amazed once he got to their planet. But it seemed to be the opposite. Everything they saw inside the pyramid-house was pure *ho-hum*. Jack dropped his shoulders and looked around, exhaling loudly in disappointment.

Why bother bringing us here if there's nothing to see? Jack expected something mind-blowing. Instead, we seemingly got very little. Four blank walls. *Wow.*

The large, tongue-poking Pianif to his left, held something small in his hand, and pressed a button quite deliberately. One entire wall, side to side, became a high-definition television screen. It showed a game, much like Gaelic Football, watched by a massive crowd in a packed stadium. Jack watched in awe – they played sport, just like us. *Amazing*, he thought. Then he thought, *why wouldn't they?*

Out of the wall behind them, was pulled a full, ready-to-use kitchen, replete with cooking utensils, devices, white-goods, drawers, a pantry, table and chairs. Before that, the wall was entirely blank and presented as a normal wall. The Pianif then put it back in the wall again with a flicking motion, using their fingers. *Wallah*...the house was empty again. Pietr stood tall, with a gleam in his eye. A huge reptile towered over them. He, and the rest of the Pianif were clearly very pleased with this technology..

'We can do the same with bedrooms, and the rest of the house,' leading guy said, who seemed keen to talk with Jack. The creature that stood next to him, towered, with green, scaly, skin, and was vociferous, toning proudly into his brain.

'...Laundry, toilet and living rooms. When you leave a house, everything folds back into the wall. This is new dimensional technology and came as a spin-off of dark energy and being able to fold space.' The large Pianif continued to make a flicking motion with his paw, showing the humans how he did it.

'*Amaaaaazing*,' Jack piped loudly and enthusiastically. 'Absolutely incredible.' John let out a huge gasp. Despite his pain, he recognised it for what it was. A giant step forward for humans if they had it.

Everything is cleaned by automation,' the Pianif said, 'including clothes...we use AI, which is provided to our people, free of cost. The days of cleaning and washing have been over on our world for some time.'

Jack followed the line of beings through the greasy wall, to stand on the long black grass at the rear of the house. The vessel sat proudly, glinting brilliantly in the afternoon sunlight, like a polished supercar. Jack was dazzled. They were upright lizards, no doubt, but they had tech to die for. And there was probably more to come. If only humans had it, he thought passionately. Earth would be super-amazing. *Alien tech*, he thought incredulously, beaming with wonder about what could be.

Against his will, Jack peered at his dad and could see that he needed to sit down. If he didn't, he'd fall down.

'Dad, *dad*? He shouted hysterically. 'What -can I do?' Jack ran up to him, his voice cracking with emotion, knowing he could do little.

Jack could take no more. He turned and pounded up to Pietr. '*Pietr*,' Jack shouted, and pointed with a stiff finger. *My dad needs help right now*. He has cancer, which has returned. *Please, for God's sake, help him*.' He yelled desperately, with feverish eyes. His voice was a potent high-pitched cry for help. Jack stuck his fist against his mouth, to hide the emotion, but made sure Pietr could see how hopelessly distressed he was. Pietr was a brick wall, made obvious by his empty eyes and lack of reaction.

Pietr turned away and ignored Jack, focussing on the black radio.

John wiped tears from his eyes, and nodded his head, and smiled brokenly at his son. He too, conceded that the situation was dire indeed. It was clear from Pietr's lack of reaction that the Pianif wouldn't act. John knew his situation was grim but still he tried to be philosophical about it, at least he got a last holiday with his son. That brought his mind straight to his wife, and John could feel his eyes fill with tears.

'I'm, uh, okay Jacky...but thanks for trying.' The last thing John wanted to do was worry his son. His son was assessing him with terror and love in his eyes.

John was determined to lift himself, for his boy's sake. He looked at his son, who wore a mask of hopelessness, as he gazed back. John smiled weakly, and Jack grinned back.

A few hours ago, they were on Earth, enjoying themself. Now, they had been forced to travel through folded space, and were on God-knows-what planet. For the purposes decreed by the Pianif's Ruling Council apparently.

The way his dad's face twisted with pain, told the awful story. *Oh God,* Jack thought. What to do? His dad couldn't go on like this, that was obvious. Jack glowered at Pietr, and swallowed the fuming lump in his throat. Jack simply had to confront him, for his dad's sake. *Get in his face.* He glanced at his dad and smiled weakly.

He would confront Pietr, but he'd have to pick the right moment. The quixotic pilot, was horrendously busy, navigating the craft and organising and directing the crew. He'd confront him at the most opportune time. He knew it had to be soon, or he might lose his dad.

Jack and John slowly filed back into the craft. Pietr sat in the pilot's seat and did something to the knobs. The craft rose steadily into the sky, and headed further inland, where a number of vessels seemingly lay waiting. Again, they felt no inkling of movement or any sound. Like an electric car, Jack reckoned. Some craft they saw were starkly red in colour, but most were white, and shaped distinctly like a tic-tac or a flattened tablet. Very un...aero-dynamic, Jack thought curiously. They didn't look right. They looked more like train-carriages than something abled for travel in the sky. Human-bias, he knew. It was impossible not to do it.

None had wings or a tail, ailerons, flaps, or any surfaces that humans would normally associate with aeroplanes. No surfaces to alter air pressure and encourage lift. These vessels did not rely on air-pressure to hold them aloft. Anti-gravity and Zero Point Energy were theirs, just like the ones that buzzed Earth.

Being able to characterise Dark Energy was a huge advantage for these reptiles. It unlocked *negative mass*. The same thing that caused the expansion of the Universe, allowed them to avoid gravity and propel their ships *without* relying on an engine. By onboarding Dark Energy in the amount equalling the mass of their ship, and the occupants, they could float to orbit. A bit less would see them float in the atmosphere like a helium-filled balloon. A little less or more would add velocity or slow them down. This knowledge belonged only, sadly, with non-humans. Humanity were children amongst men.

Their own vessel landed near the swarm of landed tic-tac's, and a wheelchair with several small wheels was rolled in for John. The wheelchair looked odd, because it had four small wheels, but it still managed to do the job. John was placed in the seat, and they followed him out of the vessel and into one of the white tic-tacs. Jack was pleased to see the wheelchair, even though it looked a little strange.

It meant these creatures were thinking about his dad's illness and disability. And could see his dad wasn't well, and was generally struggling. That he required assistance to get around. Jack smiled and relaxed a bit, despite the horrific circumstances. The fact that they wanted to look after his dad was comforting.

He wondered if the tic-tac was controlled AI? If it wasn't, how the hell was vision actuated, Jack wondered sceptically. Because from the outside, Jack could see no windows. Perhaps they weren't needed. Jack put his mind in neutral, and just let it happen. This was crazy. It was just a lump of metal, devoid of anything aerodynamic, that would normally be needed to help something fly in the air. It was even devoid of windows. Was this thing supposed to fly? Jack had seen videos about anti-gravity and ZPE so the likely modes of air-flight weren't unheard of. Astounding yes, but not totally unfamiliar.

Jack noticed that the tic-tac object they were in had taken to the skies, and they weren't alone. *Definitely not.* Outside, there were no windows. But *inside*, it was a very different story indeed. This was insane, Jack thought incredulously. There were panoramic windows down each side of the craft. And small windows that looked forward, into what was presumably the pilot's area. He could see two lizards in front of a black radio device. There were seats for maybe 600 creatures in the main section behind them, and there was more than one level. Welcome to air transport – *Pianif style,* Jack thought, smiling tentatively at John, who continued to be in pain.

As open-minded as he thought he was, Jack reckoned it looked totally wrong. These creatures were primeval lizards, but their ability to decode the Universe and physics was nothing short of dazzling. In a moment of blistering realisation, Jack conceded that the Pianif were far superior to Mankind. Like an adult to a newborn.

Put in our place by a race of lizards, Jack thought, bewildered. Their tech was stunning. Humanity should aspire to it. But human jealousy, pride and arrogance would get in the way, he was certain. As a species, generally, we were far too emotional and closed off.

Beyond the panoramic windows were fleets of flying tic-tac's. They were everywhere - the sky was literally teeming with them. All points of the compass were accounted for. All were separated by clean air, and every one of them were going in the same direction. Apparently, there was a rule to maintain a certain distance from other ships at all times. Whether it was automated or manual, who knew? Presumably, there was another part of the sky dedicated to a different direction. Or maybe direction of flight was organised by time, Jack thought. These details were unknown to humans. Similarly, their laws and social structure remained a complete mystery to Jack.

Still, Jack was intrigued by this superficial peek into the extraordinary, which was severely tempered by his dad, who wasn't going so well. He was clearly entering a phase, where hospitalisation on Earth would be a must. Opiates were a similar *must*. He needed help to cope with severe cancer pain, which he was fearful, would soon prevent him from moving at all. What then? He wondered morbidly. What happens when he slips into a coma? Jack reckoned their plight with the Pianif was akin to an ant trying to stop an elephant with bad language.

Looking at his dad, the wheelchair was too big, making him look like a child. His eyes were narrowed in pain, and he was bent over in the chair and constantly massaging his back which was clearly giving him hell.

Jack thought that *surely*, they'd noticed that his dad was suffering. But maybe they didn't have the right mind-set to recognise it. He looked at Pietr desperately as he hunched over the control-panel. Jack shook his head in despair. He could feel his own heat rise, knowing that the crisis-point was nearly on them. Jack glared at Pietr, there was zero help and clear indifference in those dead, vacant black eyes.

Jack felt so sorry for this man who had read him stories in bed, when he was little, and taught him how to play football. And looked after him when he was sick.

Now, he needed a serving back. His dad was light years from medical help, and a hospital that suited him. *A human hospital.*

The situation with John was now beyond dire. Jack knew that his dad was being maudlin and histrionic, but it was fair enough, he thought.

John was sitting in his wheelchair, practising self-propelling, using the front wheels, near Jack's bed. He looked through the rectangular window, and saw a nest of tall, light-bluish pyramids below, one bigger, taller and bluer. It actually had markings on it, inside a huge circle, for the first time. Every other structure they'd seen was totally blank. They were heading straight toward it. Their trajectory toward it, was very obvious indeed.

Flying toward their engagement with their Ruling Council no doubt, Jack thought. Pietr said we were flying to their home, to execute the meeting, for which we were apparently taken from Earth. Jack whispered to his dad, 'Fine, let's get this over with.' He was keen to see what happens then. Everytime, he thought about it, his heart raced, and pounded like it wanted to break his ribs. *Then what?* Post-meeting was a huge source of panic and dread.

Every building on their planet was a four-sided building, a polygon, according to Pietr, by law. Because their race gathers health, vitality and energy from the pyramid structure, which mechanically amplifies incoming EMAR. Without the morphology, females become infertile and the general population can't live long and healthy lives. They become depressed and ultimately, suicidal. Very different from humans indeed.

John's pain was nearing the tipping point. He tried to stifle it for Jack, but the pain racking his insides ratcheted up. He was out of everything, including the ability to stifle his emotions.

John wept with great shuddering sighs that finally got the attention of the Pianif. But instead of doing anything to help, they treated his outburst as a curiosity, surrounding him, poking him, and looking closely, making chirps and squeaks.

Incredibly, it appeared like they'd never seen such a display before. Jack watched their curiosity with horror. He never felt as isolated and hopeless as he did at that moment. He gawked at Pietr and realised that none of them understood humans even a bit. We were a deep, dark mystery. His dad and Jack were truly alone...without any help, any hope, or any sympathy.

Understanding was zero. They may as well be surrounded by a pack of dogs.

Jack watched his dad navigate the trip to the window in his wheelchair and saw how bad he truly was. His dad was still crying, clutching his back, and was barely conscious. He'd given up all hope, Jack could see it in his barely open eyes.

'*Dad, dad...what do...I do?*' Jack blurted in panic, knowing that he could do stuff all, because of where they were, and who surrounded them. All he could do was be with him and provide whatever psychological help he could. Medically, he could do nothing.

'Unless you've Morphine in your pocket, forget it Jacky.'

'This is mine to deal with. *Mine alone.*' John said forcefully. 'I don't expect much help from *them.*' John scowled at Pietr hatefully and was met with a bristling brick wall. Pietr was oblivious to everything and most everyone and everything except piloting the ship and directing his crew. That was his sole priority. John shrugged his shoulders and closed his eyes. He thought of his wife again, and deep sobs attacked his insides, which made the physical pain worse.

Take us home, he thought desperately. Saying that out loud, to Pietr would be a waste of air, he thought uselessly.

The Pianif had travelled a long way to get us. So, they valued us, in some obscure, soul-less way. Related to us, being an example of different life...*intelligence*, to be introduced to their Ruling Council. Pietr would have to care, if one of us died, wouldn't he? We had to use that to our advantage, Jack thought tactically.

Time was their number one enemy, John thought weirdly. He didn't know how much time had elapsed on Earth. But he knew their arrival back home was going to be very late indeed. Jacky said we occupied different time-frames and travelled FTL for much of the trip here. So, unfortunately, time-dilation could be significant. After he'd said that, John was nauseous.

Jack's bewilderment and terror was turning to boiling hot anger. *How dare they,* he thought, flaring his nostrils. His feet were planted wide and he cracked his knuckles. *Something* had to change. *Right now.* It was time for a little love to be directed our way.

Jack bared his teeth. Anger and heat grabbed him and pushed him toward Pietr. He pointed angrily at his dad, and knowing they understood spoken English poorly, he got straight to the point.

With a pounding heart and sweating like a dog, Jack said, 'this man, *there*,' he pointed with a fist, '*must* get urgent medical help. *He has advanced cancer.* I know you've read our internet, so you know what that means.' Jack started to yell furiously through tears. '*If you do nothing, he will DIE, in front of your friends here.* And if that happens, I will *refuse* to cooperate, in terms of "meeting your Ruling Council." His voice had risen to a cry of hysterical venom. '*So, I strongly suggest you take us both home.*' Jack shouted and spat the last part at him, at the top of his voice.

'It is obvious that you respect your Ruling Council.' Jack said, less venomously. 'You want this "contact" to be cooperative, and not forced. So, that depends on how my *dad* is treated.' Jack's voice was again a cry of anguish. Tears poured down his cheeks, right in front of Pietr, who turned away coldly. There was little doubt, he understood the gist of the statement by Jack.

Pietr considered Jack's words while turned, and then shook his huge head quite dramatically, and glared at his co-pilot, conversing silently. He pushed on the side of the black machine, and they started flying steeply and quickly toward the starboard. Destination had clearly changed. There was no increase in gravity. All they felt was the normal pull, but they'd clearly turned. Extra-inertia from turning was extraordinarily absent. Jack ran his hand through his brown hair, and puzzled about Pietr's lack of response, and the changed trajectory.

Pietr turned fully to front the humans. 'We will *not* take you back to Earth.' He said firmly. 'We will have you treated here.' With that, Pietr turned back to the black machine, and the sound in their heads stopped.

Jack was exasperated - he got the distinct impression that Pietr was annoyed by his words. He glared at him and sighed with contempt. His lack of empathy and sympathy was in keeping with his physical form, Jack reckoned irately. *How dare he?* He thought hatefully.

"Treated here," Jack thought frightfully. What the hell do they know about humans? The response by Pietr did nothing to quell Jack's fury and unease. One look at his dad was enough. He fronted Pietr again. 'You don't under-understand...this man...is my father. *I only exist because of him*,' Jack pleaded. 'I, you, need to return him to Earth, to be treated properly. He requires *human* medical care, urgently.' Jack made the sign of the Cross on his chest and then brought his hands together and interlocked his fingers, literally praying to Pietr, to take them home. Jack was now entirely beside himself, and overwhelmed with grief, and desperately needed Pietr's help. He was the only one that could help them now.

He stopped praying and exhaled loudly, sitting down on his dad's bed, with his head in his hands, sobbing so violently, his shoulder-blades were shaking. Jack felt as though the battle was lost. Talking to Pietr seemed useless. He was an impenetrable brick wall. Pietr's response was no, and very brief.

It appeared he had not one ounce of empathy in that green, carbuncled body. Jack was desperate, and ready to fight him, which was ridiculous, he knew. Just look at him, he thought devastated. Jack was literally at his wit's end. He had nothing else. They just didn't get it. There was no understanding. Looking at him was like looking at a bronze statue, and expecting it to act. He knew that whatever he chose to do, was futile.

Pietr could see that we were frantic, yet he remained stone-cold indifferent. Jack glanced at his dad and sighed dejectedly. 'Dad, I don't think they understand...even a little bit.' His dad nodded despairingly, before gawking around the craft dismally, seeing no possibility for help, knowing they were nearing the end.

John glanced back at his son and smiled, 'It's fine Jacky...do as they say, I'll be fine. It's not worth aggravating them and bringing forward something possibly worse.'

Jack scowled at Pietr. There was nothing more that could be done. He could say more, but his dad advised against it, because they might just throw them out of the craft into space.

Jack had no idea where the line was, he didn't know how valuable they were. Even if they *were* valuable. The Pianif wanted us to meet their Ruling Council, but if we didn't work out, maybe they'd get rid of us, and get another two. Afterall, they could get to Earth in a few hours. The next step by the Pianif, was a giant mystery.

Jack saw they were now approaching a large nest of tetragonal buildings...a medical centre hopefully. But their ability to treat a human being had to be questionable at the very least. They landed softly, like a bee on a flower, on an indent in one of the pyramids. After they were set down, Jack saw movement inside, everywhere.

A hatch opened and four upright lizards in blue coats, entered and took John away, bed and all. They knew he was coming and were waiting for him apparently. The creatures inside the building were all wearing similar, dark-blue attire that resembled a uniform. Many of them had cards hanging from their waist. Jack wondered if they allowed entry to somewhere that was restricted from general entry?

Jack went to go with his dad and was stopped by the ponderous paw of one of the orderlies. He pushed through it, and went anyway, jumping onto the end of his dad's bed. No-one, human or not, would stop him from going with his dad. His dad's so called "treatment" filled Jack with dark, painful images of torment and suffering. Whatever happened, would require both of them to be present. Jack would fight tooth and nail for his dad. Important, because John was in no condition to do it himself. He was a single sick human, amongst thousands of Pianif. *Hope* was something they'd have to fight for together.

Looking from the bed, Jack noticed that everyone in sight was watching them, or taking short, shocked glances. We, the *humans*, were the aliens...in a Pianif hospital. No attempt had been made to disguise us. In a sea of reptiles, Jack and his dad's *humanness* stuck out like a sore thumb. He wasn't sure what the lack of concealment meant. They didn't care, or it was a common occurrence, maybe.

Jack noticed that many of the creatures were holding a long green card. Some had bright yellow cards, and a few who looked particularly ill, had a black card, mostly held by others. Jack wondered if it was a different way, to triage the ill.

John and Jack were whisked into a room, through a large door this time, dominated by a single strange machine. This thing looked like an outdoor spa. Except it was covered at the top by glass or at least a transparent dome. It appeared to be slightly filled with some sort of fluid that was bright yellow in colour. The object looked like it had a layer of lemon cordial. The surface of the fluid showed it to be thick, viscous fluid, that had a texture similar to partially set jelly. Very odd indeed.

The operator of the device was a spindly, hunched-over creature, who didn't look like he had the energy to do much at all. He fiddled slowly with the metallic control panel, while humming a strange tune and tapping a foot. He was very close to the panel, almost touching it, as though his vision was poor. Jack could see that that the glasses he wore were very thick. Even with them on, he clearly struggled to see properly. This made him look more like a human, more than any Pianif they'd seen so far.

The brightly coloured fluid, that was now uncongealed, drained from the device and once almost drained in full, the lid popped open, with the sound of a lolly jar opening. It seemed that the fluid lost its viscosity, and drained like water, when they wanted it too. Jack watched, as the last of it drained away, leaving the machine dry as a rock in the desert Sun.

'*John,*' the hunched-over creature unexpectedly squealed into his brain, as three creatures picked John up and placed him in the device. He squealed in pain when he was touched.

'*W-What...are you doing?*' Jack yelled panic-stricken, petrified that some torturous procedure was about to be unleashed, without his approval, or even their acknowledgement. What the hell was this *thing*? John's feverishly blinking, wide eyes and scrabbling fingers said everything. *What, why, where*?

The machine looked like nothing they'd ever seen. Was this supposed to help him, or perhaps more likely, was it purely for research? Jack's heart thumped unevenly in his neck, as he watched his dad struggle to sit on the uneven bottom of the machine. The smell of iodine, or whatever this fluid contained, was overwhelming. Jack felt powerless and helpless, and glanced at Pietr who looked back with vacant, soul-less eyes.

'My name is Rendn,' said the spindly operator. We need to know exactly what is wrong with him. Before we can do anything about it.' He said, adjusting glasses on his small, almost non-existent, green nose.
Jack was relieved to hear it. That was the first statement of intent, he'd heard. At least they intended to help him. If it was just research into the human genome, he'd be furious with Pietr for misleading him.

His dad desperately needed help, but this machine worried him. It didn't resemble anything on Earth – it wasn't even close. We used imagers, X-ray, CT, MRI, surgeons and radiation guns. This looked nothing like any of those. Jack would go with it, only because of Rendn's words, and because there was no other option, and his dad needed *something*. Jack knew they were grabbing at straws with this machine, but he honestly didn't know what else to do. Nothing else was on offer. His dad was at the end of his tether, *something* needed to be done.

Jack just hoped that whatever was proposed turned out to be positive. Even a dose of Paracetamol would do. Anything that lightened his dad's load a bit. The poor sod couldn't go on as he was. He knew desperation shouldn't drive decision-making, but what else were they to do?

There was another problem that stood out like the proverbial. This machine wasn't made for humans. His dad was inside a machine made for Goddamn lizards. It was a clear compatibility issue. Surely, he wasn't the only one to recognise it. Jack gazed at the machine angrily, and then glanced at Rendn irately. DNA was specific to a particular species, wasn't it? Jack was bewildered, wondering what manner of sideshow he'd stumbled into.

He didn't know what sort of machine it was because no-one had told him. But it definitely wasn't made to treat *humans*, so he wanted him out. His dad looked so small and patently uncomfortable inside the thing. He was lolling about in a foot or so of yellow, smelly fluid. John was just dropped on the bottom, like a stone. Jack felt as if a hand had closed around his throat, as he watched his dad treated like a sardine. Jack turned away from the machine and crossed himself. His dad needed help and attention, but he wasn't sure that this was it. In fact, looking at it, and seeing his dad's reaction, he was pretty certain this was *not* it.

Jack gritted his teeth, and conceded that his dad had to go through with it. That was the worst part. If we couldn't get home, someone had to do *something* for him. Assuming this thing actually *helped,* which was a huge assumption.

Jack thought about grabbing his dad, and making a run for it. But where the *good fuck* would they go? His dad wouldn't last a few days out there. This machine was his *last hurrah*. If Jack lost his dad, he'd just give up, and concede utter defeat to Pietr. Become his pawn.

As his dad's remaining carer, he hoped like hell he was doing the right thing. As a carer, uncertainty could be a killer, he knew that. And he was deeply uncertain. Doing it might kill him, but doing nothing might kill him as well. Maybe this thing might extend his life a bit. The more he thought about it, the more uncertain he became. Genetics were particular to a species...then, how on Earth is this thing supposed to help a *human*? Hope and optimism were great, he thought, but *not* when they're premised on pure desperation.

Before Jack could do anything, the operator of the device lurched back in front of the control panel. He made a few pressing motions and the lid closed and more bright-yellow fluid started pouring in. 'Heated to the temperature of his blood,' the aged operator said. 'It will thicken around him in due course.' He said to Jack, who glanced at his dad, and wished he hadn't.

Jack watched his dad in sheer panic, claw at the lid. John's hands were now clenching and unclenching, as he lay there, and his eyes were wide, showing all of the white's. John was staring at Jack without blinking, and glancing at every lizard in the room. None of them seemed perturbed, or even interested, and did nothing to help him. Jack looked at his dad's twisted face and brought a shaky hand to his forehead, wondering if he should try and intervene. Jack was bereft of opinion or advice.

Jack snapped his eyes to the operator, who raised a paw, cautioning them not to take any action. Jack stifled a loud scoff, while focussing on his dad's panicky, flailing hands.

The fluid shut off with a thud, and Jack had his hands on the dome, pleading for his dad to calm down. There was also a deep noise he could hear, that was absent before. This machine obviously used audio as well as the fluid.

Once the fluid stopped gushing in, so did his dad's clawing. He just lay there, staring wide-eyed at his son, the fluid full to his chin. Jack did his best to look *ho-hum* and failed badly. His dad's lips were pale and quivering, and his eyes were twitching. He wanted to get his dad the hell out of this thing. But equally, he knew this was the last chance. Pietr and Rendn had both said, this machine will help him. So, Jack backed off, knowing that this peculiar machine would rightly or wrongly, be his *last hurrah*.

'He needs to have his feet, *both* of them, touching the cube.' Rendn said firmly. Jack relayed that to his dad. The noise stopped and the fluid lost its viscosity and drained out, and the dome popped open and rose to 180 degrees. Jack immediately retrieved his dad from the machine, with Rendn's help. 'Come here dad,' Jack said, as he lifted him gently out of the pod.

****

'We, er...have the results,' the short, aged Pianif said proudly, after a few minutes. His dad was now out of the device and back on his bed. The fluid on his clothes was removed by a small hand-held device that was attached to the larger machine. It dried wet products by simply touching them. Earth would eat it alive.
The verdict on his dad's health was coming, and Jack could feel the thump of his own heart get more obvious. Jack didn't expect a rave review, and even wondered if he'd get anything at all, given his status as *human*, and the indigenous origin of the quixotic Pianif machine. Genetics meant something, Jack was sure of it.

3

Non-Human Tech

**"Earth is a very small stage in a vast cosmic arena.
— Carl Sagan**

The machine was about 15 feet across and 10 feet high. The whole thing was a perfect circle, and looked totally unlike any human medical devices. Jack reckoned it was more like something recreational. He tried not to let his human bias have a say, but it was hard, simply because he was *human.* Jack couldn't get passed it – he was adamant, *it didn't look medical.* This thing looked great for toddlers to splash around in. But that's it, Jack thought, smothering a gurgle of laughter.

It sat only a few feet in front of them. Internally, the metal alloy was soft like plasticine. It had the visual qualities of a metal but was malleable and soft to the touch. The inside of Pianif space vessels was similar, but not as soft.

Rendn looked up, adjusted his glasses and said, 'this device detects genetic diseases, and is 100% reliable.' The hunched-over creature said. Jack wanted to say that they knew nothing about human genetics, but didn't, instead he swallowed a *humph,* and gave his statement of perfection, the benefit of the doubt. His dad was fairly much comatose, perched in his rather unique wheelchair. Jack was next to him, and patted his unresponsive hand. No device is perfect, he thought, skeptically. He knew that was home-grown bias, but he honestly didn't care anymore. Some Earthly beliefs were sticky, and hard to move.

'Dad?' He asked, and then said it louder and more urgently, when he received no response.

His father slowly roused, and eventually took an elbow and sat higher in the chair, mostly awake.

'I'm, er...okay Jacky. I-I think.'

He said that while massaging his side deeply. *Like hell,* Jack thought, gawking at him. He didn't look or sound okay. He hoped like hell that they had some serious pain relief. Looking at their tech, he was sure that analgesics existed on their world. Hopefully, they could supply something strong, like Opiates, that would hopefully help him.

Jack saw his dad's twisted face, and watched him massaging his back. He felt like screaming. Jack felt beyond powerless. They, as in the Pianif, had to do *something* for him. It couldn't go on. The Pianif put all their faith in this curious machine, but he was far from convinced. It didn't look right, probably because it was so different from Earthly devices. Desperation, drove Jack on. Dad would die in agony unless they did something positive for him...*quickly*. Putting all their money on this machine, seemed wrong.

Because they did what they did, the stress probably caused his dad's relapse. The doctor and the oncologist told mum and Jack not to expose John to stress under any circumstances. Jack was furious, and reckoned it was all the Pianif's fault. He was sure that, left to his own devices, remission would have continued for his dad. The Pianif had a lot to answer for. As far as Jack was concerned, it was totally their fault.

Jack was fired up and ready to rumble. He was scared of these reptiles, but his degree of desperation, emboldened him to the point where he just didn't care about the outcome.

Jack used to worry that aggressive behaviour might get them killed, but right now, he didn't care. The only priority he had, was getting care for his dad. Because if he didn't get painkillers, John would die in agony. And no-one, much less his dad, should go like that. Jack had conceded that his dad would die here – there was no life-extension treatment here, he decided mournfully. It was all based-on genetics, and the Pianif had never come close to humans before this mission. So cross that one off. To Jack and John, it seemed that successful treatment wasn't available on this planet.

Jack glanced at his dad, and thought how unfair this all was. What he would say to his mum, was a question debated during his nightmares. In the daytime, he just blocked it out. He had no answer. If and when he got home, there would be no words for his mum. This ridiculous, unscheduled journey was totally unexplainable.

Rendn, the operator of the device, crept over to them and stood tall, which for him was difficult, because he was unusually short. The Pianif were a tall race, but not Rendn. His deeply carbuncled, moist green skin and split red tongue was in their face. The operator toned directly to Jack. He was already bent over. He looked directly into John's and Jack's eyes, like a frustrated schoolteacher.

Looking at John, he toned loudly, 'AVA has detected cancer in his stomach, liver, kidneys, lungs and bloodstream. It is advanced and has metastasised. Our system is programmed to provide time to death for our species, unfortunately, it will not do so for yours.' Rendn glanced grimly at the control panel, and clearly expected more.

'It is telling me that John's time of death has already passed, which is clearly not correct.' Rendn looked grim, then his face broke into a wide smile, which seemed odd, given the circumstances. Jack chastened himself because he expected Rendn to act more like a human.

At least they knew what cancer was, and by the sound of it, they were intimate with the disease. Jack was pleased – at least some decent pain killers could be expected. Perhaps some Opiates might even eventuate, Jack hoped. Ease his dad's suffering. Jack managed a brittle smile. That was better than nothing.

Jack was going to mention the human genome. Because surely that was central to any treatment. But so far, he hadn't found an opportunity. He wondered if human DNA had been collected during the current mission? Maybe one of the devices they called "scanners" was the vehicle?

'*Fuck*,' John blurted, knowing for certain now, that cancer had invaded some of his organs...*again*. He thought of his future in this non-human place, and almost retched. John knew he needed help, dumping it all on Jacky was so unfair. He glanced at his son, and swallowed the despair that rose in his throat. This mob would be zero help. They were clearly focussed on their own list of priorities. Which were very different from Jack and John's. John reckoned his poor health, was just an inconvenience. Pietr knew what he wanted, and it *wasn't* related to his dad's illness.

Rendn squinted at Jack who turned to him. Jack brought a shaky hand to his forehead and spoke with a voice choked with tears. So much for being determined and unflinching, he thought. Jack was close to breaking point, and getting closer, everytime he looked at his ailing dad. Or thought about his poor old mourning mum back on Earth.

Jack glanced heatedly at Pietr, his entire face twitching nervously. His skin was flushed and sweat was pouring off him. Everyone knew that his dad had active, life-threatening cancer. For the Pianif, there was nowhere to hide now. They *knew* he was deathly ill. Jack was sweating and ready to explode. He could take their indifference *no more*.

Jack ran up to Pietr. '*Y-You have to take us h-home*.' Jack pleaded aggressively, sobbing with terror, thinking his dad could keel over and die at any second, on *his* watch. '*Please...please*,' he begged, crying openly, literally praying to this aggressive, indifferent lizard.

Jack could see that his dad needed chemo, radiation...and a shitload of good wishes, to try and slow down the cancerous onslaught which had again enslaved his body. The disease had returned, probably because of the stress afflicted by the Pianif. They were seemingly doing their very best to kill him.

Jack felt like swearing at Pietr, but instead, looked aggressively at him, thinking irately, "*YOU people are responsible*." He was the only one who could help them, so he tried to remain cool, taking the deepest of breaths.

Pietr waved Jack away, in response to his demand to be taken back to Earth. He would have none of it. His prime directive took precedence. He would do what he could to ameliorate whatever obstacles came his and their way, but the prime directive took priority. His commitment to the Ruling Council remained.

Jack let out an uncontrollable sob, and clenched his jaw to hold it in. What could he do? They were held captive by seven-foot reptiles who were built like NFL players. Jack was certain they couldn't overpower them, which left negotiation, as the only hope of getting home. And Pietr had just confirmed that he refused to even consider it.

Jack had nowhere to go, and he knew it. He felt powerless and useless, literally wrapped tight in a feeling of utter futility. His dad was dying, and he was surrounded by callous and hideous non-humans, on a planet that was all theirs. Appallingly, nothing in this hospital, or on this planet, was remotely *human*.

He knew what it meant – his dad was deathly ill and now distinctly yellow and, in some light, a bit green. He was doomed to die from an uncontrollable terminal disease, and stuck light years from home. Could it possibly get *any worse?* Jack wondered morosely. He glowered at Pietr and knew he may as well address a brick wall. His unemotional black eyes were a garish stop-sign.

Jack watched his ailing dad, and was terrified for his future, and then he thought of his poor mum, back on Earth. Jack's face twisted with anguish, and he broke down, bending over and crying in a rush of grief and anger. There was literally no-one to help him. The nearest human was light years away. No-one here *wanted* to do anything – their priorities were elsewhere. Jack had never, *ever* been so forlorn.

They were the only two humans on the entire planet – and that's how he felt. Isolated, *secluded,* on a lonely Godforsaken rock. Like being the only two people on a remote, uncharted island, with everything indigenous wanting to injure or kill them. Jack felt like sitting on the ground, and refusing to move like a rock. But then, who would look after his dad? Circumstances had him manacled.

The operator turned to look at Pietr, then swivelled back to John, who was hunched over, yellow everywhere, and whimpering like an injured puppy. Jack could do little, apart from hold and rub his hand. His dad's back, near his waist, had erupted with pain, so doing anything else only made it worse. Jack knew that now had to be the time. If the Pianif were going to offer anything, it had to be now. Or it'd be too late. His dad would soon slip into an irreversible coma. John's eyes were burning under tightly shut eyes. Jack eyed his dad gravely, and saw how close he was.

The operator glanced at Pietr and he nodded back at him. Rendn could see that Jack was beyond distraught, so, Rendn toned, 'the machine can *assist* you as well my friend. It has two modes. 'Identify' *and* 'Rectify'.' Jack straightened, and his eyes lit up. *Surely not.* It was way too much to hope for. Advanced race was one thing, but this would put them in the realm of the Gods.

Jack steeled himself, not to get his hopes up. He remained deeply skeptical. By Rectify, it might mean applying pain relief, which would still be useful, if it was opium-based. *Whatever*, it was probably worth trying. They'd come this far.

If his dad was definitely stuck on this planet, which they appeared to be, it was worth doing. John couldn't go on like he was. Something *had* to give, and it looked like it was about to. Hopefully, his mum would agree, Jack thought miserably.

If the device proved one thing, it was that *time* was definitely not on their side. The operator and two other Pianif, grabbed his dad from his chair, and he screamed in pain, all the way to the machine. They placed him carefully in the bottom of the machine, to lie down face up, still moaning and groaning pitiably. Everytime he was touched, his dad would scream in pain. Clearly, the cancer and the pain, had spread almost everywhere. Jack watched on, drumming his hands in panic, once again, not sure whether to intervene or not. Jack pulled back, and let it run its course, relying on Rendn's words.

The operator ambled slowly back to the control panel. Before he did anything, he said to his dad forebodingly, 'this time, it will be a little more uncomfortable.' John widened his eyes and clenched his toes, and tried to prepare for what was to come. He had no idea what this machine was, or even what he was doing in it. It was supposed to help him, that's all he knew. He couldn't go on like he was, so, *bring it on,* he thought desperately. But now, he second-guessed that *gung-ho* approach, but stayed inside anyway, in sheer desperation.

Jack looked like he'd seen the devil himself. 'W-What do you mean, "u-uncomfortable"? Jack said anxiously, glancing down at his poor dad, who's eyes were wide-open and questioning.
'Wait...you will find out...it's not an invasive procedure.' The operator said casually. He put his hand up to Jack, to mean, *wait*. Jack was incensed by the hand, and walked over to the machine anyway, seriously considering pulling him out of the machine. His dad had endured huge amounts of pain just getting in. Pulling him out would hurt just as much, so Jack reluctantly decided not to do it. Telling Rendn and Pietr to go *fuck themselves* would be nice, but not at the expense of his dad.

'John, this time you must hold the cube with both hands and face upward toward the dome. The fluid will enter the machine from below and will cover your body entirely, and thicken. While this momentary procedure takes place, you will need to hold your breath for 20 seconds. The fluid will temporarily thicken around you.'

Jack looked at his dad seriously, frowned, and gaped incredulously. '*He's over 60, and seriously ill.*' He gawked at the operator skeptically, and then turned and did the same with Pietr. Jack was incredulous, and got no response from anyone, throwing his hands in the air and walking over to his dad, lying in the machine.

'Piece of piss Jacky,' John said to Jack.

Jack peered at his dad, and was incredulous. 'Dad...what are we doing? You might drown or even suffocate in this thing. There is no-one that is going to judge you, if you want to come out. You might die in this crazy thing. What would *mum* say?'

'T-That's exactly it, Jacky, I think she'd say, g-go for it. *Do it.* And don't forget what Rendn said. According to the makers of this machine, the advancement of the cancer, means goodnight-time is only a stone's throw away. Anything it can do to slow the damn thing down, or supply pain relief, has gotta be good, doesn't it?' John looked up at his son with an expression of pained tolerance, asking for help. John knew he was on his last legs.

'Yeah...I suppose,' Jack said hesitantly, still deeply unsure. 'But this thing right here is a total unknown. It might work for them...but for us, I'm not sure about it. *It could kill you dad.* Our

DNA is slightly different to theirs. Therefore, genome diseases should vary.' Jack looked at his dad with huge, teary eyes. He didn't want his dad to risk his life on a bad bet. This thing before them was a total mystery. Both of them knew there was nothing close to it, on Earth. So, it probably favoured the reptilian form of life. Jack saw the sense in that. He frowned at the machine grimly, and just didn't like the look of it.

'The fact that the Pianif want us to go through with it, shouldn't be taken as a sign of confidence dad. Xeno-psychology is a totally closed book. Who knows how they think? *Common-sense* may be a human-thing, who knows? His dad was ill, no doubt, but betting on a longshot is *never* warranted, when it came to your health. Jack knew his mum would agree. She had several out-there theories on common-sense. Krissy thought some humans, especially politicians, just lacked it. So, was this *thing* worth it? Because it was all that was available? Jack looked at his dad, and realised that it might not be his decision to make.

'Jacky, I'm not sure that you've noticed, but the cancer needs to be slowed down.' His dad's voice had lost its lightness and gained some dark sarcasm. 'Without treatment,' he croaked, 'I'm a goner. So, I say, *do it*. Anything is better than nothing.' With that, he screamed in pain and turned around, and looked down at the yellow fluid.

Jack came closer to his dad and whispered in his ear. '*Not here dad...I cannot lose you here*. This is a different planet, with tech that's made for *them...for reptiles*, not for humans. Who knows what this thing will do to a human. I am your son, and your remaining carer. And I say *no*; the risk is too big. I need to emphasise....to *re-demand*, that they take us back to Earth.' Jack's mouth was clamped, to imprison a sob. He would use the mum-card again, if he needed to, and he reckoned he did.

'That is what mum would say.' Jack said morosely. 'I can't lose you here, dad,' he said again. 'Simple as that.' Tears blinded his eyes and choked his voice. He began crying bitterly, looking at his dad in this strange, circular alien contraption that purported to help him.

Jack shook his head and closed his eyes, unsure how they got into this insane position. What had started as a weekend away to celebrate his status as a "cancer survivor" took a very odd and dark turn indeed.

'Well Krissy *isn't* here,' John started, 'and I cannot go on without some sort of help. The pain is too much, Jacky,' his voice faltered, then cracked, as did his face, which fell into a broken pit of anguish. John closed his eyes, and tried to stifle the sobs that threatened to overwhelm him. Tears poured down his cheeks. John knew he was at the precipice of darkness. It was too much for him to face unmedicated. John looked at his son with narrowed eyes, that were burning with pain.

'I need *something Jacky*. Help me, the pain is too much.' John's face turned distinctly darker and greener. His hands dropped to his lap. 'I -I agree with everything you've said,' John croaked. 'But it's a chance I *have* to take. *I want to take.* Holding my breath will be difficult, but so is being boxed inside this thing.' His voice was a hiss now. 'I reckon we gotta hope that this does something positive. Even though it's quick, I don't have time to get back to Earth anyway.' John stared vacantly over Jack's shoulder. His dad was going to try this thing, irrespective of Jack's decision or indecision. He'd tired of the constant blinding pain. This thing he had was eating him alive.

Jack exhaled loudly. 'Okay...fine dad, we do it...and hope for the best. But, if this *fuck's* up...' Jack stopped talking, knowing where he was heading. 'Anyway, there is no time to do anything else...right?' His dad wasn't getting out of the machine for anyone. John's money was on the machine, whether or not it was a good play. His dad was prepared to bet with his life, because he'd reached his tipping-point with the pain...which had become white-hot agony, that now touched most parts of his body.

'Right.' John said. He positioned himself in the pod, facing up and holding the cube with both hands, like he was told. Jack showed a thumb to the spindly operator, and to Pietr, and the dome closed. Jack broke down, crying dismally, while holding onto the side of the machine. The sight of his dad in this alien thing, hoping against hope, and the turbulent yellow fluid, was too much for Jack to handle. He doubled over and lost all control, crying hysterically for his dad, who was now surrounded by yellow fluid. For Jack, hope was gone, replaced by faith.

The dome closed with a click, and the fluid rushed in from the bottom, as promised. Jack knew the fluid was blood-temperature, so the temperature-shock was minimal. It was mainly the claustrophobic effect once the dome was shut and the fluid crystallised. He knew it would be nothing short of horrific to be under all that foul fluid and have it thicken around you. Jack glanced at his dad - severe pain had etched deep lines in his face. Jack made the sign of the cross on his chest, and crossed everything he could.

Jack watched him, panic-stricken, and glanced at the operator for hope, and he showed Jack a casual thumb.

Easy for him, Jack reckoned, furiously. He was terrified for his dad, and fully expected him to die right there, in front of him. *And Rendn shows me a thumb.* Jack looked back, and he still had his stupid thumb in the air. *Seriously,* what was wrong with him? Confidence was one thing, but with his dad's life in on the line, some concern would be nice. Rendn continued to look like a carny, overseeing some scary carnival ride, while John kept thrashing around in sheer panic.

Thankfully, the fluid was now thin, and draining from the machine. His dad had survived the hardest part. He was saturated and bedraggled, and looked as though he'd been tormented by Satan himself. But incredibly, he was okay.

'Get him out.' Jack demanded loudly. The poor sod looked tiny, cold and dishevelled inside the Godforsaken machine. Three creatures helped him out and ran the "dryer" over him. He was then deposited back in his chair with a thin sheet over him.
Jack looked straight at him, then up and down, to check him out, and his dad suddenly flashed a wide toothy grin at him. 'I feel good Jacky,' John said upbeat... no pain anywhere. The pain in my back and side has just... gone.' He continued to smile curiously.

'Probably the result of what was essentially, a warm bath, dad.' Jack said, thinking, massive Placebo effect. Jack fussed over his dad to make sure he was truly okay. John's eyes narrowed, and he gave his son a rather surly look.

'I'm *fine* Jacky...just back off a bit.' he said loudly, hoping that Jack would stop worrying and fussing so much. He had to admit, he liked it, but Jacky needed to slow down...to relax. Who knows how long this journey would go on for? When so many of his friends were reporting a worsening of their relationships with the kids, his experience was quite the opposite. Jacky was a kid among kids. He still loved his parents and continued to live with them. Probably because of his illness, he thought. Although, Jacky and he had always been close. From reading, and telling stories at bedtime to, introducing him to Mario, Luigi and videogames generally. From there, it was always on the up, taking him to soccer and footy games with school, and then the local club. And now, the pièce de résistance, taken by non-humans, together. What a fucking story. A total mashup, he reckoned. No-one on Earth would believe it. Jack recounted it in his head, and agreed, it sounded like a bullshit story of science fiction.

***

After another "swim" in the pod ten minutes later, John waited for the results, from the rather avant-garde machine, for which there was no parallel on Earth. Probably suits their genetics, he reckoned. Which would make it incompatible for humans. *Christ*, Jack thought, totally exasperated, running his hand through his hair. Maybe genetics aren't important, but that was against everything that Jack knew. For cancer, genetics were everything, weren't they? He had argued himself into a shoelace bow.

The operator came out from behind the control panel of the device, and looked John squarely in the eyes, like the reptilian version of Mister McGoo. He seemed to be smiling, but Jack doubted that was the correct emotion. He didn't seem to be a happy being, probably related to his job, he thought. Intense, certainly - happy, no.

'The news is good.' Rendn toned drolly, looking rather disinterested, with his large black eyes and orange pupils. They were hidden behind thick reading glasses, that were in his dad's face. Jack looked at his dad and shrugged, waiting for this supposed "good news."

'All traces of the cancer have been removed,' Rendn toned evenly. 'You are completely cured, John. The machine has treated you like a Pianif, and you have responded similarly, as we expected.'

Jack glanced quickly at Pietr and he nodded coldly. It was clearly no shock to him, as a Pianif - he'd seen it many times before, and he was therefore rather *hum-drum* about it. Notwithstanding, it was a stunning moment for the humans. Jack was speechless. He turned his head rapidly, and gazed at his dad, eyes bulging, and taking a step backward. '*W-What?*' He stammered in disbelief.

Back on Earth, millions died each year from exactly what John had, and Jack knew it. Cancer had killed a billion humans in recent years. Somehow, *he'd* beaten the odds, which were vanishingly small. No-one defeated cancer. It was a chest-beating, bicep-crushing, son-of-a-bitch, that few on Earth shrugged off. Most simply died.

To defeat it permanently, all John had to do was visit another planet. Some people will go a long way for good medical help, but Jack conceded happily that what they'd achieved was plainly ridiculous. He made the sign of the cross on his chest again. Jack looked back at his dad who was beaming, and realised that somehow, he'd been blessed with a miracle.

On Earth, he would have been terminal, and soon enough dead, but here, on this planet, they had the understanding and the skill to cure cancer. So, you could live your life, rather than become an unfortunate statistic. And the most stunning part, *no-one here was surprised*. The Pianif, *incredibly*, took it in their stride.

Jack's eyes bloated, and filled with tears, at the astounding realisation that his dad had been miraculously cured of something that should in all probability, have *killed* him. Being kidnapped was bad, but this was *unbelievably, amazingly* good. Jack felt like cheering at the top of his voice, and dancing. Jack was so happy for his dad. He desperately wanted it to be true, but there was something sharp that was digging into his brain. He refused to acknowledge the doubt, and bathed in his dad's newfound health.

Jack started moving drunkenly, falling at the feet of the operator, overwhelmed with emotion. '*Thank you...thankyou...y-you're sure?*' Jack asked, suddenly, questioning him, biting the inside of his cheek. He knew, if it was true, it was a genuine, untainted *miracle*. Curing advanced cancer was impossible, based on what he knew. On Earth, terminal cancer was just that. Here, it was like the common cold. Walk in, get cured. Jack stared at John incredulously, with huge, tear-filled eyes, walked closer and hugged him tight, the tears coursing down their cheeks. Incredibly, the Pianif barely acknowledged it.

'You're sure? Dad is cured. Jack croaked to Rendn.

'100% certain Jack. Your father is cancer-free.'

John turned his head, and gazed at Jack with brimming eyes, smiling brokenly. Then he closed his eyes and grinned to himself. '*Who would have thought?* Jacky,' John purred. 'What we thought was a threat to kill me, has, er...cured me. They don't seem to realise how extraordinary and ground-breaking it is,' John gazed back at Rendn curiously, who stared vacantly back. Jack shrugged, and smiled, ear to ear at his dad. Cancer was a death sentence when you had it like John did. But he had escaped the hangman's noose by a stone's throw, and Rendn effectively shrugged his shoulders and yelled, '*next.*'

Jack flashed a grin at his dad and his eyes smiled. None of the humans could truly believe it. The news was too good to be true, *surely*? Cancer had been a problem ever since they left, now it had apparently been magically spirited from his body. Could they believe it? Jack was jubilant, but suspicious.

John put both arms above his head and shouted, '*I'm back baby.*' Jack clapped his dad on the back, while Pietr and Rendn looked on, curious and mystified. Such celebrations were brand-new to them.

The Pianif treated the incredible news with condescension. As though it was a daily, *expected* outcome. On Pianif it may be. But for humans, it was nothing short of staggering. On Earth, cancer couldn't be cured, and killed millions of humans. John wished the Pianif could get their heads around the horror on Earth. Just the mention of the word can bring humans to tears. But on Pianif, it was in the same basket as the common cold.

Jack thought of all the doctors, nurses, hospitals, medical checks, treatments and appointments, that were now finally and permanently behind them. *Somehow*, his dad had beaten the infinitesimally small odds, courtesy of advanced tech, developed by non-humans. Jack felt like roaring with pleasure, but sensed the pull of uncertainty. But they were *reptiles*, *lizards*...everything he hoped for, was dripping with craven human bias. To Jack, it seemed so unlikely. He needed faith in Arthur C Clarke.

Jack knew he had to get with the program of the Universe. Humans could treat cancer, maybe slow it down, but the Pianif could cure it, lock, stock and barrel. And they could do it quickly and easily. *In a finger-snap.*

Jack felt dizzy, as he pondered how many ways it would change medical care on Earth. How much misery and suffering could be avoided. Jack's mum's mum had died of breast cancer that had metastasized and lodged in her ovaries. She died young, and suffered badly before the end came, before modern drugs, according to Krissy. She wished she could have helped her more, and was heartbroken when she finally died.

This tech - how many human lives would it save? Lives cut short, would suddenly get back on track. Families broken today, could be re-formed tomorrow. His brain was whirling and spinning. *My God*, he thought with awe, Earth needed it so badly. He imagined curing all the poor sods back on Earth.

There were millions of them. Chemo and radiation wouldn't be required. They would instantly be superseded. It would be straight to cure. Too good to be true, *surely*? Jack reckoned disbelievingly. He shook his head grimly, and remembered the long sorrowful lines of people waiting for chemotherapy at his local hospital. Well, if this tech landed, those long, sad lines wouldn't exist. *Period*.

* * *

Jack and John followed the line of creatures to an elevator, or their version of one. Pietr pressed a button with strange markings on it. Eventually, the doors to a car opened. But rather than sliding apart, this door was singular, and rolled open like a garage-door. Inside was a large car with white metal seats in the rear, and standing room at the front. They all piled in to the seats, and the standing room. The elevator went down rapidly and stopped gently. The door opened from the top, down and revealed the base of the great pyramid behind them, red ground, in front of them and similar though smaller structures appeared in front of them, for as far as they could see to the horizon.

All of them moved toward an object in the distance that looked like a glinting, bone-white structure, shaped like an egg. Jack watched his dad in the wheelchair, and was pleased to see him *not* holding his back and rubbing his side. His face, normally twisted with pain, was smiling, and gawking around curiously. Taking in the strange sights of a new planet.

The smile on his face was ear to ear. '*YES*,' Jack blurted jubilantly. He thought his dad was going to die in this distant alien place, which would have been very ugly indeed. Instead, he was unexpectantly and astonishingly *cured*. Something had finally, *finally*, gone very right.

Jack was super-relieved, and very thankful. He wondered what he would have done if the machine *wasn't* successful. Jack scratched his chin and the top of his head, and had no answer. Without his dad, he'd have no link to home. Jack tried not to stew on it, or dissect it. He knew what massive distress lay in that direction.

'How're you going dad?' Jack asked happily, seeing the smile on his face, and pretty much knowing the answer.

'Unbelievably good Jacky - the pain has just...g-gone.'

'I can't help feeling it's just a placebo effect dad. I hope not, but things that seem too good to be true, normally are. If you start feeling pain, you tell me straight away, right?'

'Of course, Jacky...I will. I will. You'll be the first to know.'

'To think they've nutted out a cure to cancer. It's tough to believe, especially in a crazy machine like that.' Jack was stunned, but so far happy. 'At least we've got something positive from this whole sorry story dad.'

Jack watched his dad closely, but he also took notice of what they were walking over. It was sort of like a road, but it was ruby red in colour and had a different, rougher texture, compared to either concrete or bitumen on Earth. Pietr looked at Jack curiously, because he was kicking at it, to see how slippery it was.

Standing close with an obvious smile, Pietr toned proudly, 'our roads are filled with plant sterols and micro-processed plastic. It absorbs carbon dioxide when it cures. If used in your USA alone, for new buildings and upgraded or repaired roads, it will absorb all of Earth's excess carbon in the atmosphere, six giga-tonnes of carbon-dioxide. And remove all your waste plastic – *forever*.' Pietr stood to his full height of seven feet and had a gleam in his black eyes. He knew how important this was to Earth. It could literally save the planet from the effects of climate-change, and he knew it.

Pietr could sense their disbelief and bewilderment. 'We have your internet remember?' Pietr toned. Having heard his words, Jack stumbled backward a couple of steps and stared at Pietr with wide eyes. He was floored by the revelation of this concrete. And what it could do. Jack was blown away. He knew immediately what it'd mean to Earth. Jack saw stars, rich rainbows, black and white spots and globules of stunning colour, before his eyes. It'd mean...incredibly, no more *climate-change*...which governments globally were currently plagued by. Unbelievably, on this planet, was the answer to Earth's primary woes.

Pietr knew they'd both love the concrete, because he had the human internet, and knew what a horrendous and convoluted problem it was. Pietr realised that Earth was wrestling with climate-change, and fairly much losing the battle. These carbon-fixing roads would change the scales in human favour. It'd cure Earth's climate-change just like *that*. Excess carbon would be permanently fixed. Earth would be beholden to Pianif, and he knew it.

Jack's mind was gyrating and filling with brilliant white light that permeated his entire body. These non-humans were like magicians and conjurers. He and his dad had been on their world for a couple of hours and were already gobsmacked by their incredible abilities, and what they took for granted. The Pianif could amazingly, cure cancer, and had an off-the-shelf remedy for climate-change. People had spoken about the likelihood of wondrous tech being "out there." But to actually come into contact with it, was nothing short of stupefying.

Those two things from Pianif were stunning by themselves, but were treated as *ho-hum* by the Pianif. Earth's biggest issues, that threatened death to the globe, were incredibly, cured by the Pianif with pure scientific knowledge. Different planets – different abilities.

But Jack knew that wasn't all - they could also fly FTL, and understood anti-gravity and probably zero-point energy. And their houses boasted extra dimensions. This civilisation was nothing short of epic. Earth was far outpaced by a race of reptiles. Jack felt like screaming in frustration. All those wars back on Earth, if you look on the internet, most say they were good for an evolving race. Jack thought it was odd when he read it. Now he knew for sure. The Pianif are only as old as humanity. And look where they are...curing cancer and climate-change. Regrettably, despite what the internet says, wars and crime have held humanity back.

Imagine Earth, similarly endowed, Jack thought, awestruck, gazing into the sky with eyes stretched to their fullest. He was genuinely stunned by what he'd seen, and heard about. Earth would eat these things up, like candy to a ravenous child. Their tech would be inhaled like air. New industries would rip into being, the world over, many wondering where it had been all this time. Earth would become a different planet.

Jack gawked at his dad elatedly, wanting to share this incredible moment with him - and found him slumped to the side of his chair, staring down at his hands with a vacant expression. He looked exhausted, or depressed...the *opposite* of where he should be at. *WTF?*

'*Fuck me...what's wrong dad?*' He said terrified, wondering why he wasn't similarly cocka hoop. He'd just been cured of a fatal disease. He should be up and about. Yet, looking at him, he was on a major downer. His dad was slumped all the way to the left, with his eyes half-closed. Jack poked him for signs of life.

John looked up at his son, eyes half open, and smiled weakly. In a hollow, mono-tone voice, he said, 'nothing's wrong Jacky, I was just, um, thinking of mum. In a faraway voice, he said, 'she thinks we're dead, you know. Dead...and gone.' John wiped at his nose, and spoke like he was dying for real. Clearly, he'd been sobbing off and on for some time. His mum's appalling situation played hard on his mind. Jack looked at his twisted and deeply lined face, and felt the sob in his own throat. If he hadn't clenched his mouth, out it would've come, for his dad to hear. For his dad's benefit, all shows of emotion were to be avoided. Because they would destroy his dad for hours.

Jack thought about his mum all the time, magnify that by 10 and you had John, he reckoned, seeing the black circles under his dad's eyes. Which weren't due to sickness, but to constant worry and grief. Jack looked at his dad and knew he had to keep it positive. Otherwise, surrounded by non-humans, it would devolve into something intolerable. For both of them. His dad had been cured, but his main worry, his *major* source of misery, still remained.

'Won't she be surprised when we get home,' Jack said upbeat. His dad looked up at him incredulously, with tears in his eyes. 'I don't think they have any intentions like that.' John covered his face and turned away from his son. 'Going home would be nice, but I don't think that's in their playbook, Jacky. We can kid ourselves, or accept the truth,' John said sombrely.

Jack gazed at his dad disbelievingly, and shook his head. He felt like grabbing his dad and shaking some sense into him. '*They cured you dad.*' He blurted, incredulously, like a cannon-shot. 'You have to give them credit for that. They wouldn't bother curing you, just to off you.' His voice was loud and heavy with irony. As soon as he said it, he knew he might be wrong. They might have cured his dad, just to *shut us both up.* He'd keep that to himself though.

'We'll keep asking to go home dad, pushing and demanding, and we'll see how we go,' Jack said firmly. 'They wouldn't cure you, and then kill us. Nup...*no way.*' He'd convinced himself. 'I reckon we're on pretty solid ground dad.' Jack said, with his fingers crossed behind his back. He had to keep it positive, even if he wasn't fully onboard.

Jack walked into the interior chamber of the triangular ship. He thought it was intriguing how it was sharply triangular on the outside, but purely circular inside. It didn't seem to make sense from an Earthly perspective. Jack wondered if the Pianif did this with their understanding of extra dimensions? He didn't have a clue, but he knew it was something humans didn't have, or understand.

His dad, in the wheelchair, was rolled up the silver-tongue-like entrance by two of the creatures, and was taken into the craft proper. Jack and his dad were together again, one in a wheelchair, and one sitting casually on a stretcher.

Being cured of cancer was hard for either to get their heads around. Cancer was so complex and insidious, and that yellow fluid that smelt like antiseptic. The humans were stumped. It all seemed too incredible, and ridiculous for words.

To Jack, it was just sad. That one world should suffer, and another doesn't. It was nothing short of a travesty. *Cie la vie*, Jack supposed, after thinking about it. The Universe was probably like that. Only the truly smart, with alpine technology, prosper.

Pietr ambled up and came close, smelling of cloves, and appearing ready to tone. He stood tall and looked directly into their eyes, resembling an effigy from their darkest nightmare. He gestured to the two creatures who stood at their side, guarding them. The two guards deliberately took two steps backward.

The noise was headache loud between their ears, and with it for the first time came colour, which danced formlessly before Jack's eyes. It was blue and green, like the ocean. The colours took the form of globules and splotches, and grew in size when the words came.

'We intend to take you both to meet our Ruling Council.' Pietr said loudly. 'This is what we agreed to do for them.' He flourished his arm and paw at Jack and John, who stared vacantly, captivated by the moving colour before their eyes.

Aboard the craft and sitting down, Pietr filled them with voice once again. 'We didn't arrive near you on Earth by accident,' Pietr said loudly. 'We were there primarily to collect Molybdenum. Then it was realised that a far greater resource was on offer. *You,*' he pronounced loudly.

'We promised the Ruling Council, that we would bring examples of intelligence back to Pianif. They were eager to meet you. So, we gathered two specimens. You have nothing to fear from them. They do not mean you any harm. They have observed your beautiful planet, curiously. Simple contact is all they seek.' With that, Pietr sat down on one of the seats near a window.

Jack could see intersecting red roads, and dark vegetation through the window nearest him. Then they went almost instantaneously higher in the sky, where below him, all he could see was a bank of yellowy clouds. There was no inertia, or feeling of movement at all, but clearly, they had shot upward in the opaque atmosphere. Below them, the clouds parted, and Jack spied a nest of distinctly pyramidal structures, below. The craft banked, and they started descending.

The structures on this planet were all polygons, required to satisfy a biological need. They were totally unlike the living and working structures on Earth, which tended to be multi-form buildings and Earthly houses. The Pianif produced the precise opposite. A sameness...*omni-tecture*, Jack thought curiously. He'd expected much to be different on a different planet, produced by a different species. But houses and buildings, not so much. *Live and learn*, he supposed. The contrasts went further and deeper than he thought.

All the buildings they'd seen on Pianif were isosceles triangles...tall, stretched pyramids with three or four triangular faces. The nest of pyramids, Jack could see from the craft, were surrounded by landscape like New York back home. Nests of pyramids surrounded by tall grey trees, pale paths and black plants. This planet seemed highly planned, much more so than Earth. Whether these were primary or secondary structures though, who knew?

Inside an outer square of vegetation, were large pyramids, analogous to a planned city, on Earth, Jack thought. Polygon-houses surrounded them, much like suburbs on Earth, with one very in your face difference. Sameness or uniformity. Everything was three or four-sided pyramids – even the houses. There wasn't the intermingling of different architectural styles. Some were short and simple - some were taller and some were multiples. Large structures, that were essentially joined pyramids, many ringed by beautiful ornate fences. But *all* were three-or four-sided polygons.

Jack watched the planet below, as their vessel went higher in the sky. They were flying over glowing blue ocean and then dark vegetated land. It looked like a humid regime, as they passed over vast tracts of dense, twisted black rainforest that looked like South America, apart from the colour.

A mighty river, like a huge snake, wound its way over the landscape to empty its contents into the glowing ocean. South of their current position and looming larger, was a huge nest of tetrahedra. Their Ruling Council must be close at hand, Jack thought.

This place was nothing like Earth, Jack reckoned. The same looking three or four pointed houses were everywhere, on different continents and on small islands. Jack and his dad were surrounded by pyramids, and triggered Jack to ponder Egypt and Giza...and he let his mind wander. Afterall, the Egyptians had tools that could barely cut wood, and some of the stone blocks weighed over 200 tonnes. Jack was convinced that the Egyptians had help. Their technology simply wasn't advanced enough. Jack wondered reverently – did the pyramids on Pianif have a relationship with Giza?

Jack tried not to think about his mum, but when he did, the tears weren't far away. The gulf of space and time between them was overwhelming. The need to get home was growing in intensity. It was top of mind for both of them. John had almost run out of tears, crying himself to sleep almost every night, since they'd been ripped away. Jack could hear him, and wasn't far away, himself.

Jack thought about his mum, and her being on Earth, and being totally in the dark about their location. All she'd know was that we'd vanished into thin air. No-one would find a trace, FBI, private investigators, CIA. *Poof...we'd gone.* Pacing around the house, she'd wait for the knock at the door, or the squelch of tires on the gravel. Which would never, *ever* come. Poor mum, he thought agonizingly, bent over and nearly vomiting with grief. She would be powerless, and probably never recover. PTSD, he reckoned, her experience would be similar to being in an active war zone. It was all the Pianif's fault.

Krissy had been through the wringer with John's illness. She had visited John in hospital every day, with Jack, for four months straight, when he was struggling with cancer. They were on a first name basis with all of the staff. Krissy was even friends with some of the bloody cleaners. Her old life was on hold, while she tended to him. Now *this.*

After discharge, at home, his mum fussed and worried about his every move. To say her current loneliness was undeserved, was an unholy understatement. John prayed for a reunion every day. He was desperately worried about how late they'd be, and what it would do to his wife's beautiful heart.

The best they could hope for, was to cooperate with these creatures, and hope that they eventually did the right thing with them. Which would be, to take them back to Earth. It didn't take long to get *here*, so the reverse should apply.

If Jack knew more about the Pianif psyche, he could come to a more definitive conclusion. Nothing he'd learned so far, put that thinking out of the question. The Pianif seemed concerned about his and his dad's well-being, but that might have only been related to our ability to meet their Ruling Council. Again, xeno-psychology? Contact with another species had not yet happened, so humans knew nothing. All we had was humanity. We were our only sound-board. The rest was just guess-work.

His dad's cancer pain was one thing, but her's was pain of a different sort, but just as harrowing. Both physical and psychological pain could be debilitating and excruciating. But only one sort was eased with analgesics. Jack and his dad knew that reunion was the *only* solution.

The Pianif probably didn't realise that they were dealing with an emotion-laden species like humanity. They had most of our internet, so they should have known who and what we were. They saw that we had engaged in warfare, nearly 8,000 times and had a crime rate that was far higher and more serious than theirs. Jack reckoned you didn't need much intelligence to work it out.

Maybe, the Pianif just didn't care about the consequences of their actions. *It was what it was*. Krissy would beg to differ. It was completely life-changing, for her. She would never be the same again. Jack and John too. Life would be *very* different, now, and in the future. Perhaps the Pianif weren't wired that way, so empathy was absent. They did what suited them, everyone else could take a number.

They were now approaching an indent in the tallest and brightest, golden pyramid, in their egg-shaped craft. From where Jack was sitting, and the trajectory of their flight-path, it looked like the craft was going to land somewhere on the indentation. The vessel sat down lightly as expected, and there was renewed activity on-board. Jack reckoned the craft should roll once it landed, but it didn't. After setting down, balance was firm and immediate. Pianif were walking quickly everywhere in front of them. Getting ready to de-board, apparently.

Two creatures stood up from their chairs around the outside of the craft and slowly approached his dad. Without even looking at either of them, they grabbed his dad's wheelchair and rolled him out of the vessel, and straight into a brown corridor. This corridor was as large as a train tunnel but was illuminated like it received direct starlight. It seemed to be lined with dark-brown, polished wood that showed grain and large knots. It was at least thirty above their heads, which made Jack wonder what it was made for? Just walking through it, seemed a waste, and they didn't appear to be that sort of species. Maybe it was for emergencies? Jack put that on ice, and continued to follow the line of creatures.

Jack was wondering nervously about their destination. Was it to meet their Ruling Council, or something else less pleasant? His heart started beating loudly in his ears, as they plodded onward. Here in crazy town, *anything* was possible, Jack thought fearfully. In this place, he felt like their next step could be their last.

After they walked about 200 metres up the same large corridor, they turned immediate right, and hit a part of the wall that looked no different from the rest. The line of creatures moved easily through the wall, and the humans tentatively followed, hoping the wall treated them the same as the Pianif. After pushing through the sticky wall, they found themselves in a rather small room that was coloured light-blue, and the wood was replaced by something resembling metal. It had a single picture of a tall, golden pyramid hanging on the wall. It seemed to be a painting, and not a photo, and the subject looked like the building they were currently residing in.

All the creatures left through the wall behind them, so Jack and his dad were by themselves in the small room. It seemed to amplify every sound they made. Jack looked squarely at his dad, and was gratified by his rosy, healthy colour.

'Not a thing to sit on,' Jack said, curling his lip and wrinkling his nose, wondering why they'd been deposited here. He hoped they would meet their rulers, soon enough, get it over with. John looked at Jack caustically. 'Yeah, but remember what Pietr showed us? What looks mundane, ain't necessarily so.' Jack smiled and nodded at his dad. He was right. The Pianif's ability to muck around with dimensions, transformed a boring room into something quite incredible. The same probably applied to this one. Potentially, it hid items, that would essentially become a treasure-trove. On Earth, what you see, you got. Not so, here.

John got out of his chair and started prodding and pressing the wall, getting up close to it, like a private detective. He tried to elicit some movement from it by tapping and pushing. If their situation wasn't so serious, it'd be comical.

Jack was sure his dad was going about it all wrong. 'Er, dad...I think you need a remote control to activate it first.'

'I thought, maybe, I could find something...like wiring,' John said. 'Some evidence of the tech...but...there appears to be nothing. You are right Jacky...a remote or similar is probably needed.' He continued to push at the wall. Jack nodded, and suppressed a gurgle.

A creature appeared through the bluish wall that was definitely a Pianif, but was distinctly different from the one's they'd seen. The creature that emerged through the wall was dazzling in its appearance. It wore bright orange, ultra-crisp clothing, a golden bread-tin-like hat, and a large, loose top that hung to shoulder-length. There was another three of them, that appeared, and wore similar, unusually bright clothing. They almost walked in slo-mo, very graceful and elegant.

They were very different from any Pianif they had previously encountered. Jack was sure that they were the rulers of the planet. Underneath the hats was super-thick translucent, white hair that was braided and hung to shoulder-length on each of them. The clothing set them apart, and so did their amazingly braided hair. Jack had seen girls in Tucson with similar, loose braids, but the intense white and thickness of their hair, really made them stand out.

Regular Pianif had no hair at all, anywhere that they'd seen. Jack wondered if the Council were a slightly different species. Clearly, reptilian...but *different*. Their skin was similar, with its scales and bumps, but it was a much lighter shade of green. Their movement, despite being lizards, was slow and ethereal...*sensual* almost, Jack thought, stunned. Must be getting used to them, he reckoned.

The first girl that came through the wall seemed to be about to tone to them. Jack assumed she was a girl because she was shorter than the other Pianif he had seen. Also, she had a heart-shaped face, despite being covered with greenish reptilian skin.

'My name is Swann,' she said in a forthright manner, which hit them hard and loud. This creature was clearly used to talking to crowds. The noise caused John to flinch. He expected it, and Jack had gone to pains to warn him, but the loudness and suddenness got him. 'I am part of the Council that rules this planet.' Came the words in his head. Wonder what she does? Jack thought.

Fancy a species that had no serious crime, Jack thought incredulously. Most on Earth wouldn't believe it was possible. America without police and the DOJ, no courts...*nothing*. Not possible, most would say.

'We are very pleased to meet you,' Swann toned. All of the Council held their clothed arms straight out toward them like a sword, looking like it was an unfamiliar movement. 'We knew of your existence, and have known for numerous cycles.' Swann gazed deeply into Jack's eyes, and he felt like his mind was being caressed, from the inside. 'We have been anxious to meet you.' Swann said, smooth as honey, looking confident in herself.

All of them shook hands, even though their paws were wet and cold, a bit like dead fish. 'Welcome humans, to Pianif,' she said formally. 'We are rulers of this planet, and our species is also found on a world called Ranf which is 400 light years away. A different Council rules that planet.' Swann inhaled deeply and then continued. Jack reckoned it was odd because Swann's language to humans, was breath-free, requiring her focus only.

'We know of Earth,' Swann toned firmly. It is a particularly beautiful planet in a nearby system. Detonating nuclear bombs interferes with our world and the additional dimensions that we access. Burning fossils, such as coal and oil, is affecting the operation of Earth's biosphere. Humans know that, but are not aware how quickly your atmosphere is degrading. You under-estimate your human impact on the planet.'

'*This is where we have a real problem,*' Swann emphasised. Jack was nervously blinking, praying that the solution wasn't annihilation of the species. Because there was little doubt that they could do it. Swann looked at the humans like an irate schoolteacher. She bent over and stared directly into John's eyes, who swallowed a burning mouthful of stomach acid. He felt as though he was being personally berated. The way Swann leered at him, was enough to loosen his bowels. Swann looked unhappy.

That's why we're here, Jack reckoned. To be told what we're doing *wrong*.

'Take this with you, and give it to someone who understands.' Swann said firmly. John accepted a huge wad of paper that was held within a fat blue folder. Swann handed it to him, like she was handling hair-trigger explosives.

'Er...o-okay then...er, t-thanks,' John said uncertainly, accepting the bloated file with two hands 'W-What is it?' He asked, looking bewildered at the gift. His eyes were wide and round, like boiled eggs. He didn't expect to be given anything by the Ruling Council, especially something so big and unwieldy. The pile of papers must have been a foot thick. He expected to be rebuked or harangued, not given, what amounted to a gratuity.

'It's the secret to our technology,' She toned seductively. John did a double take, ending up staring closely at Swann. '*What the...?*' Jack blurted, gawking at the bloated file. Jack looked at Swann and she seemed to have the beginnings of a smile on her face. One corner of her small mouth had pulled slightly higher. Jack looked at her, incongruously, what the hell was going on here?

Swann glanced at the papers, then looked proudly at Jack and his dad, smiling happily. She then proceeded to tell them what had been conveyed. Swann told them that Earth and humans needed help to survive, and to grow. If left to themselves, their future was short indeed. The planet itself was expected to be uninhabitable within 150 years. This was a *last hurrah* by the Pianif. If this fails to save us, Swann said humanity would fail. Jack knew that was a polite way of saying *extinction of the species*.

Humans had insufficient time to save themselves, if left to themselves, Swann told them firmly. They needed a course correction. With these papers, she maintained that humans should be able to extricate themselves.

Jack thought about it, and was floored. He saw these incredibly ugly creatures in a new light. *They were trying to save humans*. An entire species - a whole planet. A helping hand to allow us to defend ourselves from extinction. Fireworks started going off in his brain, as he reached a wonderful and glorious conclusion. That all the unpleasantness should lead to this? Jack was floored.

Armed with our internet, the Pianif realised that humans were heading irrevocably toward oblivion. Rather than visit the planet and show us how to do it, rub our noses in it, as it were, they preferred the remote, *gracious* way. The internet told them that incorporating this technology was the only way it could work, long term.

They took two humans from Earth, back to their planet, and threw papers at them, and weaponised them with the needed intel. Jack nodded to himself, it all made perfect sense now. The Pianif didn't take us for selfish purposes, like we thought. *They were trying to save us.*

The internet they procured from the Mars OT satellite, told them where we were going, and they determined what we'd need to move in a different direction. Without it, we were doomed in the very short term.

Jack swallowed the lump in his throat, and realised that these creatures, this race of lizards, should be venerated. They were fully benevolent - generous, caring, *kind*, call it what you like. Jack was stunned, and smiled, ear to ear at Swann and she smiled back, walking forward and hugging Jack tight. 'It's our pleasure Jack,' Swann purred.

'The papers show you how to move FTL,' Swann said soothingly, 'and how to find, and characterise, dark matter and dark energy. Also, critically, there is information on how to access the quantum energy field, you know as Zero Point, which energises virtual particles, to fizz into and out of existence. It is energy created by the big bang Jack. The energy of creation is clean and limitless.' Swann became suddenly still, then she dragged in a quick breath. For some reason, she'd been holding her breath.

'Oil, gas and coal, the resources that promised extinction, will be made redundant.' Swann said. 'Using Zero Point, there is no discharge into the atmosphere Jack. It is clean, free and unlimited.' she said smugly, 'and there are *many* on Earth who need it.'

Jack realised that the Pianif had access to our internet, so they knew our problems, and the holes in our knowledge. Which were less like holes and more like chasms, and led humans to an unhealthy reliance on dirty, atmosphere-killing energy. Which compromised the entire biozone, to the point where the whole planet was at risk. We were almost at the point where the atmosphere of the planet wouldn't sustain the global population. Burning fossil fuels is depleting free oxygen. Including animals, there were just too many oxygen breathers on Earth. ZPE would give us a lot more time.

Jack thought about it, wondered, hummed and ha'd, and rubbed the back of his neck. Would that intel paint cross-hairs on their forehead? There would be a lot of people with vested interests, that wouldn't want that sort of intel to see the light of day. He knew it would be fantastic for Earth and humanity, but not so good for oil and gas companies. They made humungous profits from what was underground, and under the ocean. And dirtied the atmosphere and reduced oxygen levels as a result. Earth's killer.

'We have included the recipe for a new type of concrete, that has stronger properties than yours.' Swann said. 'It has the enormous advantage of absorbing carbon dioxide from the atmosphere.' She emphatically pronounced the words, and stepped closer to Jack when she said it, almost shouting. If it was done for effect, *it worked*. John felt his bowels loosen once again. All this was *big stuff*, especially for a couple of back-woods country-folk.

'If you used it in your USA alone, to repair roads and build new ones, and used it in the building industry. It will absorb six giga-tonnes of carbon dioxide Jack. And remove climate-change, *lock, stock and barrel*.' Swann didn't smile, but she stood taller and had a proud gleam in her eyes. She knew what this would mean to ailing Earth.

Jack turned his head and gawked at John, smiling incredulously, ear-to-ear. He knew there was a lot of people back on Earth who would be stunned. Climate-change was a huge source of consternation, the world-over. Governments floundered to meet new regulations, and each year, the world continued to get hotter. Everyone on the planet knew there was a tipping point.

And most knew that Earth was very, *dangerously*, adjacent. But with this new concrete, we could nip it in the bud permanently, and make Earth sustainable *forever*.

To get rid of climate change so easily, would make many on Earth embarrassed and a little ashamed. The United Nations, G7, Five Eyes and many groups and governments on Earth, believed a staged approach to curing climate-change was best. Where green alternatives like solar and wind turbines are blended with fossil fuels, to gradually reduce humanity's reliance on dirty energy. There were several Emission Reduction Acts currently in place, but Swann knew that these weren't strict enough. Earth would die before they had the impact they sought.

With this new concrete, the entire supply of carbon-dioxide would be fixed forever. And waste-plastic would similarly be removed from the planet, in a finger-snap. Several gargantuan problems would be fixed on-the-spot.

Swann was still going, her level of passion increasing as she spoke. This was clearly something she'd been looking forward to. Her eyes were now sparkling. 'The keys to Anti-gravity, inertia-evasion and atmospheric propulsion from Dark Energy are also provided. The secrets to new technologies are handed to humanity, because our race is benevolent, and we wish humanity and Earth to survive for the long-term.' Swann made a complex signing above her head, with her hands and fingers. Then she said, 'Earth itself is unrivalled in the Universe,' Swann purred, 'it is *peerless* in its aspect.' Jack snapped his head around to his dad. His eyes were enormous with wonder, matched by John. '*What?* Jack blurted. He knew humans were captivated by the image...but them too?

'Your planet is gorgeous Jack, *one of a kind*, unique, and *must* survive,' Swann toned loudly, over the top of Jack's further exhortations. 'Everyone on our planet knows about Earth. The blue planet, with oxygen and satellites. And a civilisation. They are all in favour of it enduring. What you hold there, in that blue folder, is the result of a planet-wide vote. It is a gift from the entire population.'

Swann's head almost touched the ceiling. She deliberately looked at the other Council members, smiling widely and signing above her head again. The others in the Council clearly agreed.

Every Pianif in the room made a similar, but slightly different signing, in return. Jack looked closely at Swann and detected a bright gleam in her black eyes. She clearly held out the Pianif, as the *saviour* of humanity and Earth. She was proud of her civilisation. And proud of its ability to help humanity and the planet she described as unique.

'Weaponization with dark energy will naturally occur,' Swann said, 'rendering your nuclear tech unnecessary. Some species take a more hands-on approach. They visit your nuclear sites, and try and push you toward a certain goal. This is not our way.' Swann glanced at the others in her team, and continued her loud toning.

There was a certain undertone in what she was delivering, Jack reckoned. He listened closely and tried to read behind what she was toning. Swann had an agenda, he was sure. There was a reason for their benevolence, Jack thought, he just didn't know what it was, yet. It didn't seem to be benevolence for no reason. Jack reckoned *quid pro quo* was involved somewhere. But what would they want from humanity, a clearly inferior species? Jack was stumped.

'Humans and Earth deserve the technology that we have. Without it, your planet is destined to quickly become uninhabitable. The strategy of your governments shows no discernible improvement in climate-change. They are too concerned with having enough energy to power their economies. They are not willing to forgo any part of their financial system. They believe everything and everybody *must* have sufficient power at every part of the day and night. With that attitude, burning high density, fossil fuels for energy, will always remain. ZPE is absolutely critical for humanity, but there will be transformation pain, that *must* be accepted.' Swann looked grimly at Jack, knowing that this would be a sticking point for Earth. A necessary, although uncomfortable, transition period, where fossil fuels were exited as a source of energy.'

'In the opinion of the Council, humans need our technology simply to survive. Without it, climate-change will kill the planet and kill humanity. We brought you here, so that we could make contact with ordinary humans, but this meeting has become much more than that. Because humans and Earth need help to simply survive.'

'Humanity's understanding of physics and the Universe is less than required to survive. Your internet has told us that. And there is little hope of that changing in the short or medium term. So, what you have inside the blue folder, is what you will need to survive and flourish.' In what appeared to be a momentous happening, Swann signed above her head, again. A longer, even more detailed signing. The other Pianif did an abridged signing back at her. Swann gazed at Jack and her reptilian face rearranged itself into a wide grin that she shared with the entire room. All the Pianif were now smiling at them...even Pietr.

It seemed to Jack that this was the genuine meaning of the mission. To meet with humanity, and provide them with technology and understanding to both save them, and to elevate them. Jack reckoned, Earth and humanity, should count their blessings. Because, according to the Pianif, without their intel, we were *gone*.

Swann smiled as she spoke. 'Humans and Earth must be successful, and we are not the only species to believe that. The skies and oceans of Earth are home to many species, who wonder about Earth inquisitively, pondering if they will, indeed survive for the long-term. We have done our own research, and believe, if left to their own devices, humans and Earth will *not* survive. It will be made extinct by its lack of knowledge of the physical world.' Jack swallowed uncomfortably, and hoped she'd finished talking. He'd heard enough.

Swann continued though. 'It appears that everyone in Earth's skies and oceans have tech that Earth itself does *not* have. The planet has a potent attractive quality, but species are disappointed when they get to Earth once they learn about you. To have humanity in charge of the destiny of such a gorgeous and rare planet, is disturbing to many.'

Jack felt as if a hand had closed around his throat.

'You are provided with this intel on behalf of the Pianif, and it is hoped that you know what to do with it.' Swann toned firmly. 'You and Earth depend on what you do with the intel.'

Jack nodded knowingly at Swann, but in reality, he had no idea. This intel was great, but it was like a nuclear trigger. If enacted, it would lead to a brand-new world, and by his face, his dad recognised it too. John got off the bed and walked slowly up to his son, shaking his head, his eyes as wide as they would go. John was horrified.

'*Holy shit Jacky.*' John blurted into his ear. 'This stuff is beyond *explosive*. Imagine Earth, with no oil, coal or gas.' John huffed and puffed disbelievingly. 'It'd be a brand-new *fucking* world.' John was gasping in terror. 'Once it's out – we, as in the whole family, could be in massive trouble.' John's face twisted with agony. 'Think of the Arab states, the Middle-East, big oil companies. Vested interests would spend billions to keep a lid on this new intel. And it's us, you and me, that brings these trillion-dollar companies to their knees. John's eyes looked ready to pop out of his skull. 'I don't like it, Jacky, it could be the family's death knell.' His dad's voice was deep, the harbinger of doom.

John looked at the papers he was holding, that took both hands to lift and carry. He felt like dropping them and saying, *no fucking thanks*. But equally, he knew how important this was to Earth and apparently, to the Pianif.

But...what about *our* family? He wondered anxiously. What about Krissy? Sweat started running into his eyes, and he glanced aghast at Jack, who was staring vacantly back at him, thinking and sweating. Jack gestured to him, to say stay cool, and we'd discuss it later. This stuff was a naked flame, and Earth, a powder-keg. Jack and John both knew that big trouble, *maybe death*, lay in that direction. And the Pianif had handed it to Jack, as though it was simply a gift. Rainbows and teddy bears.

'Big Oil would kill anyone, anywhere, and their family and their family's family, if anyone threatened their livelihood. Jacky, we need to be ultra-careful, and put a lot of thought into it.' His eyes were wide, and he was terrified to the point of paralysis. John's breath was heavy and rasping, and his eyes bulged from his sockets like boiled eggs. He could see the murderous potential of this stuff. It was getting more unpleasant by the second, and they both knew it. Their planet was *acutely,* addicted to oil. God help anyone, who had a better, cleaner and cheaper alternative. And it happened to be *us. US!* John and Jack Stevens of Tucson, Arizona. The ridiculous and comical had somehow become fact. We lived our life in an out-of-the-way desert, and had no impact on the world. And now *this.*

John thanked God and wiped his brow, thankful that his son had the beginnings of a plan, to *safely* provide Earth with the intel. It wouldn't be straight-forward or easy, quite the contrary, but according to Jacky, it could be done.

***

'The journey to Earth started as a molybdenum drive, but through coincidence, ended up with you two, Jack and John.' Swann said, looking directly at Jack.

'Coincidence or...engineered?' Jack whispered to John, under his breath. John nodded, both doubting the veracity of the words. They both reckoned that humans were always the primary targets. Pietr had said as much. Coincidence was zero, Jack thought. But it was supposedly to our benefit, which Jack now agreed with. Things were now a whole lot better than they were a few days ago, when simple mortality was questionable.

'We know Pietr and his crew were aware of our strong desire to meet humans on our planet. They took you for that purpose. Right Pietr?' Swann asked.

'Right Swann. We knew of the Council's wishes. And we wanted to fulfil them.'

'Okay then.' Swann said. 'Meeting over. Please return them to Earth.' Swann demanded. She was like a king. What she wanted, she got. All the orange-ones vanished through the wall. Jack watched them go as they walked into the bluish wall, that turned canary yellow when they hit it, and transitioned back to blue after they exited. One after another, they exited, until they were all gone, and they were alone. Pietr and his friends didn't move. They had agreed to take us home, but remained seated. Perhaps they were waiting for us to make a move, which seemed unlikely. Maybe they were giving us time to get used to the idea, which also seemed unlikely...

John was ebullient and out of the wheelchair, and felt like cheering and dancing. To use their own time to return us, didn't seem to be the Pianif way, but with recent events, it made good sense. The smiles were ear-to-ear. Incredibly, it looked as though they both got to go back to Earth. They handed us the intel, so returning us to Earth to implement it, seemed only logical.

That told them something very positive about the Pianif mind-set. Jack was sure that they lacked empathy, but now, it seemed like he was wrong. Going home was a surprise, no doubt about it, but it led John to a maudlin image of his poor wife. They *would* be re-united, it seemed, but there were so many questions around it, he felt sick, and worse, he was starting to tremble. As he thought of Krissy, he felt his heart start pounding like an iron mallet in his chest, and sweat started pouring off his forehead. He was terrified of their first meeting. They'd been married for 44 years, but still, he was petrified, and as nervous as a mouse in the final moments before a cat pounces. *How* on Earth would he explain *why* they had vanished?

Also, and *critically*, what in God's name would time-slippage do to their homecoming? The very concept of it, horrified him. John didn't have a clue how it would impact, or even if it would impact - he would have to defer to Pietr. They'd been away about a week, according to his phone. But what might extreme speed and traveling through warped space add to that? John chewed the inside of his cheek, and was on the verge of panic, and his son, not much better. The ghastly, devastating image he had before his eyes, was Krissy as an 80-year-old. The potential was life changing. Possibly, a horrible, overwhelming catastrophe.

John clenched his jaw to trap the sob in his throat when he thought more about his wife. Her distraught image was everywhere he looked. His temperature was off the charts, and he kept sweating, like he'd run a marathon. The image of his wife in the kitchen was always front and centre. He tried to squash them, where her ageing was off the grid. But some got through, that made John scream in fright.

Now, he saw her in the veggie garden – she loved it there. When she wasn't tending to John, that's where you'd find her. Picking tomatoes, or digging up carrots and potatoes. It was Krissy's own piece of paradise. Jack ran his hand through his hair, and could see his mum bent over, and picking out weeds. She would come inside with a tray running over with fresh veggies for the family.

Another love she had was singing to her cows, that they raised for milk. That was an image and a melody that was engraved into John's brain. Mum would sing, Golden-Brown to her cows and they would moo back. Each of the three cows had a name, and she would start calling them as soon as she left the house. Jack would bet London to a brick, that all that had stopped. The motivation to do it would be gone. Home would have quickly devolved to a house, cold and devoid of love and sound.

'H-Home? John said incredulously, glancing at Jack.
'We're going home, dad. Jack smiled and grabbed his dad by the shoulders and reeled him in. Jack and his dad embraced, knowing that one massive problem had been solved, and one still remained. They were both pretty certain that Pietr would space them, but they had just learned that incredibly, they were to be taken *home*. At least this potentially murderous issue was solved. And Jack and John couldn't be happier.

Her face was still sharp in Jack's mind. He was looking forward immensely to their reunion. But was deeply concerned about the date when they finally got home to Earth. There was no way to calculate it, but Jack expected time-slippage to be a problem.

At least he'd return with a newly cured father. Cancer would no longer be an issue. Krissy would be floored, firstly by us walking casually through the door, and secondly, by John no longer having cancer, in any organ. Both would set off fireworks in her brain. Remission would be replaced by complete cure. Her jubilation would be unequalled. But would it, Jack wondered? He knew it was more complicated than that.

The first question, once they were back on Earth, in a human hospital, had to be - was her husband really cured? Or was it just some elaborate hoax? A human doctor would tell them straight between the eyes. And it would be based on human imaging, and human research.

The more he thought about it, the more cynical Jack became. Human knowledge of other races was nil. *Misleading* might be exactly how they rolled. Empathy is one thing, but that doesn't automatically invoke honesty. Xeno-psychology was an untouched discipline for a reason.

We'd be home some time in Earth's future. That's all John and Jack knew. John burst out crying, when he thought about Krissy *dying,* before she ever knew what happened to them. *Surely not*, John hoped, wiping way tears. Jack embraced his dad and tried to sooth him, saying, "it was, what it was" and that the outcome was beyond anyones control. 'Space-time will decide it, dad.' Not very comforting – but true.

His dad was still sobbing bitterly, so he held him tighter, and repeated to him that at least they got to go home. His dad was shaking, he was crying so hard. Jack's attempts to calm him hadn't work. His ability to help him, was sadly lacking, and Jack knew it. Platitudes were useless, his dad's fears were clear, present and real. There was little anyone could do, but try to assuage him with inanities, which really didn't work. Jack knew it all came down to the date on Earth when they finally got there. Both of them were deathly afraid of significant time slippage because they knew how much it would affect Krissy.

Without knowing the date on Earth, the real nature of John's reunion with was impossible to predict. His dad shared different scenarios with Jack, all the time. John worried about it so much, Jack was afraid that he'd get sick again, and we'd have to go through it all, again.

Jack turned around and looked back at his dad, who was thankfully regaining some control of himself. He had red eyes and dark circles underneath, and still whispered for his wife, but the continual blubbering and sobbing, had thankfully stopped. For how long, he didn't know.

***

Pietr, and the rest of his team, remained seated. But they had re-arranged their chairs and now huddled together, discussing something in private. The trip to Earth, hopefully.

Jack loosened his grip on his dad and returned to a seat to sit back down. He looked at his dad who was still a picture of abject sadness, but at least he wasn't crying. Although separated by light years, his love for his wife remained as strong as ever. John was determined that she know the truth about these non-humans, that had taken them. He remained heavily date conscious and hoped against hope that time-gain was manageable.

The bit that hit Jack the hardest, was the new silence that would have hit his house. It wasn't even a probably, it was definite. There would be no talking, chat, or banter. With one person, there'd only be silence and deep black hole misery. Jack could see Krissy, gazing vacantly, lurching room to room, looking, but never finding, listening, but never hearing. Her's would be a forever life of searching and hunting but always coming up empty-handed and behind the eight ball.

The thought brought him to tears at night. His mum, of all people, didn't deserve it. Not now – *not ever.* She treated her husband like a God, attending to his every wish. *In sickness and in health,* was a marital clause, a way of life.

She tried the hospitals, the hotels and hostels. Even the men's sheds...and there was zero trace. They had just disappeared into thin air. Krissy had reported them to the Police as *missing*. She was told to wait, while they conducted their checks. So, she went home and cried some more. No-one cared it seemed.

Krissy went to the local Tucson police station and was met with indifference and apathy. No one seemed sympathetic or interested. The girl who took her details acted like a robot. So, she reluctantly entered her own private hell in Arizona, with no help from the community or the police. Without her family, she was nothing but a shell and a number.

For Kris, they knew life would devolve into an agonising, tormenting nightmare, day after day, week after week. She lived for her family, and now they had evaporated without a trace. There was no possibility of closure, and each day was full of lament and hardship. Just getting out of bed, was hard. Walking from place to place became a slow stagger. Lurching and staggering became the new walking.

For Kris, one day morphed painfully into another, and all she was left with was a knot in her stomach and a pounding in her head, from the insomnia. Krissy's life became one of listening, for that knock at the door, Jack's whistle, or the sound of rubber squelching on the gravel of the driveway. To say, someone was *home*. Short of that, Krissy Stevens didn't exist.

What a terrible, morbid travesty, John thought sadly, wiping away tears with his hand. He desperately needed to know what she was grappling with. John finally held his breath after asking Pietr what the potential for time dilation was, expecting a genuine horror-story in return.

John closed his eyes and stood to his full height, holding his breath, as he waited for the answer that would decide his fate. John opened his eyes, and looked at Pietr closely, and didn't see an iota of concern in his wide eyes. For Pietr, it was all business. For him, there were no shades of grey.

Pietr thought about it long and hard, and turned to look directly at him. 'John...we will return two of your weeks after we left.' He toned.

'Two weeks,' John said evenly. 'Just enough time for Krissy to get really worked up. Great. *Good*, he said, sarcastically. John spun to look at Jack, 'better than two months, I guess. Or two years.'

Jack's mouth fell open; he was stunned that the time difference was as good as it was. 'Better than I expected dad...much, *much* better,' Jack said thankfully, 'I don't know how fast we went to get here, but it was *damn* quick. We are light years from Earth, dad. They must have a way of obviating time difference. Something to do with that wormhole, I suppose.' Jack's face broke into an irresistible smile.

4

Earth

**"Extraordinary claims require extraordinary evidence."
— Carl Sagan**

They sat in two chairs, beside a large rectangular window, and similar ones encircled the entire craft. The chairs were light blue, and tightly woven, with similar backs, which were also arranged in a perfect circle. Pietr said they were on their way home – back to Earth.

Jack grinned across at his dad, who was smiling irresistibly. All John could think of, was the look on his wife's face, when they came traipsing through the door. It'd be classic, he thought, ecstatic that time-slippage was so tightly controlled. Of course, Krissy would be pissed, at least initially. After the jubilation of a return, it might get a *lot* more challenging.

If they revealed the intel they'd been given, oil and coal would be suddenly worth a lot less, maybe close to nothing. Natural gas would be a giveaway. Vested interests would stop at nothing to veto the delivery of the information. Then the issue would become revenge. *Vengeance.* John knew his whole bloodline could be in massive jeopardy. Even the family's family was in trouble. So, it had to be released *anonymously*. No one could know it was them. Do it secretly or die. As soon as he laid eyes on the papers, Jack knew anonymity would be key.

The wad of papers was now in Jack's backpack, with the wulfenite specimens and tissue paper. And would stay there until a satisfactory process was agreed to by the entire family. If a safe way of revealing it wasn't found, the papers would be shredded. The intel was critical, but the safety of the family came first.

***

Jack looked out the closest window of the vessel and could see the blackness of space rapidly envelop them. They were coming close to a huge structure, that looked like the familiar mouth of a gigantic whale. The craft's ability to create it was now confirmed, because Pietr went to pains to hit two small levers simultaneously to generate it. Jack witnessed it all, stunned that they had the tech to turn space into a semi-solid and then punch a hole through it. The structure acted like a wormhole.

Jack could see it through the side window, and it appeared that they were heading straight for it, again. He knew it was the Pianif method of travel over long distances - a ship-wide hole though non-Euclidean space. This craft was able to turn gravity on or off at will. And treat space like a fabric, and punch right through it. It was amazing what you could do when 100% of the Universe was in your back pocket.

Rockets were for *shmucks,* here on Pianif. On Earth, we used them routinely to pierce the gravity well of the planet and take our astronauts and equipment into the vacuum of space. On Pianif, to access space, there were no spacesuits or tight harnesses required. There was no burning fuel, petrol trucks, or noise at all. No flying by the seat-of-your-pants, inertia, or the threat of death by explosion. And importantly, no residue left in the atmosphere, as they tore through it at will.

In a *finger-snap*, the Pianif could be in orbit, like catching an elevator, and pressing "o" for orbit. Understanding everything was a huge advantage to a space-faring race.

*****

After about five minutes of gawking at a mottled red structure whizzing past the window, the noise began, a *noise* that had *no* equal. It was a horrendous, *grating* sound that rattled teeth, and buffeted bodies like a strong wind. *Now*, they felt inertia, and it hurt. The deafening noise was something new. The humans had never heard it, or felt it before, and by the shocked looks and panicked movement of the Pianif, nor had they.

It started as a roaring high-pitched shrill, like air being released from a gigantic balloon, in short busts. Then it became deeper and more vibrational, slowly morphing into an outcry of pure rage. It was as loud as a football siren, set off in your inner ear. John was sure something about this craft was deeply wrong. All the Pianif ran up and looked as one at Pietr, waiting for information and guidance on this new noise. They wanted to know what to do. He gawked straight back at them, vacantly, clearly having no immediate idea what it was, or why their passageway through space had broken into little pieces.

Jack looked outside and could see stars, instead of the gaudy redness that had previously been there. He was now convinced something was very wrong, not only from the sight of the devastated wormhole. But by the bulging eyes of the Pianif, and their panicked movements around the craft. Jack was suddenly terrified, and felt the heat and the sweat coming, as he waited white-knuckled, for the pull of the freezing vacuum. He unfastened his top button and snapped his head around, and gawked wide-eyed, at a scene that was getting more chaotic by the second.

Jack and John were now drop-dead frightened. Whatever was wrong, was *super-serious,* and out of control. Being sucked into the vacuum, seemed a real possibility. An inglorious ending to this whole event. Just when his dad was cured and allowed to go home, into the vacuum you go, and dead.

Jack glanced at his dad; he too, looked mortified. John was holding onto his wheelchair for grim death, ready to be whipped into the vacuum, through a ragged hole in the hull.

None of the Pianif seemed to know what was going on. Several Pianif, including Pietr, were examining one of the cubes, which was in Pietr's paws. He had removed it from the floor and now inspected it.

Pietr put the cube back in its housing on the floor and hunched over the radio. Presumably trying to work out what the hell had happened to leave them without propulsion. Several of the creatures had seemingly given up, and taken seats near the humans. Pietr spoke to his remaining kin in an angry, unintelligible language, that sounded harsh, and at times, Arabic.

Pietr turned his large head and looked directly at Jack. He had a red crest on his neck and head, which was now erect...and deeply chilling. Then, it deflated and was thankfully hidden by a flap of green scaly skin. He was obviously panicked by what had happened to the craft and *bang*, out it came. The toning by Pietr was abrupt, and seemingly angry. They reared back, expecting notice of imminent death.

'Slip-space has expelled our craft and broken up. We will need to find an alternate way of getting to Earth. Travelling in flat space is out of the question,' he said. 'Thankfully, a second mode of transport exists, which we will now take advantage of.'

Jack looked at Pietr with a questioning gaze. He hoped they had something reasonable in mind. He wasn't keen on spending months in this ship, or worse. Jack watched Pietr walk forward and prepare to address the ship. 'Spacetime will be wrapped into a bubble, around our craft; gravity and electromagnetics, do the rest. We fly to Earth FTL, in about five of your days.

John said, 'five days sitting here...what does that do to time slippage?' Front of mind for John, was the experience of his wife, and John was adamant, he didn't want it worsened. John was clenching and unclenching his fists and his eyes were almost closed. Time-dilation was at the very top of mind. He'd pray and beg if it would do any good.

'The date on Earth, when we get there, is of c-critical importance.' John said, terrified and anxious, crossing himself while he spoke. He pulled his hands into fists again and waited with bated breath for Pietr's reply to hit his brain. He anticipated the worst and felt his heart start revving up in his chest. Every hair on his body stood to attention.

Pietr looked grim, and John's heart cracked. 'Blows it out I'm afraid John,' Pietr said, 'by years probably, but we get back to Earth safely, and quickly.'

John was horrified; his face instantly twisted with grief and agony. He knew exactly what it meant. '*YEARS?*' He shouted at the top of his voice. John snapped his head to Pietr, '*No...no, NO,*' he yelled. '*Please,*' he begged at the top of his voice. '*No, no, no,* John trailed off and began crying bitterly. '*Please,*' he begged, knowing it was unavoidable, yelling through an intense wave of tears. John begged, like Pietr could somehow hit a button and fix it.

John was close to panic, he knew years were insufferable, but Pietr was indifferent to his agony, stating mechanically, it is what it is. *Holy good fuck*, he thought. He begged Pietr for another way, but was met with cold alien eyes that told him there wasn't one.

There was nothing anybody could do about it, apparently. John felt faint and saw brilliant white light in front of his eyes. Jack thought his dad might die of sheer stress before they got home. *Poor, poor Krissy,* John lamented mournfully.

John was inconsolable, making a noise like the agonised cry of a child. The thought of his wife putting up with so much hell, was killing him. John blamed the Pianif, their unfeeling, selfishness was unforgiveable. John shot Pietr a withering scowl, knowing that was the limit of his powers.

'Dad,' Jack said dejectedly, like a rifle-shot...'we have little, er...no choice. The main prop ain't working. I'm not happy either...but like Pietr said, it is what it is. There's no point begging and whining. He can't do anything about it. It's how space works.' Jack's face was twisted with regret, and he pleaded with his dad to understand, because there was no choice.

John nodded toward his son. No point getting angry or impatient with him, John thought. Jacky was right. Pietr's kind had cured him of a fatal disease, so complaining and moaning should be nil. The time-thing was a killer, but, somehow and someway, they'd have to deal with it, because it was unavoidable. Even the Pianif had no answer to it.

John turned his head and stared at his boy, who was standing next to Pietr. A human and a Pianif side by side, he thought. The Fermi paradox answered. John had a gleam in his eye, and despite the gruesome situation with his wife, he had a grin on his face. He loved his son. Jacky was his secret weapon. And soon, he'd be deployed in full.

***

Krissy would spend years on her own, to drill down to the weathered nub of her own existence, worrying, and lamenting the loss of her husband and son. Vanishing like smoke, from the Arizona hills. It was supposed to be a two-day trip. But litres of tears later, she realised they were not coming home. Despite Jack's assurances, Murphies law won, and they'd lost.

Jack wondered what she thought about during all that time on her own. He was consumed by it, during the daytime, and it filled his dreams at night. He constantly saw her image, and frequently dreamed of her face during the daytime, while still awake. Jack knew his dad did as well because they talked about it, and compared their thoughts. Krissy's appalling situation was a constant topic.

Neither knew how they should approach her, when they finally arrived home. For them, it was such a painful topic, that it physically hurt to talk about it. So, they left it alone. Or at least, they tried to.

Years, both were horrified and sickened, and found it hard to believe. It sounded like one of those dark fairytales. But once we got back to Earth, Jack knew the time-slippage would be right in their face. They'd hate it, but they'd simply have to deal with it.

Out of the rectangular window, that was closest to him, Jack continued to see bright points of light that were distorted by the bubble of space, they were looking through. Pietr was occasionally tapping away on the black radio. He obviously communicated with that thing, probably FTL with Pianif.

Looking at his dad on the alien bed, Jack crossed his fingers, and held his Christian cross tightly, in the other hand, trusting that Pietr knew what he was doing with this alternative prop. They were close to Earth now, so we only had to survive a bit longer, and they would be back on their own turf. The thought of getting home was melodic music to his ears, and tended to block out the chaos they could expect when they got there.

***

Five days of eating instant noodles was too much for Jack. John was the same. He couldn't take any more. He was totally over them. He liked instant noodles, but not *every* meal of every day.

By pointing to it, he didn't realise that it would be the only food they got for eternity. Noodles for breakfast was a brand new and unpleasant experience. He tried to explain it to the Pianif "chef," by using his fingers and pointing to it, but to no avail and Jack eventually gave up. This guy just didn't get it. How hard was it to understand that we don't want this *all* the time?

His dad said, 'good talk,' with a cynical grin. Maybe it was only humans who had a varied diet, Jack thought despondently.

John wrinkled his nose and curled his lip when he received it yet again. He didn't want it, but that was literally all there was. It was that, or nothing. And *nothing* was repugnant and worse. John had already decided never to eat them again when he was Earth-side. He also realised with a sigh that his dietary choices would be the least of his problems.

The Pianif ate something that was very different to the humans. It looked and smelt like a fish, but apparently, it wasn't. Pietr said it was a land animal that the Pianif corralled for food on their planet, and that humans could not digest. We didn't have the required enzymes, Pietr said. Irrespective, John and Jack were ready to give it a go. But apparently, severe dysentery would be the result, so they backed off with their demands.

When Earth became visibly blue, even though it was severely distorted, both humans became nervously ecstatic. They worried again about how much time had elapsed on Earth since they left? That would partly determine how Krissy would react when they arrived. If it had truly been years since they left, then severe emotional distress and more, was likely when they arrived. John had worried himself into a stressed, sweating knot as a result. His expectation was epic disaster when he confronted Krissy. Jack's reunion with his mom was something to look forward to. For John, it was the opposite. He was frozen with terror.

Pietr said about 2 ½ years would have elapsed, but when pressed, he couldn't be exact. This was a qualitative science apparently. We wouldn't know exactly how much time had been side-stepped, until we got there. *Be prepared*, he said emphatically to his dad. Jack was sure the date on Earth wouldn't be pretty.

Jack was horrified internally. His stomach was already making strange noises. He was certain his dad would be a basket-case, if he got news, he considered *bad*. And Jack would have to help him hold the fort.

Jack wondered grimly. Had we been declared dead? Enough time had passed to make that horrid scenario a reality. Was his dad's wife still even alive? Was his house still standing? Every nasty option or scenario Jack could think of, was increasing his fear of approaching the house. His dad was cured of cancer, that couldn't be lost sight of. That was truly extraordinary, so their journey to the stars was a steep story of mountainous highs and cavernous lows.

But the reality of life, was now on a rocky planet that had aged years without them. Earth would complete 2 ½ revolutions around the Sun before they came back from Teegarden. What would his mum think when she laid her eyeballs on them? Krissy would be stunned, shocked, and totally dumbfounded to see them come traipsing through the door, like they hadn't been lost at all.

But that was still only the very beginning, Jack thought miserably. There was also the small matter of what they brought home with them. Jack knew that the pages, the intel from the Pianif, could kill their family's bloodline on Earth, if not handled carefully. It shouldn't be like that, *but it was.* It was Earth. *Good news* was not always good news, for the establishment.

The information Jack and John brought home, had the potential to totally unbrick the establishment, and create a *brand-new Earth.* New industries, using new technology, and existing industries using alternate production methods, would rise across the planet. Batteries would power all transport, in the medium term. And all electricity, including that for batteries, would be produced from the quantum Zero Point. It would eventually be goodnight to petrol, oil and coal.

And Krissy might have simply moved on. New husband, new house, new life. Jack doubted it, if only, because she loved his dad so much. You just had to look at them, together. They mooned over each other. His mum was only 59, but she looked 45. She was deeply devoted to John.

He'd never suggest it to his dad. He was sure he'd come to the same conclusion, as a possibility. Like Jack, he'd probably dismissed it as ludicrous. They'd been happily married over forty years. John and Krissy were from the generation that mated for life. They were like two penguins, holding flippers. *Lifelong mates.*

* * *

From orbit, the world rotated, until the Atlantic Ocean disappeared and America was directly below them, and it looked truly gorgeous. They waited until the bubble of space disappeared and the continent, and Earth, went from blurry and indistinct to focussed and minutely detailed.

Below them was a dry desert, and it rather suddenly took up the entire rectangular window. They zipped out of orbit and through the atmosphere, and in a finger-snap, they found themselves out of the craft, and in the desert. John and Jack were standing in sand, next to the broken wooden headframe of the old Yuma mine. They were unexpectantly back where they'd started from!

Jack and John were standing next to a cracked block of ageing concrete that used to support an ore-sorter, the Sun just inching above the short-treed hills in front of them. Jack looked up, but the sky was clear. The craft was nowhere to be seen. Already, there was heat in the Arizona Sun. Welcome to Earth. You *fucking* beauty, John thought rapturously, with tear-filled eyes. He never expected to see it again.

Neither of them had any idea how they got there, especially standing inches from the dilapidated headframe. They remembered the trip to Earth intimately. But they could remember nothing of how they got out of the vessel and onto the planet. Presumably, that would've taken some fancy flying, and input by a few of the Pianif. Their recollection was zero.

'We're back,' John blurted, looking both of them up and down and giving a slow, ironic grin like a cowboy. Jack looked stunned, gazing at his dad nervously, and then glancing at the gorgeous low hills around them, trying, but failing to recall their trip to the ground. Both were dazzled and shocked to be home, and amazed they were out of the craft, and felt so...awake. He thought at the very least they'd be drugged, drowsy, and ready for a sleep.

Method – unknown. Memory – zero. Did they land... presumably they did, but who knows? Maybe we teleported here, or were deposited, using a beam of particles? Facts were elusive.

His first thought was for his wife, seeing that they were now back on home territory. Her image hit John like a truck. The closer he got to Krissy, the deeper, sharper his thoughts were. He was still worried about the first sight. What in God's name would he say? He'd thought about it, contemplated, cogitated, weighed it up, but was still at a loss. Thinking of her, gave him a heavy feeling in the pit of his stomach, getting worse, the closer he came.

'The date. That's our first priority Jacky. We must know what it is. We need to know.' His eyes had fire in them, and Jack could see it. '*We must.*' John continued to mutter the same thing, over and over, like a nutter, trailing off to a broken whisper.

Jack imaged his mum in the veggie garden and nearly collapsed in a slobbering heap. Jack bit his lips and his cheek, terrified by the possibilities. He just hoped and prayed that time-slip wasn't too bad. If it was over ten years, then, God help us all. His dad would be finished.

Pietr sounded unsure and hesitant about time-dilation. He didn't want to be exact because he just didn't know. His dad pushed and pushed him, and Pietr eventually said 2 ½ years. But realistically, Jack knew, it could be *anything*. As long as his mum was still alive, he thought, they could work through anything. If not, if she wasn't, his dad would never, *ever*, recover. Nor would he.

'First thing we're doing,' Jack said loudly, 'is get you assessed by a *human* doctor, see if they concur with the Pianif diagnosis. Any pain, anywhere?' Jack asked and held his breath.

John shook his head. 'I'm fine Jacky, I feel good as gold, for the first time in yonks.' John felt his side and smiled, then said to Jack, 'the first thing we do, even before that, is find out what the fucking date is. See how much time we've missed down here, and how much shit we can expect. And then track down my...wife, and your mum as soon as we can.'

Jack looked at him cynically and shook his head. 'Y'know dad, you'd be dead without them...and look what we brought home with us?

John smiled widely at Jack, who also wore an infectious grin. Both hugged tightly. The outcome was better than expected.

'Jacky,' John pushed his son back and looked at him seriously. 'We need to work out a way to release all the intel, *without* being marked for life. The oil people are naturally, super-protective of their position.' John rolled his eyes and bit his lips. The pressure was on. Several things vied for full attention.

They were both terrified of the date. It equalled the amount of incredulity, disbelief and anger that Krissy would have. Of course, those emotions would be through the roof when we mentioned the nature of our kidnappers. She would think we'd been sniffing glue.

John's eyes were so wide, they bulged from their sockets. 'What we have in our back-pack Jacky...will change the world. It will render oil almost value-*less* and create massive earthquakes on stock exchanges around the world. John drew in a quick, painful breath. 'Our backpack will blow humanity and Earth to kingdom come.' John's mouth dropped open, as he stared at his son, like he'd just started a nuclear bomb ticking.

'Energy is currency dad, and we've got gazillions, courtesy of the Pianif. Releasing it must be done *very* carefully. Their ability to cure cancer and other genetic diseases is truly staggering. But the ability to access unlimited, free, clean energy will impact *every* person on the planet. Nobody on Earth will be unaffected.'

Jack gazed morbidly at his dad. 'Because of us and this intel, hundreds of millions of people will need new jobs dad. They won't be needed by oil and coal anymore. That's a hell of a legacy.' Jack squeezed his eyes shut, and instantly reopened them, and looked horrified.

'*Fuck me.*' John whispered in disgust, looking up at the sky. John was breathing in shallow, quick gasps. 'It's for the greater good, no doubt, but in the shorter-term Jacky, it will cause massive tsunamis across the world.' John started grinding his teeth loudly. He knew what was in front of them. It was great for the world, but possibly fatal for them and theirs, and horrendous for the millions of people working in oil and coal.

They had to remember that *revenge* was a dish best served cold. Quite simply, Jack thought anxiously, if they were fingered for this, the Stevens bloodline would cease to exist. Big-Oil wouldn't stand for it. Someone would pay for their missing billions. And if found, it would be the Stevens family, out of Tucson, Arizona. They would be *kaput*. All of them.

5

Krissy

"Humans are the legacy of 15 billion years of cosmic evolution." — Carl Sagan

Jack and John stopped talking, and made their way east, down the hill, ecstatic to be home on Earth. For a while, Jack thought, things looked grim, they held no hope of returning. All hope was seemingly lost, several times. And here they were in beautiful Arizona, surrounded by low hills, saguaro cacti and extraordinary Joshua trees. *Paradise.*

Jack noticed how bloody hot it was out here. And it was still morning, but he knew they were in the Arizona desert, so heat should be expected, he supposed. There were few clouds in the now blue sky, and there was a real bite in the large, yellow Sun. On Pianif, he never felt the heat from the star. It was a baby, and ours, a fully-fledged adult.

As Jack walked past desert cactus and rock daisy, he noticed how differently our star presented to the pre-schooler that warmed Pianif. Even though ours was a lot further away, it was still bigger and brighter than theirs. It was a totally different star, and Pianif was a lot closer to theirs. The Pianif star was crimson and dull. Ours was yellow, brighter and bigger.

In the back of both of their brains, was the issue of Krissy. It was deeply incised, and impossible to remove. The date on Earth was the first rock to kick over. They now *expected* it to be bad.

Jack looked for his Daihatsu, but it had gone, there weren't even any tire tracks that he could find. Rain had washed any evidence away. Jack felt something heavy drop into the pit of his stomach. It was the horrible realisation they hadn't been in this spot for years, though for them it had only been about a week. The disconnect with timeframes, was never more in Jack's face.

Neither of them had a charged phone with them. What to do? Jack wondered frantically. We can't phone for a taxi, or an Uber. John was of the same mind. Hitching a ride out here, was just asking for trouble. But they had little choice.

'We'll have to hitch it to Tucson, dad.' Jack said reluctantly, knowing it was just asking for it. Out here, it could be a nightmare. You never know who might pick you up. The desert was just a rotten place to stick your thumb out. As John said, it was a great place to be attacked with a shovel.

'Don't have much of a choice Jacky,' John said slowly, gazing at the pristine empty desert in the distance, and the heat haze that hid a lot of the detail. It was as though the desert was throwing up an eerie veil of secrecy. Neither of them, liked it, and felt deeply alone.

The intel provided by the Pianif, was good for the planet, and in the longer-term, for humanity. Because of the way humanity had built its civilisation, this stuff had the power to transform, and to create catastrophe. Jack reckoned Swann didn't know that. She didn't realise Earth's depth of addiction to fossil fuels. That's exactly what Jack and John had to confront. And, if the intel wasn't released just right, there would be murders and violence.

Swann was a different kettle of fish though. When he thought off her, Jack felt warmth in his core, and incredibly, feelings of *tenderness, devotion and love*. It felt like he'd known Swann for his entire life. Meeting their Ruling Council, was a glimpse into Pianif life, and *how* it was ruled. Obeying Swann's mandates would be easy because she was loved across the globe.

John knew that Jack was a staunch advocate for the intel to be released to Earth, with the highest degree of anonymity, to protect their family. Jack had told John over and over, that this intel was critical to humanity's future.

It was super-critical to Earth and humanity. And now that we'd received it, *our responsibility* was to upload it properly.

***

They both walked down the hill, the mine was positioned on, and along a trail near a parched and cracked riverbed. They stopped when they reached the road that connected them to Tucson. John was puffing and panting already and sweating like a sheepdog. It was a dirt road, but it was a fairly good one. Silverbell Road wasn't sealed until you hit Tucson itself.

Thankfully, the City of Tucson kept the dirt roads in pretty good order. That didn't mean they were easy to walk on though. John found it hard going, he lurched along, and knew he couldn't keep it up in these oven-like conditions. His tee was wet through with sweat, and his legs were already cramping.

John loved the hills around Tucson, but was second guessing walking through them, because of the heat, the sweating, and the waves of flies that attacked him. Jack watched him, with his thumb out, as he deviated all over the road like a drunk, desperately in need of a ride and a place to lie down.

'Dad, I'll do that,' Jack insisted. 'Come and sit down,' Jack said, pretty sure that he wouldn't last half an hour out there, as he was. He was definitely a liability. Now, he wanted to take his shirt off because he was so hot. Jack eventually convinced him not to, to avoid sunburn and likely heatstroke. He reckoned it was like walking with a pre-schooler.

There was bite in the Sun, and Jack reckoned it wasn't even midday. He grabbed his dad and sat him down under an old Ash tree, on a log that gave him at least some respite from the Sun. He wished there was some water left, but all he had was an empty bottle. They'd drunk it all, getting down the picture rocks trail. Now they had nothing.

Jack stood on the side of N Yuma Mine Road and waited to hopefully flag a car down. Traffic up here was almost non-existent. A Volvo full of young people nearly ran him down, forcing Jack to run for his life, and then jump out of its way.

'*What the h-hell is wrong with people?*' Jack heaved, shaking his head, and deciding to sit with his dad for a while. '*Fuck*'s sake,' he blurted bitterly, annoyed that he had to take hasty evasive action in this heat. Jack looked closely at his dad. He wasn't sure if he was just hot and tired, or sick again. They'd walked a fair way in hot, desert conditions. So, being stuffed and sweating was fair enough, he thought nervously.

Jack didn't want his dad to know how worried he was about him. The more he thought about the medical treatment his dad received on Pianif, the more skeptical he became. Was it simply human-bias, or was the treatment really questionable? Maybe it was *legit*.

***

A silver vehicle was approaching in the distance. They could both see a cloud of dust approaching. Closer up, the cloud of dust morphed into a Mercedes sedan, Jack saw excitedly ... two in it.

Jack was on his feet in the heat, with his thumb out. The other hand alternately pointed toward his dear old dad, and he prayed by touching his fingers to his chin. Jack was literally begging them to stop and pick them up, deliver them into the bowels of their vehicle.

The Mercedes blew dust all over them, but came to a stop a few metres in front. 'Thank *fuck*,' Jack cried happily to his dad, and ran for the rear door, and safety for his dad, from the oven-like Sun in Arizona. Jack reckoned it was closing on 40 degrees C. Far too hot to be in the desert, for someone like his dad.

He opened the door and jumped in, with his dad in front of him. '*Thank you, thank you, thank you,* Jack blurted to the two good Samaritans, who sat in the front seats.

'It's our pleasure...you sort of look like my dad and my brother. I would hope that someone would help them if they needed it. So, er...here we are.' They introduced themselves, and so did Jack and John. The air-con made the interior of the car heavenly. John was downing water from a bottle the driver had given them. In the front of the car were Jo-anne and Shirley. They lived in New Mexico, but were having a day trip to Tucson, and surrounds. They had literally saved John's life. Without water, and without a car, he was in deep trouble on a day like this. His lifespan was a few hours, out there.

'What brings you boys to our backseat?' The question hung in the air for a while. Jack looked at his dad who was twitching and sweating all over. Jack held his palm up, to say to his dad that he'd field it, and John should try and relax.

'We were fossicking for minerals at the old Yuma Mine, when someone stole our car. *Can you believe it*? Jack said indignantly.

We were up top, taking care of business, and they were below, hot wiring our vehicle.' Jack shook his head, as if to say, *how dare they.*

'So unfair,' Jo-anne said. '*Fuckers,*' Shirley blurted. She was a take-no-prisoners type of girl.

'By the way girls, what is the date? Jack asked nervously.

'23rd of June,' Jo-anne replied.

'The *year*?' Jack burst out, trying his best to keep urgency out of his voice, but failing. He held his breath in anticipation. John looked terrified, despite his best efforts to hide it. His eyes were so wide, and protruded so far, they nearly fell from his skull. What these girls said next, would literally set the scene for the rest of their lives.

Both girls looked at him quizzically, and Shirley quickly put her eyes back on the road. 'You want to know the *year*?' Jo-anne asked incredulously.

'We've been, er...out of touch, for a fair while.' Jack said, and John nodded furiously. Then there was only the droning sound of the air conditioner filling the car with cool air. Jack smiled at John and waited anxiously for the answer he knew Jo-anne had. Jack and his dad hoped like hell the answer wasn't as bad as they expected. John held his breath.

'Makes you two sound like bloody time travellers,' to which Jo-anne and Shirley laughed uproariously. Jack and John joined in, but their laugh was brittle and strained. Jack looked at his dad, and silently agreed, that they weren't very far from the truth. Too *fucking* close, Jack thought grimly. They weren't time travellers, but wouldn't they be shocked to learn that we were from 2024.

'2027,' Jo-anne said slowly and casually, as if she was reading the 9 o'clock news.

'*Holy fuck,*' John blurted before he could stop himself. Jack snapped his head around to his dad and jabbed a finger in his face and harshly whispered '*sssssh.*' John swallowed his consternation and the wail of grief, that grew in his throat.

Their worst fears were confirmed. Incredibly and shockingly, Jack and his dad had gone fossicking for minerals at the Yuma Mine *two and a half years ago.* The horrible scenario was bitingly real. They had left his wife, against her wishes mind you, in December 2024, for a two-night trip. Now, it was half-way through 2027. *Fuck*, John screamed at himself.

Jack looked at his dad and saw how deeply affected he was by the news.

Now, him and his dad were part of a disaster that made the Shakesperean tragedies look like a picnic.

John closed his eyes and tried to blank his mind.

'So, where are you boys going?' A now suspicious Shirley said. She saw the impact of the date on John. He definitely wasn't expecting it. Or, he was, and Shirley's words really cemented it. Whatever was the truth, it was a giant shock to John in particular, and Shirley noticed. She wondered spuriously if time-travellers was close to the mark. *Surely not*, she thought.

'We're, er, looking up an old friend of dad's...Lorraine Wigley, on route 77, not far out of Tucson.' Jack lied. The address was correct, but not the name. No need for them to know.

'We'd be happy to drop you off,' Jo-anne said. 'Not far out of our way really...we're going to Pheonix.'

Jack looked at John and nodded tentatively. If they didn't drop them off, they'd have to bus it from Tucson. 'Er, okay, thanks...we need her help to ring the Police, and so on. Whoever stole our car, needs to be caught.' Jack said, looking serious. John found it hard not to smile. His mouth twitched with amusement, watching his son spin a story that was nothing short of broad poppycock. Incredibly, Jack did it all without missing a beat.

Jack turned his head and looked at his dad and smiled.

The closer they got to home, the more nervous, stressed and anxious his dad became. His breath got louder, and his eyes grew wider. The lines on his forehead grew deeper, and his fear was now palpable in his eyes.

They'd just passed Mammoth and the pine forest, so, not far to go now. His dad looked him square in the face. Jack thought he was going to cry because his chin and lips were quivering. Instead, he whispered, '*what the hell do I say Jacky? She thinks we're both dead.* Krissy's possibly re-married. Maybe she doesn't even live there anymore? *What a shitshow Jacky.* How the fuck did we get in this position?' John struck his sweating forehead with a fist. Jack grabbed his dad's slippery hands and whispered to him again, to just be honest. Tell Krissy what happened. *The whole nine yards – beginning to end.'*

'*Oh, shit* Jacky, great idea,' John whispered back. 'Krissy will think I've been on a bender for two years or just flipped out...*both probably.'*

'No, she won't,' Jack whispered back, 'because I'll back you up. I was taken too, remember. What *you* recall – I do too. I am your primary witness. Never forget that dad. I am with you.'

Jack told Shirley that it was two houses up, in an area that backed onto several dry riverbeds. His dad was always worried about flooding, but in 50 years, it hadn't been a problem. Every time it rained, he reckoned it was *this* time.

The Mercedes came to a slow halt outside the sprawling Stevens property. John's heart was pounding like a locomotive. In front of them was a house and future that neither of them could believe. Incredibly, they hadn't touched the gravel, or been near the house, for over two years.

Up ahead was a bungalow, set about half a kilometre off the road. His dad had used the property to rear some cows for milk. And had a veggie garden, to help with self-sufficiency now that he was retired from full-time work. Of course, he didn't expect to be away from the house for *years*. It was worse than that because he was away from the Goddamn *planet*. It still sounded absurd - the stuff of drugs gone very wrong.

'Thank-you girls for picking us up and driving us here.' Jack said sincerely. Both of them had the same problem. They were almost too jumpy to speak. Too terrified to think.

'Yeah, thanks to you both,' John waved, as they sped away on route 77. Jo-anne turned briefly to look suspiciously at Shirley. 'What the hell?' She blurted incredulously. '*Fuck me*,' Shirley blurted aghast. 'They were whispering, but I heard it all,' Jo-anne said. 'They were meeting someone called Krissy, and they'd missed 2 ½ years...what does that mean Shirl?' She looked over at Jo with skeptical, fucked-if-I-know, eyes.

John looked around, 'The hedge has *gone*...I loved that hedge.' John turned his head left and right frowning. 'Gone completely...like some huge machine just picked it up and took it for their own.'

Both of them started walking in short steps up the long, winding driveway, finding it hard to believe that they were finally here. The house was so close.

'Well, you have to expect some changes in two and a half years, dad,' Jack said philosophically, and immediately wished he hadn't. He was hammering it in. And by the looks of his dad, he didn't need it.

'*Fuck*, Jacky...what in God's name are we going to say?'

'Christ dad, we need to be thankful for small mercies. It could've been 25 years, imagine the catastrophe then...Krissy *might* be dead. Imagine 250 years, everyone you knew would be gone. Jack's voice had risen to a cry of agony. 'At least what we confront is manageable, dad. 'Anyway, Dad...just keep it simple. And do what I said. Start at the beginning, and end at the end. We've done nothing wrong. *We* are the victims, dad.' Jack finished with a firm nod.

John nodded, and wiped his nose with his jacket, then resumed walking. 'My cows are normally on the field in front of the house.' John turned around and looked critically at the yard. 'The milking shed has gone too, Jacky. That was where Krissy used to sing Golden-brown to the cows, while they gave us milk. I could hear her, up in the house, Jacky.' His dad looked at Jack tenderly, with a faraway, daydreaming look in his eyes. After a while, John shook his head, and readied himself for what lay ahead.

'My Ford from the shed has gone too,' John said. 'Your Daihatsu has taken its place. They probably towed it here and dropped it in the shed. My Ford – who knows, *sold* probably? Krissy always threatened to sell it. Now she's probably done it for real.' John had a brittle smile on his face, that was fleeting. His face was a canvass of nerves and anxiety, as he plodded up his own driveway, with his tunnel-vision directed toward the house. 'I can feel her, Jacky...and I'm close enough now to smell her...Krissy's sweet, musky perfume.' Jack looked at him sceptically.

John noted that the paint on the wood of the house was still the same pinky white, they called *Easter Morning*. He'd painted it himself a couple of years back, getting sunburnt and listening to *Icehouse*. He'd never forget it.

'Good to see some things don't change,' his heart thumped in his ears as he approached the house, which looked in good order. He realised his wife was probably in there.

John's heartbeat was pounding like a steel block on his soft palate.

Jack watched his dad come to a complete halt in front of the stairs. And now he just stared into space. Jack knew his dad well enough, he knew what the problem was.

'We're *really* here, dad.' Jack said firmly. 'We *need* to take the next step, dad.'

John shook his head, and turned to look at Jack, and eventually smiled knowingly. Thankfully, he appeared to be back.

Jack ran up the stairs to the front door, and waited for his breathless and terrified dad to join him. John slowly ascended the stairs, panting like a steam train, and noticed that the front door was adorned with a brand-new security barricade. Also new, were the windows, which were now behind ornate, but sturdy metal bars. A lot had happened while they were away.

'*Fuck me*,' John blurted nervously, wiping his brow. 'I suppose you can't be too c-careful...with one female occupant, and all that.' He gawked nervously at the new, thick bars that encased the windows. Silence followed, and both could hear John gasping for breath, and the cicadas singing in the afternoon Sun.

John took a deep, shaky breath and staggered up and down the length of the porch, and then stopped abruptly, and glanced tentatively at his son.

'I can't bring myself to knock, Jacky,' John said weakly.

Let's get this over with, Jack whispered into his ear. He walked up brusquely, and banged on the security door five times. 'That should get a reaction,' Jack said nervously.

Both had their hearts in their mouth, waiting for the door to be flung open. John, taking long hissing breaths, looked at the door and everything became bright and full of blinding splinters of white light.

What a time for a stroke, he thought, panic-stricken. John shook his head, like a dog, and his sight returned to normal. Jack banged again, five times, as loud as he could, making the door rattle on its hinges. He was sure she was in there, in the kitchen maybe, which was at the back of the house.

'Just a minute,' came a melodic call from inside.

Jack's heart was now beating like a drum solo.

The door was opening and it was just John at the door. Jack had vanished.

'Can I...'

Her eyes scanned them, opened wide, then closed, and she fell backwards, in a disorganised heap. The next noise they heard was an explosive thump, as poor Krissy hit the ground like a dead weight. She'd taken one look at them and fallen backward like a pushed shop mannequin. John screamed to Jack to help. John's hair was almost standing on end, and his heart close to exploding. He was terrified that he'd killed her. Krissy took one look at him, and it was *goodnight*.

'*She's c-collapsed Jacky.*' John screamed, gesturing to Jack to come and help. John opened the door and grabbed his wife, with the help of Jack, and took her over, and placed her on her back, on the sofa. John's eyes bored into her, and despite himself, he smiled.

Jack bent down on all-fours and put his head close and checked his mum urgently. 'She's breathing fine, must have been the shock, dad.' He could only imagine the number of times she willed us home. And for us to finally be there, bold as brass, must have been an almighty, thunderous shock. She would've given up on us, yonks ago, John reckoned.

'*Call 9-1-1, Jacky, do it now.*' John blurted urgently. He stared at Krissy and almost purred like a cat. 'I'm home darling...sorry to be so late.' John cupped her face, and Krissy continued to sleep. She was out cold, but beautiful. John looked at her and cried like a child. Then he wiped away his tears, because he had work to do. Krissy needed his assistance, and by *Christ*, he'd be up to doing it. *Finally*, we were home. What a tumultuous, bewildering reunion. At least its happened, John thought, distressed, but overjoyed to be home.

Jack told the operator of 911 all about her, and the need for urgent help. What he didn't say, was the likely cause of the shock. Jack said she simply fell over, which was true. What he left out, was the abject shock of seeing her husband and son at the front door. After they'd been gone for two and a half *years*. And been declared *dead*. That part was omitted.

Krissy was lying untidily on the sofa, coming around slowly.

'Just let her be, dad,' Jack soothed. 'Mum'll wake up when she's ready. She's had a *hell of a* shock.' He helped his dad up and patted him on the back. They both stared wordlessly at her, both of their hearts pounding.

They could both hear the Emergency Ambulance from North-Western, gradually get louder, as it got closer on route 77. Both men could hear the urgent squelch of tyres on the gravel. The paramedics parked near the house and came bustling inside with a crash-cart, a cardiac monitor, and a big bag of equipment.

In a few minutes, they had stuck her with a needle and established IV access. Without talking, they connected her to a cardiac monitor and oxygen saturation probe.

'Okay,' the paramedic said, harried, 'tell me what happened?' Jack jumped in and said, 'she just collapsed, out of the blue. Strange – it's never happened before. Er...is she okay?' Jack knew the white lies were to everyone's benefit, so he didn't feel too bad.

'All her numbers look good, but she should come to North-West, just in case.' The paramedic said dramatically.

Krissy was almost awake now. Jack knew he had to get rid of the paramedics before she awoke fully. Otherwise, their game was shot, because she would ask questions, that would lead to answers that weren't meant for their ears. Or anyone, really.

'No, if everything looks okay, we'll leave it at that. She hates hospitals.' Jack said firmly. 'If you knew mum, you'd understand.' John shook his head and rolled his eyes.

'Okaaay, if you want to go against our recommendations, you'll need to sign a waiver.' The paramedics wanted Krissy to accompany them to hospital and have a full medical work up. But Jack and John knew exactly what was wrong with her.

'No problems,' Jack said, I have full signatory rights, where do I sign?'

The paramedic produced a piece of paper that Jack duly signed, and John witnessed it. The paramedics quickly packed up and left, but not before the thin man cautioned them. 'I would recommend a doctor take some blood for analysis. Maybe she's low on something. Her blood sugar might be awry.'

'*Yes, yes, definitely.*' Jack promised, with his fingers crossed behind his back. He knew it meant bad luck to lie to a doctor.

Jack moved forward to help them out the door, and made sure it was closed behind them, and deadlocked the door. Krissy was still out, but she was gradually scrabbling toward wakefulness.

She'd had a *huge shock*, and there were many more in her near future. Her husband and son, who went missing years before, turned up at her front door like something lost in the mail.

The Police and the FBI had been mystified. In the early days, she had the local Police, and even the NYPD and the FBI at the house, interviewing her. Even the CIA had a go, because of the negative feel it produced for the Tucson area. But none of them found even a hint or a suggestion. They had vanished in the truest sense of the word. The searchers all abandoned their files, and the money, believing they'd been murdered, and disposed of, in one of the abandoned mines that dotted the Arizona hills.

After all hope had evaporated, well after the funeral, Jack and John had the temerity to just front up and knock on the door, *years* after they left.

Jack thanked God that she wasn't dead, or in a house elsewhere, or God forbid, with another man. Her eyes were closed, but she looked glorious, lines and all. They had waited so long for this view. They *were* more than twelve light years away, 120 trillion kilometres. But now they were arm's-length. It was too close to believe. Too close to properly conceive of.

John couldn't help the tears that coursed down his face and fell onto the sofa. Her face was perfectly heart-shaped, and her auburn hair still reached her waist. John's wife was a beautiful woman.

The noises Krissy was making were louder than before. She sounded like the noises were the stuff of her own dreams, coming out as jumbled, muffled whimpers of despair.

Then her eyes flicked open and opened wide and kept widening until they were bulging.

'Mum...it's me, *Jack,* and that's dad.' Jack pleaded. He swallowed his tears. 'We were taken from Yuma by aliens. Sounds ridiculous and insane, *I know*, but our travels with them caused a slippage with time. What was a week for us, was actually over two years on Earth. Timeframes are just *different*.' Jack looked directly into his mum's eyes, and what he saw wasn't good. She didn't believe him, but it was worse than that.

'*No, no, NO...I don't believe you,*' Krissy screamed at the top of her voice, casting terrified, sidelong glances at both of them. Her voice was a cry of disbelief, and her eyes like pieces of granite. 'I spent months waiting for you two to walk through the door...even after the cops said there was *no* hope.' Krissy's eyes welled up, and the tears ran down her cheek like a river in thaw. 'A funeral was supposed to bring closure.' She said harshly. It hadn't come - it was clear, Krissy still mourned. Hardly surprising, John thought knowingly, they'd been married for over forty years, and Jack was her only son. She had nothing else. We were *her* family. Her beloved family.

Jack walked up and took his dad's hand. This was even harder than they thought. She was a brick wall. They knew it would be tough, but this was off the grid. Dealing with raw human emotion wasn't his forte, but the Pianif had forced it on them. Here was his mum, collapsed with grief on the sofa, all because of them, and their selfishness. Jack looked up, and ran his hand through his hair, '*fuck you very much.*' Jack saw Pietr's image, and felt like spitting at him.

Pietr had done some wonderful things for them and for Earth, but this, *right here*, was unforgivable. Bottom-line was – if they weren't taken, *none* of this would be a reality. So, it was Pietr's and the Pianif's fault. The fact that John would be dead, had somehow evaded them.

Jack watched his mum, and shook his head in frustration. Krissy was adamant and unyielding. Whoever we were...we *couldn't* be trusted. We couldn't be her son and husband...*no way.* They were dead and gone. We were malevolent imposters. Getting through to her was like chiselling through granite with a rubber chisel. Her eyes were enormous with terror. Krissy's reaction was a shock to both of them. They knew the reunion would be difficult, but not like this.

Krissy was fully awake now, and seemed fine, although she continued to be totally unbelieving. Her refusal to accept that Jack and John were real, remained front and centre in her mind. She refused to have a bar of us. 'The Police and Emergency Management people scoured four levels of the mine and checked for recent diggings in the surrounding two-kilometers of countryside.' She took a huge, whistling breath and held back tears by swallowing them down.

'They found a few dead cats and dogs and the odd Jackrabbit but not hide nor hair of either of *you.*' She spat the last word at John. 'They checked hospitals, soup kitchens, hostels and hotels. Even men's sheds and the street-vagrants from North Stone Avenue and back again, they found *nothing.*' Krissy hawked it at them. The implication John and Jack garnered was that they *couldn't* be them. *No way.* They were evil phonies, come to commit misdeeds against someone very vulnerable.

Krissy took a huge, angry breath. 'The Police loaded you on their Missing Persons Database and despite a few hits in Denmark, they came back *nil.* There are signs on every vertical surface in five counties.' Krissy's voice had risen to a cry of anguish. John looked at his gasping wife and saw the harried state she was in and made to hug her. She wasn't having any of it. Krissy pulled away violently.

'Stop...*you*...don't come near me.' Krissy cried loudly, pointing at John with a stiff finger. She inched herself backward until she was hard up against the backrest. John inched away dejectedly, overwhelmed, and on the verge of crying. Jack put his arm around his dad's shoulder and pulled him back. He could see what he was trying to do, and under normal circumstances, it would be natural. But now, it was just too early. Krissy's eyes were like nuggets of stone. She didn't want a bar of either of us...yet.

'Not yet, dad, give her some space...some time.' Jack saw her beady eyes, and could tell, she wasn't ready. Not yet.

Krissy stared at John with flinty eyes, boring into him. 'You say two-and a-bit years. '*What about your cancer checks*,' she said nastily and thunderously. 'That doctor you saw in Tucson, expected it to return, I could see it in his eyes.' You *fucking* pretenders, she thought angrily ...caught you out.'

Jack gawked at Krissy and shook his head in frustration. 'You've got to listen, mum. I'll say it as simply as possible.' Jack waited until he had Krissy's full attention. 'We were away from Earth about a week, but our speed of travel caused a disconnect with Earth-time.' Jack paused, to make sure Krissy was paying attention. Her eyes were still small and steely, but she was nodding, and he reckoned or at least hoped that she had taken it onboard.

With empathy and understanding Jack said in a soft voice, 'our journey ended up taking over two years, mum. The non-humans who took us, cured dad of his cancer. It was coming back when we left, we just didn't know.' He glanced at his dad with soft eyes and continued. 'Dad started getting pain, *agony*, in his stomach and back. The non-humans confirmed the cancer, then removed it, *permanently*. They did something amazing, that humans can't do.

Jack smiled ear-to ear, at his mum, then turned, and did the same at John. '*Now*, dad is totally pain-free. Cancer-free, we believe.' John nodded and wore a fragile smile. He gazed at Krissy lovingly, and she smiled back at him. A penny had dropped. It couldn't be...could it?

That was a huge step forward, John thought, trying to reel in his heartbeat. She sees me. She actually sees me, for who I am. He clenched his jaw to stifle a sob, but his chin twitched with emotion anyway.

'John...is that really you...can it be you? Krissy looked disbelievingly at John. She inched closer and focussed. She

touched his stubble, and glanced at Jack, with softer eyes. The nuggets of stone had gone. marshmallows had taken their place. Krissy began trembling and whimpering. 'It can't be, can it? She muttered over and over, thinking it had to be a dream. The grief of the last few years hit her like a tsunami. Krissy was crying openly then looked at them and smiled widely, before losing her composure again, and crying wildly. Every thought hit her at once, but mainly one.

'John, Jack...*why?* Krissy's voice was confounded and hysterical, then cracked into another violent sob. Her eyes overflowed with tears, and she looked at her boys with tenderness and gratitude. 'Sorry...sorry boys...I didn't, er, um...recognise you,' she sobbed hysterically, and put her head on the back of the sofa and continued crying frantically in disbelief. She shook her head briskly like a dog, and the boys were still there, near the sofa, smiling at her with tears in their eyes.

Jack pushed John toward her, and John jumped on the sofa, and awkwardly hugged his wife, who let him this time. 'Come here,' she said to Jack brokenly, holding her arm out. She held John, and then Jack at arm's-length, and touched their faces. She'd given up on them years ago. And they'd somehow come home.

After they were certified as officially dead, they stumbled in like lost dogs, 2 ½ years later. With some half-arsed story about being abducted by aliens. Who cared though? She thought lovingly, at least they were home. They could peddle any story they liked - Krissy didn't give a stuff. Home was where the heart is, Krissy thought, goggling tenderly at the two of them, who also knew how good it was to be reunited.

Krissy looked deeply into John's eyes. And held herself tight. 'I-I went to your funerals, more than a year ago,' she said, shaking her head incredulously, that pushed her auburn hair off her face. 'You were both declared dead by the Tucson court.' Her eyes were red and puffy. 'I had to get a court order, so that death certificates were issued. Quite the kafuffle. Cost me a fortune.' Krissy took a deep, exasperated breath, ending with a dazzling smile that lit up her whole face. It was the happiness that had been missing since 2024.

'Otherwise, we would continue to get letters and bills addressed to both of us. Which used to set me off. But now, that all looks pretty stupid.' She gave a shaky laugh, and looked happy, but close to tears.

'Dead?' John said uneasily. I don't like that.'

'You went to our funerals?' Jack asked. Krissy nodded.

'We'll have to get all that reversed. But we don't wanna tell the authorities why, or where we've been,' Jack said firmly. 'All that has to remain *our* secret.' Otherwise, Jack's plan was cooked.

Krissy looked muddled. Her narrowed eyes and squashed eyebrows said it all. 'Just tell them what happened love. If they don't believe you, just stick to your story...who cares? You're here, they can't contest that. While Krissy was talking, Jack thought of his backpack, and knew it was a *lot* more complicated than that.

Jack shook his head briskly. 'With what we brought home mum - we need to be ultra-careful.' Jack glared at his dad and sucked in a huge breath. 'We cannot be known as having *any* relationship with UFO's, UAPs or non-humans, mum. It has to remain a hugely tight secret. Otherwise, we'll be tracked down by government authorities. *And done away with.* We'll actually be killed, mum, for knowing too much.' Jack ran his fingers across his neck, to emphasise their grim fate.

'Oh, come on love, we won't...

'*Not straight away,*' Jack broke in, talking roughly over the top of his mum. 'But *after* we download the intel, we've come home with, they'll be looking everywhere for us. We've got to be very careful, mum, all of us, in the footprints we leave.' Jack spoke slowly and gravely, his eyes were slits, his pupils small and steely. He was *deadly* serious.

Krissy narrowed her eyes and grimaced, swallowing, and rubbing her chin, nearly choking on her own saliva, totally bewildered and scared by Jack's words. Jack saw her bewilderment and tried to help her. Again, he spoke slowly and sternly.

'In my backpack mum, we hold the power to change the world, and there's some who would do *literally anything* to maintain the status quo. Companies want to keep making billions of dollars each year from the *old way*. And the *old way* is made redundant, by the intel we have. Do you know what I mean, mum?'

'Of course I do, love. What would you like for dinner? Something nice 'ay. We'll celebrate. There's an old bottle of brandy somewhere in the back of the cupboard.' She pointed over her shoulder, and just wiped off Jack's warning, as if it was inconsequential.

Things were happening just as Jack predicted. Mum was so happy to have us home, that everything became a supporting actor, or unnecessary detail. She was on a dangerous road, one that would shortly grow teeth, and offer murder.

Jack snapped his fingers, loudly. *'Mum, for God's sake focus! Please listen to me. This affects us all.'* Jack's voice took on a new note of urgency. 'This is ultra important, mum. *Jesus.*' Jack's voice became a cry for attention. 'This race we encountered out there, wanted to *help* humanity. In exchange for us going to their planet to meet some of their rulers, they gave us a wad of papers. A wad of intel, *information*, that we needed, as a species.' Jack took a quick, sharp breath.

'*Secrets of the Pianif technology,* mum. We, *as in none of us,* can be tied to it – it's dangerous to us all, mum. We, *you, me and dad*, need to be super-careful. Or *they* will come here, kill us, and torch the house, with us, and the papers inside.' Jack had a finger to his throat again to show his mum how life-critical their anonymity was. The message to his mum was – stick your head up, and it will be cut-off, and everyone in the family dies. 'UNDERSTAND?' Jack bellowed vehemently.

Krissy reacted to his voice by rearing back, and looking suddenly mortified. Her swollen eyes and quick, shallow breathing, and nodding head told the story. She was scared of Jack's words. And he hadn't finished yet. Krissy had a B.A. from Carrington, so working out a problem, and comprehending, was well within her grasp. She listened carefully to her son because she realised how grave and forthright he was being.

'This race has shown us, how to solve climate-change, and how to find and characterise dark matter and dark energy. They tell us how their faster than light, and anti-gravity tech from Dark Energy works. That's all fine, because it doesn't replace anything significant here on Earth, it's mainly just new technology. It will still set the world on fire, mum. SpaceX, NASA, and the other space agencies will change a lot. But life-threatening, family-destruction, will not come from them.

Mum, rockets will be obsolete. Flying cars will finally be a reality. Forget going to Tucson in a Daihatsu, you'll be able to fly there.' Jack was smiling and seemed finally, relaxed, then his brow furrowed and he looked grimly serious again.

'The really dangerous intel mum comes from replacing oil and coal - *fossil-fuels*, as a power source. Gas too.' Jack's voice became choked with tears, and his breath was rasping. He hoped to God his mum was paying close attention because this could kill us all. She was gawking at her husband with distended, "love" eyes, so he doubted it.

He knew this stuff was the difference between life and death for the whole family. But his mum was making eyes at her husband, which was fair enough. But they both needed to understand that this stuff had the potential to kill them both. How does he impress that on a married couple that are still in love and hadn't laid eyes on the other for years?

Jack was angry, focussed and serious, and looked square into his mum's eyes and demanded that she understand it, like he did. 'These beings, *the Pianif,* have given us the mechanism to access zero-point energy. Quantum energy. Clean, free, unlimited energy from the air around us. The oil industry has murdered and maimed before, mum.' Jack made sure his dad could hear him too, because he had the same old-school attention-problem, as his mum.

'The middle east and all the Arab nations are literally built on oil.' Without it, they will freefall, their macro-economics are just gone.' Jack said firmly. 'In fact, the whole world is screwed. Earth is oil addicted.' Jack was breathing heavily with flared nostrils. 'We need to be ultra careful in releasing the intel guys. Everyone in this room,' Jack declared, using his hands for emphasis, 'could be at real risk.' Jack brought a shaky hand to his forehead and looked bitterly at his mum. She needed to really understand that these people didn't play games. One wrong move could mean death to everyone she loves.

Anything that threatened Big-Oil's livelihood was an enemy to be expunged. And we and our intel would be it and if large oil companies lost their profits, they would take vengeance on our family. He'd spell it out to her again tomorrow morning, so he could think about what approach was best, to hammer it through the thickness of her head. Because sure as hell, his words today, didn't do the job.

Jack had a plan in mind which he had been formulating since they stepped foot on Earth. He walked up to his mum and dad, and first made sure they were looking at him and paying full attention. 'Dad...*dad*, there is general agreement on Earth,' Jack started, 'that non-humans are interacting with this planet.' Jack spoke firmly 'And that their vessels make use of anti-gravity, electro-magnetism, gravity drives, FTL and zero-point energy.' Jack stopped and took a huge, whistling breath to feed his determined voice.

'Despite what they say, the federal government is all over UFOs and UAPs. If they connect us with them, no matter how slight, my plan is cactus. Anonymity is gone.'

'Sooo, being associated with UFOs, UAPs or non-humans is out of the question guys. There can't even be a whiff. *Nothing*.' Jack held a finger to his forehead like the muzzle of a gun and looked closely at his mum and dad. 'We cannot use the real story – we need to come up with an alternate, that explains why we were away for two and a half years."

Jack continued, 'We'll have to first come up with it, agree to it, and learn it every which way, because God knows how much separate questioning and interrogation, etc. we'll be subjected to.' Jack looked his dad full in the eye. 'It needs to be something simple, that won't spark a full-on investigation. Our stories must match,' Jack said, still looking at John gravely. 'It's critical dad.' He said sombrely.

"After we've devised the 'cover story' and agreed to it, mum, you ring the police and tell them we are home. They'll want to close their file.'

'Okay Jacky – something simple and believable. Got it.'

Er, me too.' Krissy said. Has to involve kidnapping, I think.'

John and Jack both nodded, while John and Krissy kept holding each other tight. Her family had somehow, *incredibly*, been re-booted.' Ironically, she thought, it was a bit like time travel.

***

After ten minutes of mental gymnastics, Jack smiled, and turned to his mum and dad, who were still locked together on the couch. 'Whatever we decide on guys,' Jack said, 'has to be ultra-simple.' Both parents nodded effusively. 'Otherwise, one, or all of us, will slip up somewhere. And then...we're all gone.'

'So, with that in mind,' Jack said, 'we say we were taken, *kidnapped*, by a couple, from the Yuma Mine, who held us under armed guard for two and a half years. They threatened to kill Krissy, if we tried to escape, and they told us her address. They eventually let us go, *as long* as we never, *ever*, revealed their location to the Police.' Jack wore a grin like a Cheshire cat. He reckoned that should satisfy everyone. He'd repeated it to himself, several times, and reckoned it ticked the requisite boxes.

'That sounds really good love, but why'd they take you? I mean, why'd they kidnap you in the first place.'

'Er...yeah...well, we could say we never found that out. Jack looked at his mum and dad quizzically, 'are you, er...with me?' Time was of the essence. This had to be bedded down asap, so Jack could move onto his dad's health, and then uploading the intel.

'Yep, definitely, love,' Krissy said. 'If you're sure that we need a cover story, that's it, I guess.' Krissy peered at John, and he nodded tentatively in agreement. Jack saw the doubt in their eyes but was pleased with the decision.

'I'm absolutely positive we will need a story,' Jack said firmly. 'There're people out there, who'll stop at nothing to keep a new product off the market. Especially, one that so deeply affects their business. And believe me, this one does a number on all oil, coal and gas companies.'

'I'll, er...follow you, Jacky. If you say it's the way to go, that's good enough for me. John held his thumb up to his son.

Jack walked up, and threw his arms around his dad. No point being annoyed. '*Yes*,' he said lovingly, hugging him tightly.

'So, dad, *focus*,' Jack held his dad at arms-length, and said to him seriously. 'We were kept in a dim brown room, about five metres square, and fed twice a day, by plates that came under the door. We knew our captors as *Jill* and *Bob*, who we hardly ever saw, and when we did, they wore clown masks. Commit all this to memory and repeat it to yourself ten times.' Jack stared at him, knowingly. He said the same to his mum. She had to be onboard as well.

John was still biting his cheek and looking down at the carpet. He lifted his head and frowned at Jack. 'I uh...don't know Jacky. It's a bit much, I've never misled anyone deliberately, in my life. I know it's needed, and it's for the greater good, but I feel bad.' John said, in a breaking voice. He wasn't a liar, and obviously didn't want to start now. He peered at Jack and could feel the heat of his stare.

'*Well*, we begin now dad.' Jack said sternly. 'It's for good reasons dad, to save our lives. If we live this lie, we *might* get away with it dad. If we don't get away with it...well, we're arrested, and God knows how the release of the intel will happen, if it happens at all.'

They practiced the story until they believed it themselves. 'Okay,' John said nervously, 'Ring the Police darling. Your husband and son have been found.'

'Yay.' She chimed and dialled the number for Police attendance.

***

Two Policeman attended their house from the Santa Cruz station at Tucson. One was huge and overtly over-weight, with a large, white cowboy hat, and the other was achingly thin, and quite short. They drove up in their Ford Expedition Police cruiser, with the thick blue line and Tucson-Police written on the side. They parked brazenly at the front of the house.

Knocking heavily at the front door, they were let in, and sat on the couch, opposite the family. Jack and John were sweating, anxiously waiting for the grilling to start.

'Okay,' Big-man said, breathing like a locomotive, 'I've looked you two up on-line, and see that you've been missing for over two years.'

'Yep, that's right,' both agreed.

'Now, you're *back*,' he continued, still breathing loudly. Jack and John both nodded.

'What, er...happened?' Big-man asked curiously, while thin-man took notes in a small blue covered book. Jack proceeded to tell him the concocted story. Big-man pushed and pushed for the location of the kidnappers, but Jack said, and John furiously nodded, that they didn't know. They'd promised not to tell what they knew, and they intended to keep their end of the bargain. Big-man grunted at that, but didn't say anything that was language.

When Jack and John ventured in and out of the assailant's house, they had dark hoods over their heads. They guessed they weren't far away from home, maybe New Mexico, but didn't really know. They were very vague, by design. The agent's both seemed to accept their versions of the truth. Either that, or they didn't really care.

They didn't separate them and question them individually at all, as they'd feared. They expected the worst but got way better than that. Both got the impression that they didn't really care, whichever way the cards fell. They were just there to collect information and close the file. There'd been no crime committed at their end, so interrogation or questioning, wasn't required.

Jack finished by re-stating that they promised the kidnappers they would not press charges. And that was the way they wanted it to be. As to motive, Jack reiterated they had no idea. John tried to look as confused as possible, which he did well, mainly because it was authentic. He was scratching his cheek and looking muddled. The older he got, the vaguer he became, so it came naturally, even though he was still relatively young.

The Policemen said they would amend their records and update the Missing Persons Database. Case solved, they said. Kidnapping was a felony, so it would have to be investigated, they said. It would be handed electronically to the FBI, who would eventually come calling, in about six months, they said. Big-man told them they would mark it as low-priority, when they uploaded it to the FBI database.

Then both the Policemen were escorted out of the house, and back to their car. In a spray of dust and gravel, they were gone. Once the interview was terminated, they were keen to get out, and back to the station. The policemen clearly had another appointment to go to. Impatience seemed to be the name of the game.

Back in the loungeroom, Jack glanced at his dad, 'seeing you outside, in the full light of day, you didn't look so good. No offence...but you were pale and seemingly low on energy. You lurched a bit to the left...are you, okay? Jack peered at his dad uneasily and continued to look him over. Something was clearly wrong with him.

John knew Jacky kept him on a tight rein. He appreciated it, but occasionally, his close attention became a bit annoying. Ever since he got cancer, his son treated him like his next step could be his last. It was great for him to be so invested in his health. But his depth of concern occasionally became too much to bear.

'Dad, we need to get a human doctor to look you over, confirm your cancer status. You know...see where you're at. See if what the Pianif said, was actually true. I know you're pain-free, which is a great sign, but we need to truly confirm it, here on Earth.' His dad was smiling lovingly, and had a beaming expression, while his son spoke. John was proud of Jack and agreed with almost everything he said.

'Agree Jacky. I certainly don't suffer from back pain, or any pain...so, I assume that at the very least, my remission continues. At one stage, in their craft, the pain was almost intolerable, and I thought I would die...but now, *nothing*. Zero pain. There's been no pain since I took the non-human dip.' John smiled ear to ear.

'I'll make an appointment with Dr. Friedman love,' Krissy said. He's still there, you know. She stole a mischievous glance at her husband.

***

The family sat in the waiting room of Milagros Family Healthcare on 12th Avenue in Tucson. Waiting to see Dr Friedman who knew all about John's medical woes...and there were many. He was a surgical oncologist and specialised in cancer of the kidneys and liver. Jack had huge faith in him, as a kind and highly qualified doctor. He'd been seeing him ever since they moved into the area five years ago.

After their name was called, the whole family piled into his room and took up every square-inch of his room. 'This is fantastic news,' Dr Friedman started with, 'to have you all home, is really terrific. I remember seeing you, Krissy, several times, early on. For some tranquilisers.'

'And a kind voice to talk to.' Krissy said wistfully.

'Of course,' he said, smiling kindly. So, you want to check on the remission of your cancer. You've missed many scheduled CT's John, while you were away. These, we understand, were out of your control...but it's a *great* idea to check now.'

Any significant pain, anywhere?' The doc asked.

'None,' John replied happily. He'd been free of pain since his non-human dip.

'That's a good start John. Normally, I would give you a form and send you upstairs to get a CT done. But I'll do yours myself. Come with me,' the doc said happily. 'I haven't done one of these since med school.' They all filed out of his office, and in a single line, they walked down the hall to the front of the surgery. From there they took the elevator, and went up one floor.

***

'Please come back in,' Dr Friedman said brightly, pointing at the empty chairs in his office. 'Okay, results are in.' He still sounded happy, but more guarded than before. John could feel the sweat break out on his forehead. His life depended on the next few minutes. It was *live* or *die* time. *Right now.* Jack was almost ready to pass out. He saw stars and bright white light before his eyes, but he maintained focus on the doc's computer-screen. The doc read the summary silently, then looked at the images on his screen. John stared at the wall, wishing he would hurry up, and get to the result. He prayed to God that the Pianif were telling it as it was. He hadn't doubted it, *until now.* Jack's words that miracles were rarely true, rang in his ears, and danced uncomfortably before his eyes.

After magnifying a few areas, the doc turned to look at John grimly, to tell him whether, chemo, radiation, and the likelihood of death returned to envelop him and his loved ones. John was gasping and shivering violently, almost slipping off his chair. The doc could see he was struggling, so he pushed his glasses up on his nose, and hurried with his diagnosis. The doc focussed on the scan and searched for the tumours in his kidneys and stomach.

'Well, well, John...seems incredible, but the lymphoma in your stomach and kidneys has completely *gone*. Not inactive or dormant but *gone*. You were in remission John, but now, it seems, you are entirely cancer-free. Somehow, since our last consult, you have been *cured*. One for the books, no doubt. The doc looked at him, jubilant, but puzzled by his miraculous recovery. He smiled, ear to ear, but couldn't help wondering how this ridiculous marvel had occurred. Jack saw the doubt cross his face like a shadow. The doc had never seen this in 40 years of Oncology. It was way beyond extraordinary. The docs first thought was, the scans were mixed up, but he'd know John's scans anywhere.

John heard the news and was speechless. *Floored*. So was the doc. Friedman looked numbly into John's wide-eyes and his mouth dropped open in pure disbelief. Jack felt like cheering at the top of his voice. John realised in a moment of thundering realisation, that the Pianif had actually cured him. Everything they said to him was *true*. All the dreadful things he'd thought about them, evaporated in a micro-second. All that was left was gratitude and appreciation for a race that possessed some pretty spectacular advanced tech, humans couldn't hold a candle to.

Well, *fuck me,* John thought gratefully. Cured by non-humans...confirmed, *absolutely amazing.* Their technology, their medical expertise, was nothing short of extraordinary. Incredibly, they could cure *different* species. For the primitives on Earth, it truly was...*a genuine miracle.* The very real embodiment of advanced technology that presents as magic.

John crossed himself, thanked God, then got up from his chair and thanked the doc effusively. Jack and John hugged tightly. Their hopes and prayers had been answered. Krissy stood and joined in, putting her arms around both of them.

John had readied himself for a bad diagnosis, but incredibly, he got the opposite. A clean bill of health. What the Pianif said was true. He had no cancer – none *anywhere*. He was ecstatic, for himself, and especially Krissy.

He was happy for Jack too. He had been with his dad every step of the way. Hopefully, his son could enjoy the fruits of John's success. And relax a bit and live his own life for a while.

Dr. Friedman stood up again, and so did John. The doc held his hand out and John vigorously shook it and thanked him profusely for all his help. Jack smiled at his dad, and he smiled hugely at everyone. Krissy wore an irresistible grin. This meant everything to her. Not only was John back home, but he was cancer-free as well. The doc sat back down and looked at his computer screen.

Jack was bemused, and wondered why the unhealthy colour of his dad, if he was so well? It didn't make sense. Simply age, he thought with a shrug. *Whatever*, he was stoked with the result. It gave him faith in the Universe.

Now he knew for sure, Jack thought. The Pianif could cure genetic diseases like cancer, and probably a lot more besides. They had the answer humanity had sought forever.

One thing concerned him; he simply couldn't get his head around it. Cancer was a human genetic disease. But the Pianif didn't have our genome or DNA. John was cured of cancer, in a device manufactured for the Pianif. For Jack, and the "googling" he'd done since he got home, that was impossible. The answer was beyond him. It operated with a combination of audio frequency and fluid. It was like nothing on Earth.

The result was magnificent, no doubt about it, but something important was missing. *Gift horses*, he knew, but serious questions remained unanswered. The suspicions and the questions were always with him, day and night. Had the Pianif been to Earth before, to harvest human DNA?

Jack tried to imagine the Pianif medical tech being available here on Earth. It would start a *fucking* revolution. The number of people who died of cancer, or who contracted cancer each year, was nothing short of horrendous. That device would be a Godsend for the entire planet and save millions of people and billions of dollars. Jack wished the secret was part of his stash of papers but doubted it..

Dr Friedman looked up from his computer and his face became stern. He looked at John, then glanced back at his computer, and frowned deeply. His distinguished face became brooding. Jack did a double take at the doc and felt a chill of uncertainty.

'Now John, I am reading the part highlighted in red.' His voice was heavy with caution. The doc pointed to it with a pen on the screen. Jack looked at it, and could see the red, but couldn't make out the writing. He felt like saying '*huh*'? If *he* couldn't read it, his dad had no hope.

Dr Friedman was looking at it, and glancing at us, like it was deal-breaking. What else had the scan found? His dad's chin twitched with anxiety. Krissy went from ebullient to petrified in a finger-snap. Jack felt like his world had come crashing down. What the hell was wrong? The doc looked puzzled.

Dr Friedman frowned at the screen with blank incomprehension. Whatever it was, it clearly had the doc stumped.

'Oh, for God's sake, what is it? Jack blurted. Might as well lay it on us, he thought. How bad can it be? He wondered. Then he thought, '*oh fuck*.' This was a doctor's office.

'Radioactivity,' the doc said slowly. 'John, you've been exposed to something that has given you the radioactivity of an astronaut. It's not lethal, but it's odd...and *notifiable*. Er...John, have you been near anything that might fit the bill?' The doc was scratching his chin, and looking at John curiously, like he'd grown another leg. It was clearly something he didn't expect in a million years, from anyone like John. It simply didn't make sense.

Jack was horrified. He was speechless but gratified that his dad's health wasn't compromised. No wonder he'd been looking a little tired, and a tad pale. His father, and probably him, had received a fair dose of ionising radiation, from the tech they'd been exposed to.

'Doc, what did you mean by *notifiable*? Jack asked nervously, knowing the likely meaning. He didn't like the sound of the word. In fact, anything like it, was to be avoided like Covid. Putting us on a list, was a huge *no-no*. It was something his plan wouldn't stand for.

'I mean, it must be reported to the CDC.' The doc said. 'The requirement only recently got added, but the CDC made a big noise about it. Any cases over 15,000 millirems must be reported, or significant fines apply. So, like I said, it's *notifiable.*'

Jack frowned and couldn't believe it. They were so close. Now, *this*. It could be the fly in the ointment that brings the whole plan down, he thought, exasperated. Jack with bulging eyes, couldn't think. His brain was spinning. This could ruin all his meticulous plans. Jack looked at John, and he was met with his dad's appalled, vacant stare. He too, knew what it meant. His details would be given to the government.

John realised this would put a massive *stop* sign in front of them. Jack was terrified of the word. *"Notify"* meant they would be officially *on record.* His name and address would be handed to the Executive on a silver platter, and they would know of his dad's anomalous radioactivity.

The CDC wanted names and addresses of everyone who was captured under the new legislation. And Jack reckoned he knew why? A map of those with high levels of radioactivity would tell the government the story they sought. And that story was deeply rooted in UFOs and UAPs. Non-human intelligence had craft that were radioactive, and the government knew as much. It could blow Jack's meticulous plan out of the water, even before he started. So much for anonymity, he thought.

Of course, there would be a few who obtained their reading through nuclear energy exposure, but *most* would involve exposure to non-human UFOs. There was little doubt that their own jaunt in the Pianif's craft, did the job on John, and probably on Jack as well. And this was the government's covert way of finding out.

There was some chance the machine his dad bathed in, did it. But he doubted it. It worked using audio frequency and chemicals, Rendn said. Radioactivity wasn't part of it.

There were a large number of humans globally, that had been irradiated by close proximity to UFOs. Some just carried it internally, such as John, others developed sores, and still others developed distinct spotting. Jack knew this by the research he'd done since returning to Earth. He reckoned they were both exposed by their proximity to the Pianif vessels. Jack felt like screaming and shook his head in despair. *All the best laid fucking plans,* he thought angrily, wondering bitterly if this would bring them crashing to the ground.

The relationship between UFOs and irradiated humans was unquestionable. And the government knew it as well. The CDC could create a map for the CIA, the DSI, the NSA or whomever needed one. A map could be generated on the spot, for those that needed to be visited, and silenced. To make sure that they didn't tell anyone about their experience.

They did it because the USA didn't want it known that UFOs were a National Security, or any issue, for them. They wanted it to appear to Russia and China, and anyone else, that they knew nothing about them. That the extra-terrestrial tech, if they were real, was a complete mystery. UF-*What*? Never heard of them.

Jack was beyond frustrated with the federal government – they kept all sightings and knowledge of UFOs on the down-low. They were in a nasty cold-war with Russia and China to see who could fully reverse-engineer the tech of a UFO first.

Whoever unravelled them first, would have access to advanced alien technology. Air and ocean superiority was on offer to the winner.

Jack and his dad had the incredible, once-in-a-lifetime, chance to make sure it was America that won the war of smarts. But if they did it, they needed to do it, without putting their family at risk. The family, *all of them*, realised, what the magnitude of this intel was. It could remove them from the face of the planet if *anonymity* wasn't observed to the letter.

Jack had to think of everybody. His sister lived with her husband and young daughter in Ontario, Canada. Jack didn't want people taking pot-shots at them, following release of the information. Her daughter was a-cute five-year-old, and he owed her a secure future. Release of the intel must put *NO ONE* at risk.

***

Jack gave the backpack a rub and realised he held the power of the Gods. Good *and* bad, the wad of papers from the Pianif, *could* be glorious, or a massive rod in his back. The need to be wary, had never been more real. The image of his mum and dad hugging was front and centre, and it told him all he needed to know.

6

Intel

"I don't want to believe. I want to know."
— Carl Sagan

Jack's bag was full of pieces of paper, inside a fat blue folder. The Pianif had gone to pains to make sure it was all written down in English. Thankfully, they were in possession of the bulk of our internet. Downloaded from the Mars Telecommunications Orbiter. It had lessons on human languages therein, which were backed up by our TV microwaves. Pianif satellites In deep orbit received a lot of Earth's TV by EMAR. So, our main languages were no mystery to them.

Jack looked at the papers, and knew they were full of detailed formulae and math, and algebra. Electromagnetism and gravity were mentioned a lot. As was the Uncertainty Principle, phase space, harmonic oscillation, Casmir effect, dark matter and dark energy. It seemed that each of them was fundamental in FTL travel, and also accessing quantum Zero Point Energy. They used human terms which was a huge advantage.

The question remained. How do we get all this intel to the required people, institutions and corporations, without putting ourselves or Krissy at risk. He knew how hard it'd be. Earth was a security-intelligence nightmare.

Jack knew none of them could ever lose sight of the explosive nature of the intel they were so nonchalantly carrying. That had to be at the front of their minds at all times.

The next few weeks were momentous for their family, and to Earth. The most important decisions for Jack's parents remained, what to have for dinner? Jack didn't want it any other way. He watched them and listened to the banter and mockery and smiled. As much as he tried, he couldn't change them, and really, didn't want to.

Jack loved them both dearly but wondered if they were up for the strict discipline involved with abject anonymity. Jack would take care of most of it, but it would also involve them playing their role and playing it well.

Jack shuddered, and felt the hair rise on his arms. In his backpack was enough intel to take them all down entirely, not in the short-term, because human devices, like cars and houses, still needed electricity and fuel. But in the longer term, all the oil wells and distillation plants would vanish forever. Earth would finally say goodbye to dirty energy. And the blowback for the family, might be a killer, unless it was managed, just right.

Electricity for everything, eventually would come from a very different source, one that had been in production since the Big Bang, 13.8 billion years ago. The creation of the Universe also created ZPE.

***

John and Krissy's ongoing health were good reasons to shred the pages, but the benefits for Earth in the longer term were so good. The intel could literally save the planet. Jack emphatically believed it *had* to be released. But they needed a huge helping of caution, and anonymity. No-one must know it was them.

In his quieter times, he wondered if he was doing the right thing. Jack could walk away from it all, and his folks would be safe. But he *couldn't*, his mind wouldn't let him. He was obsessed by the writing in his backpack. It would save the planet from the terminal trajectory, oil and coal had it on. Jack knew he *had* to use it. It was too valuable to keep it to himself. Jack wanted the best of both worlds. Release the intel AND keep the source, a deep, dark secret.

That way, Jack keeps his folks away from the hangman, and Earth is saved. He wins twice.

Pietr said the new energy was clean and unlimited. It would also be free. Jack looked up Zero Point Energy on the internet, and many physicists said it was impossible to access, and countless said it didn't exist at all, *period*, prevented, apparently, by the Uncertainty Principle. These people should meet the Pianif because *they'd accessed it.* The energy from the Zero Point, powered their entire planet, including their spaceships. The physicists from Earth were just plain wrong.

Jack held all his muscles tight, swallowed hard, and was determined. This would help Earth so much.

Jack was still worried about his dad. Compared to his mum, he still had *that* look to him. He was deathly pale and sweated too easily. A side-effect of ionising radiation. John was taking potassium-iodide tablets three times a day. But he was still symptomatic. Dr Freidman said to return in two weeks if his fatigue continued. So far, it didn't look good.

The tablets themselves were crushed by his wife, and mixed with apricot jam, because John had trouble swallowing. Jack wouldn't be happy, until his dad returned to his rosy glow, and had plenty of energy. Now, he was pale, pasty and constantly hot, and lethargic, courtesy the radiation. Jack himself wasn't symptomatic of radiation, which mystified him. It might have been his age, or because he didn't receive any dose. The latter really confused him because he went everywhere his dad did. Except the bath. Maybe that answered the question.

The CDC reported regularly to the CIA and the NSA. Then those people that didn't receive the radiation through "normal" channels, were paid a visit by their agents from the CIA. Demands of total silence and threats of violence to the family, no doubt followed. This was one-way UFOs were kept quiet. All quite illegal, but that didn't stop the thugs from the Pentagon.

John would effectively, be branded by the radiation. By something that glowed brightly in the dark. A tattoo. Everything, Jack wanted to avoid, could become a reality. And it might mean erasure of the bloodline by Big-Oil. Because then, we would be prime suspects for the future event that Jack was planning.

A huge spanner was now shoved into Jack's plans of anonymity. Everything he wanted to achieve might be burnt to a crisp. The intel was supposed to be released, inside a dark shoal of secrecy...*now this*.

Jack was sitting at the dining-room table, deep in thought about their next move. His folks were fighting about which TV channel to watch. *Cie la vie*. Jack focussed more closely on them and realised he held their lives in his hands. While they fought over TV channels, he fought to mitigate their risk of being murdered. He'd warned them of the stakes, over and over. But it fell on deaf ears. Theirs were tuned elsewhere.

John and Krissy lacked any overt capacity for subterfuge or advanced thinking. It would be all up to him. And by watching them fight over the remote-control, he really knew it.

Jack had made a few landmark decisions, and he shared them with his dad and mum. Firstly, he had decided to do it. This stuff was too important *not* to release, and his folks concurred. The Pianif had themselves decided that humanity needed it, and who were we to argue against it.

***

'*No, no, no, NO,*' Krissy screamed hysterically, when Jack told her, they'd both be going on the trip. They would leave Krissy home. They emphasised that it was key to share the driving, on a very long and taxing journey.

'What in *fuck* was happening here?' She cried disbelievingly. 'You intend to *leave* me again?' Krissy shrieked. '*Surely fucking not.*' Krissy had tears of rage and incredulity in her eyes, which had now flowed to her cheeks. 'You do remember last time, right?' Her eyes were wide open and flashed at Jack. '*You can't leave me, again. I won't let you.*' Her voice was a cry of blind panic. High-pitched and full of terror.

Jack grabbed his mum and made to hug her – but she pushed him away. 'Mum, we have to do this, *both of us need to go, to share the driving,*' Jack said pleadingly to his mum. Her face was twisted in revulsion. The thought of being left alone in the house for over a week, was too much.

Jack thought Krissy was winding down from her hysterics, but no. She'd stopped screaming, only to take a deep breath. '*I can take-no more alone time*,' she screamed, half sobbing and half whimpering. 'I can't b-be left a-alone in this house...while you two go on *another* trip.' Krissy was angry now, and stared Jack down with two beady eyes. 'Don't even think about it.' She spat at Jack angrily.

Jack peered at his mum, and knew he had to be firm. To execute his plan the right way, Krissy had to transform her mind-set. Serious trouble was brewing, and Jack could see it. Her agreement with his plan was critical, otherwise, the house of cards he'd built, could come tumbling down, and then all was lost.

'*Surely...there's another way?*' Krissy begged to Jack.

'No, there's not mum - this is the *only* way.' Jack said firmly.

Jack walked up to his mum with his arms out, walking into her and hugging her close. This time she didn't push him away. Krissy knew it was non-negotiable. If Jack's plan was to work, this *had* to happen...apparently.

Sorry mum. We'll be as quick as possible.' Jack whispered into her ear.

This was how it had to be. Otherwise, the whole thing might just break.

Tomorrow, they would leave for Miami, to finally put the plan in place. Hopefully, any further visit to the house by the CIA, NSA or DSI would be made while they were away, and Krissy could simply bat them away.

The Notification to the CDC. It was constantly on Jack's mind, even at night.

As soon as Krissy understood exactly what Jack was suggesting, she said Jack should '*go for it.*' John gazed at his wife with tears of pride and admiration. She understood secrecy was important, but she was all for liberating the intel, because Mankind *needed* it.

Krissy just hoped like hell, that Jack wasn't planning, what she thought he was. Because, *no bloody way*, she'd be on-board with that. *Not again.* Liberating the intel got a huge tick, but not that. That got a gigantic *cross*.

***

Jack and John were almost ready to leave home - the seeds were in a small metal box in the boot. The brand-new laptop was right next to it.

Jack and John, intended to drive to Miami, share the driving, and stay with Jack's grandmother for a few days. Jack would place the seeds for the new plants in a small metal box and bury them in a one-foot-deep hole in the Biscayne National Park, which he had the GPS coordinates for, to be released later, while in Florida.

Growing these plants to maturity would allow removal of plant sterols, critical to production of the new concrete. That would take care of climate-change, and discarded plastic. It would fix atmospheric carbon, while it dried. Jack felt like beating his chest when he thought of doing it. It was essential for an oil-stained and smoky Earth, he thought. *Heave-ho,* to climate-change. And *heave-ho* to all the environmental poisons. Jack stood tall and with a gleam in his eye, he conceded that he truly felt like God.

In the shorter-term, the new concrete would attack climate-change, but in the longer-term, it would be ZPE. Either way, climate-change would be banished from the planet. Earth would get its pre-1750's climate back...permanently.

Jack would travel by car to the German Café, his old haunt, just off 27th Avenue in Miami central. Jack felt at home there. He would take a brand-new laptop and dispose of it after he left. Everything had been planned to the finest detail, and every element taken care of. Jack was satisfied that uploading from there, using an anonymous log-on would do the job. If he did it just so, his family would remain safe.

In the German café, he would search for *reddit.com*, which seemed perfect for his needs. Everyone who posted on *reddit* was anonymous. And the website was global. He would garner a profile and select the subject that would be either r/physics or r/energy. He noticed that there were dedicated UFO and UAP channels, but he decided against them. They attracted too many nutters and conspiracy theorists; people whose beliefs ruled their lives.

Using different names, Jack would describe his interactions with the Pianif and detail their fervent desire for Mankind to have the information, free of cost or obligation. It was provided as a gift to Mankind. He would make no reference to the Yuma mine, or anything that might implicate their location. The only reference would be to an abandoned mine. Locations, or names, would be withheld.

Jack knew that what he was about to do was super-dangerous. All the information he had was good news for Earth, in the longer term, but really bad news for many, in the shorter-term. It would eventually render the planet clean and give every human-being on the face of the planet access to free and unlimited energy from the 'Zero Point.' The quantum grid that fires virtual particles into and out of existence in the ether around us. So, it was unquestionably worth doing. Earth could be a home to humans for the next 500,000 years. But, humans, and every other oxygen breather on the planet would be gone if he failed. If he chose not to do it, Earth would be a dead husk in 150 years.

There was, however, a very catastrophic downside for a world that was built on the price of oil, and Jack knew it. Suddenly, the price for a barrel of oil would be close to $0.00. Stock markets across the globe would implode like dead stars. Unemployment would suddenly engulf the planet, like an economic tsunami. It would max out the world economy and be a problem for decades. The middle east countries and the Arab states would have nothing to support them. *Freefall.* The economy of the world would crash like an out-of-control airbus. Not one country would survive a hellishly deep depression, which would make 1930 look like a time of plenty.

It would all be for the best, he said to himself, chuckling caustically. *Like hell,* was his last thought on the subject. Jack knew Earth would be a basket-case in the short-term. But it was necessary if it was to be saved and render the planet sustainable. *Cruel to be kind*, Jack thought mordantly. Jack nodded to himself and smiled. That phrase summed it up perfectly.

Jack realised the oil industry would do anything to avoid the destruction of their world. So, it had to be released strictly, according to Jack's plan.

It was Jack and his family versus several trillion-dollar mega-companies, with thousands of employees, that would do anything to protect the status quo. These companies didn't even have to try – the money kept flowing in like a river in thaw. They had more money than they knew what to do with. Earth got hotter, ocean levels grew, and the climate got more unstable each year. Wildfires, mega-cyclones, floods, and ice-sheet thinning got worse every year – but, *hey*, profits were up!

Jack couldn't think of a nicer industry to terminate and junk. One that fucked up the biozone of the planet and only went through the motions of carbon reduction.

Pietr from Pianif, didn't plan for us to come face to face with such a potentially lethal and uncomfortable situation. He thought it'd be solely rainbows and glory for Jack and Earth. Maybe for a different population, he could well be right.

This was a simple *gift of intel* that might take humanity itself a millennium to achieve. Mankind might *never* achieve it. Many storied physicists on Earth, said that accessing the Zero Point was impossible. They were wrong. The intel from the Pianif was stunning and groundbreaking. Earth would suddenly be able to do everything it wanted to, and a few it thought were impossible.

***

Jack anxiously put the folder with the Pianif papers and the new laptop in the boot of his Daihatsu. He was nervous and terrified, but ready to roll. The journey started now. He'd fired up the computer and added what he would need - Including his email which was now set-up, and ready to go on his personal laptop.

He'd booked accommodation in Fort Stockton, San Antonio, Baton Rouge, Pensacola and Orlando along the way. The trip to Miami, and to his grandmother, would be circuitous, and over 2,000 miles. Roads were many and varied. Jack would start on Highway 10, which would get them most of the way there. Jack and John would do two hours of driving each and stop regularly to breathe and take a decent break from driving. The journey was to benefit all of humanity, so the plan needed to be accomplished carefully and on point.

There was no hurry for this, Jack knew. It had to be done right, the first time. Priority would always be *anonymity*. There could be no loose ends. He'd told his Nana they might be late arriving. Trying to guess how long it would take to get to Miami was difficult for something that was so bloody far away. His Nana knew nothing of the reason for their trip, and that was how it stayed, or she, herself would be a loose-end. And that was expressly forbidden.

Jack would then, on his own, take his papers and the laptop, to the German Café.

Jack reckoned his plan for the intel was first rate. Where he intended to place it was a very popular place that was passionate about anonymity. Every word and every formula contained in the papers would be uploaded to r/physics in *reddit.com*. Along with that, would follow a detailed description of his and his dad's non-human interaction.

Hopefully, it would be well received by countries he didn't even know existed. The bit about the cancer would blow people's socks off, around the world. It should be of global interest to a lot of people. As long as people didn't think I was peddling a load of bullshit. The more specific sites of r/UAP or r/UFO would be ignored, in favour of a subheading that was appropriate for all of it. Jack didn't know if this was right or wrong, but he reckoned it was the former, because it made good sense. The other sites attracted too many fiction writers.

Jack, John and Krissy would remain nameless throughout. Jack was still worried about the radiation, and Dr Freidman's transmission of their case to the CDC. That had the potential to destroy Jack's house of straw. It could come tumbling down if the CDC did the expected thing with the data.

* * *

Coming close to Pensacola was great, because it meant that they were finally, *finally* in Florida. After a long period behind the wheel, they were making progress. Into the home of the Miami Dolphins, Jack thought jubilantly, *his* team. With proximity, came icy sweat between Jack's shoulder-blades. Earth wouldn't know what hit it, he thought nervously.

They were slowing down to go left off the I-10 and into Pensacola itself, for their final stop. In front of them was a stationery car. It was stopped; to let a duck and its family of tiny ducklings cross in front of them. They were so cute, it hurt. Jack

145

glanced at his dad and smiled, both were keen to stretch their legs, and see the sights of Pensacola once they got to proceed.

Jack came gradually to a halt behind the stopped car and left a car length between them and the car in front. Out of nowhere, they were smacked in the rear by a hurtling plumber's utility, a guy who was on his way to work, but wasn't paying attention to local traffic.

The blow was enough to loosen teeth. The Ute had long white PVC "missiles" on roof-racks, and it struck their car from behind, without applying the brakes. The *impact* was loud enough to be heard on the coast.

Pipes punched into the back of Jack's car like projectiles from a tank, breaking his rear window into icicles of glass. The pipes pierced the back window of Jack's car and sent John's seat hurtling forward, colliding violently with the base of the dashboard.

John's leg was crushed and broken by the collision. The dislocated tibia protruded through the skin, causing massive bleeding and instantaneous agony. John threw his head back and screamed bloody murder, when he saw his leg, and felt the white-hot and nauseating pain that hit him like the insertion of a thick iron knife. 9-1-1 was already called by a local, with a mobile phone, who'd witnessed the crash. He told them that someone had probably died.

'*Dad...oh fuck*,' Jack cried, his voice choked with tears already. He saw his dad's leg and the pools of blood and was close to panic. He was comforted by the siren of an EMS coming to help them. Jack looked again at his dad and had to swallow down a loud cry of anguish. He was in so much pain and was shaking and twitching like he was in spasm. There was blood on his dad's clothes, even in his hair...*everywhere*.

Jack himself was unhurt, apart from a bump on the forehead. '*Holy...your leg dad.*' There was too much blood. The smell of wet coins was overwhelming. Jack twisted his neck, and looked for the ambulance. It had finally arrived, and two paramedics were on their way. '*HURRY*,' he shouted, through the shattered back window.

'*In here*,' Jack yelled, when they were approaching. The two paramedics opened the doors of the Daihatsu, one went to Jack, and one to John.

'*I'm fine*,' Jack bellowed, gesturing the second paramedic to go to his dad, who was in a bad way. His eyes were closed, and he'd lost a lot of blood, which was smeared over the inside of the car like undried paint.

Jack took another look at him, and shook his head grimly, wondering if this journey could have started any worse? Tears of worry for his dad, overwhelmed him. His image, covered in blood, with his leg and skin broken, would haunt him forever.

'His leg is busted.' Jack said to the paramedic, counting to ten, and trying his best not to panic. 'He's my dad, 62 years of a-age, from Tucson. We're going to Miami for a holiday, with my grandma.'

Jack wondered later if he should have used a cover-story, because he'd basically given some of the game away. Anyone who looked deep enough, would see that we'd visited Miami. '*Oh fuck*,' he thought when he realised. He batted his forehead softly with a fist. Jack couldn't believe he was so stupid.

He wasn't even there yet, and already there might be a problem. Tying us to the intel, which would soon appear on *reddit.com,* would be difficult, but *not* impossible. He placated himself with the knowledge that his dad had to be the focus – devising *cover-stories* were next to impossible in the heat of battle. Still, despite his justification, he worried about it. Jack refused to cut himself a break. If something happened to his folks, it was his fault, he knew. There was *no* justifying it.

'Okay,' one of the paramedics said, looking strangely apologetic. His dad screamed in blinding pain as his leg was straightened, to remove him from the car..

His dad was pulled out of the car, and placed on a gurney, and slid into an EMS, that took him straight to the local Baptist Hospital. Jack went with, and the paramedics were firm about it - Jack needed to be checked out too. In case he'd banged his head or suffered some other unknown internal injury.

Jack initially didn't want to go because his name and address would be registered. He eventually relented when it became clear they wouldn't take no for an answer. Jack said okay - just to shut them up. Another fly in the ointment, he thought glumly. Murphy's *fucking* law, again. He realised this time there was no way out. Murphy had them boxed in.

Jack laid a gentle hand on his dad's hot forehead, trying to ease his palpable pain. John was crying openly. The pain was carved in the myriad new lines on his face. He'd been given copious amounts of morphine, but his pain was simply too much to curb.

'That stupid car...I am so sorry dad,' Jack said, his face heavy with remorse. His dad's injury was bad, Jack struggled to even look at it, even though it was well covered. The jagged bone sticking out of his lower leg, was always front and centre in Jack's mind.

'Jacky, for God's sake, it wasn't your fault.' His dad said, choking down the pain of talking.

Jack argued anyway, even though he knew he shouldn't. 'I was the one driving dad,' Jack stuttered, yielding to the sobs that shook him. He held his dad's hand, and apologised again, feeling totally responsible. He had some more bad news for him, and Jack felt doubly bad about delivering it. Not only was he in the wrong place at the wrong time...he'd have to leave him, while he enacted the plan to help the planet.

'Dad, you need an emergency operation under a general anaesthetic, to set your leg and probably, they said, insert pins and screws. They'll be here soon to take you to the OR. He tore himself away from his dad with a muffled sob. He knew it wasn't fair, it was horrid, but enacting his plan, was literally now or never.

His dad had been through many medical nightmares, he thought. Now, he'd been handed another.

'Dad...I'll need to contact mum and tell her about it. She'll want to come and visit. There's no point in saying *don't* – she'll come anyway. So, I'll just tell her where you are. I'll, um...pick you both up from here in a week. The doc said your discharge date will be about a week away. It'll take me 2 or 3 days to upload the intel, and 2 days to get back from Miami. So, all up, it should take 7 days to get there, and back. I'll make sure I'm back in time to pick you up, dad, I'll liaise with the doctors to make sure I'm here, when you're ready to go home.'

His dad seemed so tiny in the large hospital bed, connected to the heartbeat monitor, which rang out its sonorous tune. An IV line ran into his arm...saline apparently. Jack felt like scooping him up and getting the hell out of there. But that was impossible to say the least.

Jack had a similar, although less intense feeling to the one in the Pianif craft. A feeling that things were out of his control. An overwhelming feeling of futility. He was an observer, nothing more. This was yet another one of those times.

Incredibly, his dad was still talking about joining him, for the excursion to Miami...which was steeply impossible. Then he asked Jack to delay the whole thing until he was better. He was surprised dad even asked. Saying no to him, would be hard, but necessary.

'Dad, for God's sake, you have an operation scheduled, which is essential. *No*...you are in the best place.' Jack said firmly, knowing he was breaking his dad's heart. 'The doctors will not let you leave, either. And I cannot delay the release of the intel...for a *month* until you get better. 'It might be years until you can bend that leg and get in a car dad. The doctors said you might *never* be able. I only tell you that, because going *now* is critical to my plan. Dad...please understand,' Jack pleaded. His dad closed his eyes and frowned. He wasn't happy but understood the logic.

Jack realised his dad's immediate destiny lay here, in the Baptist Hospital of Pensacola. Jack would go to Miami on his own. John felt like screaming in frustration, but he knew Jacky was right.

Three guys came into his dad's room, and said, '*right*,' like a whipcrack. They put the IV gently on the bed, and wheeled his dad out of the room, with no further words. John was headed to his appointment with the OR. Jack ran to catch up with the gurney, as they disappeared around the corner. There was no delay. The surgeons had scrubbed and were waiting. Jack's eyes filled with tears, as he ran after his dad's gurney.

'*Stop*,' Jack yelled, and the bed came to a halt. John was reaching out behind him. Jack wiped away tears, and took his dad's hand, which was held out behind him. '*Oh, thank Christ*,' John bleated, as Jack took his hand, and held it tightly. 'You'll be fine dad,' Jack said puffing, patting his dad's hand.

'Piece of piss,' John returned, smiling through the pain, as his son let go of his hand, which retreated under the covers. 'Good luck yourself, Jacky,' he said shakily, tearing himself away, with a choking cry.

'Right back at you, big guy,' Jack watched his dad's bed disappear around a corner, on its way to the OR. He felt for his phone, in his back-pocket. He needed to ring his mum, *without* injecting too much emotion, which would be hard.

Just the sound of her melodic voice was enough to get him started. This would be stressful and touching because mum would *not* be expecting it. Jack was not looking forward to the conversation which would be full of sobbing by both of them, and recriminations, negative statements and probably profanity.

He'd heard it all before – Krissy didn't need to tell him again. But she would. John had just got out of hospital – he didn't deserve to go back again, so soon. *Yeah, yeah*, Jack knew, and better, he agreed. Hospitals and his father needed to be kept apart. *No shit.*

***

Jack was terrified. His heart was pounding in his chest and he expected every step to be his last. He had already scoped out the café, and now he was there, in earnest. The Sun was shining brightly on a 30-degree-C-day, and he was finally sitting nervously in the German Café on 16th Street in Miami. To do the *deed*. To upload what would be the equivalent of a fusion bomb. It should annihilate the intellectual base of the planet. And lead to a more intelligent, cleaner, sustainable Earth.

This was the *Porto-Bello* shopping centre. A very ordinary, run-of-the-mill place. Inside the Café, was where it was all supposed to happen. He would upload all he had, and hope for the best. He saw the two girls behind the service-desk and felt like a gun carrying criminal. But he realised, to them, he was just another very ordinary and annoying customer.

He asked anxiously for all-day access to the internet. He told the girl who served him, that he was doing his Honours thesis, and attended the local Atlantis University. She really couldn't have cared less, but still, the story was out there. She replied with a gum

150

chewing and disinterested, 'really?' He expected to be tackled to the ground at any second by men in black suits from the government. Jack looked around nervously, and sighed heavily, thankfully, he was alone. There was no-one shouting, *PUT YOUR HANDS UP,* and no pinpoints of red light on his clothes. Jack was indistinguishable, among the few students, and that's how he wanted it. There were no government vans in the parking lot, and no suspicious characters at the door. Jack smiled to himself and took a deep breath. 'We made it,' he said anxiously to his backpack. Out the large picture window, he gazed at the greyness of the Miami River.

Next, he logged onto *reddit.com* and used the anonymous username he'd been given, electronic damage897, and the given password. He searched for *r/physics* and created a new post and titled it, *"TAKEN to a New World – A True Story."* Jack proceeded to tell the story of his, and his dad's interaction with the non-humans from Pianif. It sounded like complete garbage, but together with the intel, hopefully it would be believable to those who knew it to be so. Meaning a fully trained astrophysicist.

Jack could tell his concentration levels were making him breathe like a steam-train. He hoped he didn't get any undue attention, because of it. So far, by his covert screening of those in the café, the coast seemed clear. He sat in a corner, away from most of the people, so he reckoned he'd be okay.

To his *reddit* post, Jack linked a word document that contained all the intel from the Pianif. Amazingly, they'd provided all the intel in English. A lot of it was simple cut and paste. But some were re-creations of very technical formula, with intricate language that meant nothing to him. Hopefully, a seasoned physicist could understand it. Certainly, *he* couldn't, and most would be the same.

Jack looked at the pile of papers that he purported to be a version of his Honours thesis. '*Ha,*' Jack burst out, staring at it, still feeling the pounding of an anxious heart. This stuff was of such import, that it could break down the entire structure of the world. *Destroy oil and coal.* Jack was sweating like he'd been in a rainstorm. His body was shining, but he continued to type.

Jack kept gazing at the remaining pages until the words lost focus. It was just paper and letters, he thought dreamily, dumbstruck by its climactic power, that could rework the entire foundation of the planet.

He was absolutely floored by this stuff and continued to type feverishly. He had done mathematical physics in his second year of university, and some of the formula he uploaded looked familiar. But most made no sense at all.

The first piece of intel he uploaded was about the carbon absorbing concrete, designed to cure climate change. Uploading intel wasn't all that was required though. Jack had a hand-held GPS locater and he needed to bury the requisite seeds at exactly 25.8826° N, 80.1806° W. This pointed to the Biscayne National Park, and was specifically referred to in the linked documents. The seeds needed to grow to maturity, and their sterols removed, and added to the concrete mix, in specific quantities, that were detailed therein. This, by itself, was Earth-shattering. Existing climate change would be cured lock, stock and barrel. Governments, and in fact the entire planet, would be jubilant. A major bottleneck would be shattered.

His dad and Krissy should be doing fine, he figured. Jack hoped they would be ready for pickup in about four days. His dad's doc said he'd be ready, that was good enough for Jack. He'd ring before he left for confirmation. As important as his parents were, the intel itself, dominated his mind during the day, and filled his dreams at night. He hoped Mankind used it, to its full extent. The Pianif gave it to us, like a gift, now we had to take the bit between our teeth. It would be up to humanity.

***

Jack laboured over several pages from the Pianif that were dedicated to two forms of interstellar FTL drive. One was creating a warp-bubble, and contracting space in front of the craft. The other was creating special wormholes, and using dark energy to stabilise space, and gravity to dig a hole in spacetime, which is basically a "fabric" if treated right. The intel showed humanity how to turn space into a solid mass. Every space agency on Earth would have their work cut out, recreating it. But now they had the knowledge.

Jack was sweating over pages that would direct humanity to dark matter and dark energy, which were special types of Higgs particles apparently. These were absolute game-changers. Characterising dark energy would allow humanity to create anti-gravity and move on from rocket engines and propellant. They would be able to float to orbit, and float like a kite in the atmosphere. Engines, aero-dynamic surfaces and tails were yesterday's technology.

Jack had a soft spot for the TOE - the theory of everything. This was the stunning missing link between Einstein's relativity and the quantum world. He found it extremely difficult to upload. Jack looked at it and snarled malevolently. The symbols used were unfamiliar and downright *annoying.* It was several pages of detailed, complex formulae with unfamiliar, unused symbols that were totally unknown to human physics, and the Pianif said so. Jack found the symbols difficult to reproduce with the keyboard he had, requiring a lot of improvisation. Narration and explanation by the Pianif was included with the new symbols, but the Pianif made humanity seem like children. The Pianif's explanation was worded in a way where it was hard *not* to take offence. They were definitely talking down to us. Jack reworded it to remove the innuendo.

Jack was baffled and had little doubt that it was an example of different thinking, divergencies caused by varying brains, and brain chemistry. The discipline of xeno-psychology, about which Mankind knows zero, was brought into clear focus. Non-humans thought differently to humans – *big surprise*.

Now, instead of two separate theories, that were separated by a brick wall, humans would have one encompassing model of gravity. It was General Relativity, but it would directly link to quantum gravity. *One* theory – from beginning to end. *Yay*, he thought. This was a huge step forward. Jack was ecstatic about this part in particular. In his second year at Uni, he dabbled in physics and was always taken aback by the shortcomings with gravity. Gravity at the quantum level, was like building a Moonbase. You knew it should exist, but...it didn't.

Jack abruptly felt sick, knowing how much work he had left to do. He still had a towering wad of paper to get through. It sat in the centre of his table like a steel block – every page like compressed lead, supercritical with intel he needed to upload.

Jack kept typing frantically, trying to finish as soon as he could, wiping sweat away with his hand. He knew he had to rejoin his family asap, he could hear his mum and dad calling his name. Getting gradually louder and higher in pitch, until it was a scream for him to come and get them. His typing became more intense and more feverish. In many places, he edited the paper and cut and pasted direct to his *reddit* page. He tried to move as quickly as possible, but quality, he knew, was critical too. Jack made sure that every word, and every formula, was uploaded correctly.

Jack felt certain that he'd left his dad in the lurch. It made him type even faster. Guilt was eating him alive. The papers from the Pianif were spread across the table, for all to see. Purportedly, his Honours thesis. Thankfully, no-one had a clue what these pages were, or what he was doing, and much less even cared.

The Pianif had pages dedicated to dimensions and string theory. Jack knew about them vaguely. But to a very real, ridgey-didge astrophysicist, the data was gold. And that went for all of it. To those in the know, all the intel, was pure, 24 carat gold. Trained physicists would die for this stuff..

Additional dimensions allowed Pianif houses to hide tech and comforts and would be eaten up by the population of Earth. Not least, was the explanation of how they powered their world with clean, free and unlimited energy. Quantum Zero Point Energy was easy to access when you knew how. And the paper on his table, did exactly that. It told Earth how to get it. *Yikes*, Jack thought. The hair on his back and arms stood to attention, when he thought about the magnificent things ZPE would do for our planet. There were a few bad ones too.

Jack was fretting and sweating, and it wasn't just his breakneck speed, and his dad's injury, that was causing it. He was horrified by the thought that, he and his family, might be *pin-pointed*. Every noise he heard, and every car that parked, was *them*. *He was outed*. And they'd get mum and dad too. A car that backfired in the parking-lot outside, nearly gave him a heart attack. Jack was wound up tighter than an over-sprung watch. .Jack's thoughts were slowly sending him mad, he reckoned, with a nervous smile, frozen by the potential repercussions of what he was doing, right *now*.

His mind was a fertile playground. He envisioned the CIA would arriving from the Pentagon and surrounding the café. Armed secret-service agents would stride into the café en-masse, locate him, lock him with manacles, and march him, *goose-step style,* to a black van with blackened windows in the carpark. In front of a crowd of chanting, baying people. Mum and dad would never hear from him again. He would be hauled off to Guantanamo Bay with a hessian bag over my head.

It didn't happen, of course, and after 10 hours and 2 days at the table, Jack wiped away sweat for the last time and was done. He'd uploaded every word and every formula the Pianif had given him. Jack stood up and stretched to his full height. He laughed out loud and immediately second-guessed what he was doing. But looking around, it was *obvious*, no-one gave a shit about him, or what he was doing.

The closest person was four tables away. The only other person in the entire place was a morbidly obese guy in the corner who was fighting with his mouse, that had apparently stopped working.

Jack wondered if what he'd uploaded would be taken seriously. Surely, the hard science, the...*new* physics, would stand on its own. But maybe it wouldn't get that far. People might read the intro and decide this was written by a lunatic, and didn't go any further. "*Who is this idiot?*" People might say. Jack's heart skipped a beat, as he contemplated it going nowhere, being treated as 'out-there' fiction. Jack swallowed hard and held his breath. He looked out the window and fought back a wave of nausea, as he contemplated this whole thing possibly being a colossal waste of time.

The science would be irrelevant if no-one reads it. Some would understand; wouldn't they? Jack was hopelessly unsure. Word of mouth should apply, shouldn't it? Jack felt like curling into a ball and going to sleep. He couldn't stop yawning. This had sapped all his energy. The whole process had been enervating; he had *nothing* left.

Jack shook his head, bared his teeth, and muffled a grunt-scream. Literally anyone, anywhere on Earth, with the right access, could read the intel that had been garnered from the Pianif. Jack's job was done. He felt like crossing all his fingers and toes. Now, it's Earth's turn, he reckoned, it's *over* to you! Jack had a smile that couldn't be contained. He felt like screaming, shouting in joy.

Actually, he knew it wasn't done yet. He still had to bury the seeds at the precise GPS location specified in his upload. Otherwise, the concrete would not do its job. And what a job it had in front of it. With a pounding heart, he swept a hand across his forehead to get rid of the sweat, that made his whole-body shine. He'd worked hard but the upload itself was complete. His part was finally almost done. It was over to the readership of *reddit* to recognise it.

Jack tried to blank his mind, to keep his mum and dad out of his thinking. *It would be, what it would be*, was Jack's final philosophical thought. After paying his account, he fled the café and drove away unaccosted.

Despite his efforts, his mum and injured dad were high in his mind. He hoped like hell his mum was in Pensacola, with his dad. If she wasn't, there would...Jack terminated that train of thought; it was too painful. He'd pick them both up in three days.

Before arriving at his Nana's house on 29th Street in Miami, he'd visit beautiful Biscayne National Park. Per his upload, he'd bury, a foot deep, the slightly rusty tin of seeds, that had to be grown to maturity, to supply the plant sterols to the new concrete mixture. The plants were native to Pianif, and didn't grow on Earth naturally, but they could have. They would affix the carbon from the atmosphere and permanently stabilise used plastic. Jack had a shovel in the boot, all he needed was dirt, in the right spot.

When he buried the seeds, he would be careful that he wasn't sighted and identified and would remove the registration plates on his car. That would guarantee his privacy, he thought, as long as he wasn't seen by the Miami police. If he was, without plates, he'd be arrested on the spot, and that would be an apocalyptic disaster. His plan would be officially out the window. Any intrusion by the authorities was the stone-final termination of his plan.

7

Response

"If it can be destroyed by the truth, it deserves to be destroyed by the truth." — Carl Sagan

Many very smart and credentialled people thought Zero Point Energy didn't exist. They thought it violated Heisenberg's physics or was forbidden by the Conservation of Energy. It is actually vacuum energy and is everywhere and gives space its non-zero energy value.

The discovery of ZPE is a major bottleneck clearer for an intelligent race. Non-humans have known it for millennia. Humans are just late to the game.

Technology and understanding, *not physical laws,* are the barrier. The oil industry doesn't want humanity to know – but it's there...waiting to be milked. Humans continue to prefer dirty, expensive energy, that puts our biozone at risk. Non-humans shake their heads in exasperation and ask, *why? WHY* destroy your planet with carbon-dioxide when you don't have to? There is unlimited, free, clean energy at your fingertips, waiting to be tapped.

It was from the Zero Point, that the Pianif propose Earth be powered, from homes to factories and businesses, to cars, aeroplanes, harvesters and everything else. Energy would flow from the vacuum to power not only quantum virtual particles, but entire planets too. Free, clean, unlimited energy. The power of the big bang. But only for those that knew how to access it. Energy from the ZP was there for the taking, and was a major, fundamental, non-human secret.

Now, it would be available to humanity and Earth. It would no longer be a secret. Jack hoped that someone of note would take notice of what was written. Because it could save Earth from those who were seemingly determined to wipe it out.

Petrol distilled from oil, fuelled billions of cars, the world over. So, the addiction was deeply embedded in the fabric of Earth and very difficult to treat. Incredibly, Jack knew with finality now, that its days were numbered. The addiction would be broken. And it would be done cold turkey, by what he did in Miami.

Jack had just uploaded information that could stop fossil fuels in its tracks. Break its grip on the blue planet. Of course, cars would ensure a continuing demand for oil, until EVs took over completely. Then oil would be on its way to exit Earth, stage right.

Whichever way Jack looked at it, what was originally spread over his table in Miami, was the death-knell for oil and coal. And for millions of jobs on Earth but it was essential for long term survival of the planet and humans.

***

The next day, with bated breath, Jack checked on progress of the intel. There was virtually no reference to it, apart from some dude in Tuchkovo, Russia, who clearly read it in detail, and said it was the power of UFOs, revealed. He'd contacted the Moscow State University to look into it. The story was originally printed in the Moscow Times and reprinted by the Washington Post.

Jack was bitterly disappointed, and thought that the extraordinary science he'd uploaded would have gotten a nuclear reaction. He threw the rest of the newspapers in the back seat of the car, and drove to the Baptist Hospital, ready to pick his mum and dad up, and drive them home. Jack was buoyed by the good news from the surgeon. His dad was discharged to leave, anytime today.

Jack sweated and strained for days and was certain that it was all groundbreaking. But looking at all forms of the media, there was virtually *nothing*. He knew his impatience was off the grid - he'd been told enough times. But *something* was definitely wrong.

Jack was pretty sure he'd got it right. If it was important, *reddit* should work. He was no expert though, and thought, he should've researched more. Jack was flabbergasted and wondered if he'd over-estimated the site. Jack conceded that he didn't have an answer, but things *weren't* going to plan, and that only left a couple of answers.

***

Jack turned right, off Route 10 and drove up the gravel driveway to the house. His mum was in the front seat, and his dad spread over the rear, with his injured leg raised.

'What a Goddamn trip,' he said raspily, as he got out of the car and stretched. Then he went to help his dad get out of the car, and hobble into the house.

'Thanks Jacky,' his dad said, shuffling slowly inside, with help from his son. John sat on the sofa with his leg elevated on top of a pillow and kitchen chair Krissy had quickly retrieved. His left leg was covered with a cast and the leg of his pants was pulled up to rest on top. He was offered, but refused a wheelchair. Jack knew that anything like explaining or spelling out the dangers of walking, while in his state, was just wasted oxygen.

His dad was stubborn. A wheelchair implied he was disabled. John had used enough of them when he was sick. But he reckoned, he was fine to walk, with a bit of assistance. Now, that his dad was upright, he was ready to conquer the world, broken leg and all.

'We just have to wait a bit, for the reaction, Jacky...have patience,' his dad said. He knew Jack had none. Jack had to hold himself back from saying, *and you*, knowing from experience that his dad was on pins and needles too. That's where his emotion came from, he thought incredulously, eyeing his dad in utter disbelief.

'Jacky...just wait a bit, it'll come,' John piped, knowing any reaction from the intel might be some time off. Jack was again concerned by his dad's general appearance. He looked...er, pale and haggard. The bags under his eyes had returned, and his eyes were red and wet. He looked gaunt and white and was tired all the time. He knew his cancer was cured, so what on Earth was wrong with him now? Radiation...or was it something worse?

'Dad, are you feeling okay? Jack asked nervously. He had clearly forgotten that his dad had just been involved in a major accident.

'My leg is throbbing and painful, Jacky,' he said, patting it like a dog.

'Another hour, before you can have more pain relief,' Krissy added. 'Sorry love. Taking it too often can cause heart problems,' she said, pointing to the fine print on the bottle. 'Don't want you carking it,' Krissy said, with a cheeky smile.

Jack reckoned that his dad's response didn't totally answer his question. Perhaps the dose of radiation was worse than they thought. Or maybe some serious home cooking was the answer. Jack continued looking at him, positive something about his condition didn't compute. He was a worrier, through and through, no doubt, and his love for his dad, made it worse.

Jack put his mind to the Pianif papers once again. Without ZPE and the carbon concrete, climate-change would soon overtake the world.

Currently, many coastal cities and island countries struggled to keep rising sea levels at bay. States watched "mega-rains" destroy crops and homes. Fishing communities lost their catches to warming waters, and were demanding the oil conglomerates pay damages. They got nothing, no damages and no catch. And it was getting worse, by the day. Super-floods, wildfires, mega-tornadoes, hyper-hurricanes, steroidal-typhoons, prolonged heatwaves, unexpected cold snaps, were killing thousands of humans, destroying crops, and ripping Earth apart. Humans couldn't continue on the path they were on.

Jack reckoned power stations could stay the same. But instead of burning coal, oil or natural gas, to turn the wheel of power, we get the electricity from the energy of the quantum Zero Point.

With batteries, that store ZPE, every mode of transport will be run. Even agricultural equipment would use it. Anything with an internal combustion engine. Jack guessed that would include his lawnmower as well. *Imagine that*, he thought, swallowing down a chuckle of disbelief. A lawnmower running on a battery, charged with ZPE. Jack looked to the sky and did the sign of the cross on his chest.

'Dad?' John turned toward Jack. 'We'll check the major papers tomorrow. There's a newsagent in town we can visit. In the interim, I'll keep checking the socials, and newspapers, online.' Jack hoped and prayed that all his work, wasn't in vain. He was sure the data and the intel, and the words he added, detailing the Pianif-human interactions, were amazing and stunning. But they'd have to be *recognised,* as such. And not a pile of fiction. That was the sticking point.

Importantly, the intel needed to be believed and accepted as fact. Maybe I was just another lunatic uploading flat-out lies or hallucinations. Jack ran his hand through his hair and scratched his chin with doubt. He was sure the science would prove the story as fully non-fiction. But you had to get to it first ... and recognise it.

***

'Okay Jacky, sounds good.' His dad said, closing his eyes. He was tired and needed to rest his eyes for a bit. He reckoned it would take weeks for the info to be authenticated and take root. So, truckloads of patience were needed. He chuckled and chortled to himself, wondering how in God's name his son would do it. He wanted everything *now.*

Jack's mum was in the kitchen, cleaning up, and his dad had his eyes closed in the lounge-room. So, Jack checked *redddit.com* on his laptop. He went to *r/physics and* checked his link which was the Word document he'd created. His eyes widened to Moons. Jack's mouth fell open.

'*What the fuuuck?*' Jack howled at the top of his voice. '*What the hell is going on?*' He shrieked.

Jack was shaking his head bitterly. 'Any reference to Zero Point has been removed. It has just vanished. *Gone.* Jack snapped his head around to John and back again, when it was clear that his dad wasn't really fussed. Jack squealed with anger as he searched feverishly. Pages 3-12 simply aren't there. '*Why?*' He screamed incredulously.

'The pages where it was detailed, with formula and text to back it up, simply don't exist. They've been extricated by persons unknown.' Already, Jack had an inkling of who had done it, and why? *Fuckers,* he thought angrily. *Don't they realise the direction were going in?* All my hard work, down the drain. Jack was bewildered. He continued searching the upload, but it simply wasn't there. He turned his PC off entirely and started everything again. It still wasn't there. ZPE had seemingly gone for good.

All the rest of his upload remained untouched...but someone had gotten to it and had their way with it. It had to be an entity with administrative access. Probably the *fucking* US government, Jack thought angrily. Probably, some covert department from the Pentagon, he reckoned. Removed under Eminent Domain or state-secret bullshit probably. Jack shook his head and felt his heat rising.

Whatever the reason, it was a big fat *NO*, Jack thought morbidly. They are totally wrong. He pressed his lips together in anger and shook his head. '*No, NO, NO,*' he screamed. 'What the hell is wrong with these people? They are charged, literally voted in, to look after the people, and the planet. *We can't live without a planet*. What a joke,' Jack shouted angrily.

He was sure the government valued the economy and money, far higher than Mother Earth, there simply to be taken advantage of, without any thought of the future. The fact was that humanity was gone if the planet dies.

Jack was dazzled by the government's myopic stupidity. They should know better. He was surprised by their behaviour, but really not all that shocked. The government had a history of treating the public like dispensable idiots. He was certain they'd have some bullshit reason for deleting it, which would mean a whole lot to them, but fuck all, to Jack and the public.

What a bunch of clowns, Jack thought derisively. They lied every day. UFOs were real, and so was ZPE. How obvious did it need to be? Jack felt hot, angry and annoyed. Thinking about the government always did that.

There were non-human craft in the sky, using it, right now. The government had eye-balled it, they had actually retrieved craft from Roswell and other sites that *used* it. Before they off-loaded them to their defence-partners to attempt reverse-engineering, they'd laid their peepers on these machines and devices. So, to now proclaim that ZPE didn't exist, was rich. It was an out and out lie. And the public were expected to swallow it and accept it as gospel.

Given that they were only in government because of the public whim, the populations were poorly treated indeed.

The people in a democracy, had a government that in theory, was their own utility. Despite that, places like the USA, had a government that was a law unto itself. It kept its people in the dark illegally, while they hid the high-tech, and claimed, there was *no* coverup. That ruse was unravelling. Whistleblowers were coming forward in accelerating numbers. Word was out and it was reaching critical mass.

The arrogance of the government, and their conceal-first attitude to UFOs, made it harder, almost *impossible*, for Jack to succeed, as he wanted. He sought to do the opposite, literally hit the government's policy front-on. He had just disclosed how *real* they were. His upload showed that UFOs are authentic, and so is their technology that allowed them to be here. Jack stopped mid-stride, realising his upload, directly broke government policy on UFOs.

He'd coincidentally painted the government into a corner. The hide-them-at-all-costs policy was officially put to the sword. Anonymity was even more important now that he'd humiliated the USA federal government.

But why regard ZPE as a state secret? Jack couldn't work it out. It didn't make sense. Why protect Big Oil, he wondered? The obvious answer was tax dollars, which amounted to trillions. And employment and social structure, he believed. There were hundreds of millions of people in oil and associated companies across the globe. That part made sense. The rest was just wrong. Oil and coal were killing the planet.

Humanities hunger for high density energy gave us about 150 years left. And *yes*, governments around the world knew it, Jack was certain. It was the tax dollars and employment, pure and simple, that protected Big-Oil. It was a drug to governments, and they freestyled in it.

What about the public though? Jack couldn't get past it. As far as he was concerned, these government idiots were voted in by the people. Yet they did not have their best interests at heart.

So, they'd removed his pages on ZPE. Do governments honestly think it won't come out at some point? Humanity wasn't the smartest race on the block, but eventually, we'd stumbled over the answer by being forced to interact with benevolent non-humans.

ZPE *would* happen on Earth *eventually.* The most challenged idiot could see that. Many people, some of them well-regarded physicists, believe ZPE doesn't exist. Despite the fact that UFOs clearly use it. So, just because humans couldn't access it, *it doesn't exist.* Jack was agog at human arrogance.

Jack believed strongly that ZPE might as well be revealed to the planet now. Get over the short-term apocalypse. But now, his upload had been deleted, and it remained in the domain of non-humans only. A great opportunity had seemingly been forsaken. The capacity to access it, was now held by the US government, and like UFOs, it was hidden.

Jack conceded that ZPE would cause a tectonic shock, that would hit every part of the globe. Economies would be shattered, the world over. But everything in time would be rebuilt – stronger, better and cleaner. That was the way the government should look at it. Their attitude was wrong, and we were right, but that could be remedied, and there'd be no hard feelings.

***

Jack hoped that some measures were being taken by the government, to ease the shock of ZPEs introduction. Because it *was* coming. Jack knew that, through the sheer number of UFOs in our atmosphere. The government must realise the writing was on the wall. The Senate wasn't made up entirely of weak-minded automatons.

Distinct programs had started, to reverse engineer the tech that had come into government hands. Whether by Jack's intel, defence partners of the US, or an obscure country like Peru, who had more than one grounded UFO - ZPE will eventually make it into human hands. It was simply *a matter of time*. It couldn't be stopped. Hopefully, Big-Oil was on notice. The end of a dirty, smoky era was nigh, Jack was certain.

What about the rest of what he'd uploaded, Jack pondered? It was surely worth making a huge noise about. He'd heard of the massively expensive experiments, involving enormous vats of xenon in the deepest of deep mines. Searching desperately for dark matter.

Well, Jack's papers had the answer, along with a swathe of other things. FTL, dark energy, warp-drive, the TOE, string theory, extra dimensions...these things were extraordinary and super-incredible. Stuff humanity had been chasing since 1930, at huge cost.

Every physicist, whether in a university, the public domain, or the private sector, drooled over the data that Jack had uploaded. The Theory of Everything, that joined Einstein's glorious GR with the quantum world was like the Ark of the Covenant to a lot of physicists, the world over. Jack had just uploaded it. Physicists everywhere, should be staggered.

But, Jack knew, being anonymous, was critical. Profiting from this exercise was never going to happen. None of them wanted a bean in return. This was pure benevolence and altruism. That's how the Pianif framed it, and that's how Jack presented it. If they did it any other way, the entire bloodline of Jack's precious family was at high risk. The image of his parents at the kitchen table, fighting over what to eat for dinner, was enough. They were ripe for the picking. Jack knew that every step he made, had to be carefully taken without a trace.

Being known, equalled death to them. Jack might be over-playing the danger, but he had to, to penetrate the thickness of his parents' skulls. Krissy thought once it was out, they'd be fine, and John predictably agreed. Nothing was further from the truth. His parents didn't have the slightest inkling of what *vengeance* meant from a big company, suddenly bereft of its product, and the income it produces.

Feeling his temperature rise again, Jack wiped away the sweat, and struggled not to respond angrily to his parents. They just didn't get it. Incredibly, they spoke as though they were in the clear. '*Listen carefully*,' he said pointedly. 'We are *never* safe. *N-E-V-E-R*,' he said loudly and slowly. '*E-V-E-R*. Mark my words, Big-Oil will take vengeance for lost billions, and the government, for just having the temerity to make them look stupid. *Understand*,' Jack boomed, using his finger for emphasis. 'We can *never* reveal who we are.'

'Permanent anonymity is and always will be key to us surviving. The literal difference between life and death.' With wide eyes, Krissy and John nodded, now, understanding fully and under zero misapprehensions. They'd been berated by their son, and both took notice.

The event Jack was most concerned with, and which kept him up at night, was the *radiation*. Dr Friedman had promptly notified the CDC about his dad's radiation readings, because it met their rather odd criteria. Criteria, that made the hair on his back stand erect. Because he knew *why* they wanted to know.

Everyone in the know, and certainly within the US government, knew that coming into close contact with non-human craft, caused an exposure to ionising radiation. Engineered, and sorted, this data could reveal his dad as the person they sought. As the *uploader*. As the person who knew *too much*.

Jack read through the remaining intel and was a little relieved. The intel that remained with *reddit*, that hadn't been removed, didn't replace much at all on Earth. Unlike ZPE and oil, which did a number on most everything.

What was left on *reddit* was intel that humanity had been chasing for yonks, at huge expense. Jack knew he shouldn't be, but he was relieved. ZPE was critical to Earth, but at least the remaining intel wouldn't be lethal to the finder. It was just filling in the gaps of humanities knowledge about the physical world and space travel.

The theory of everything, gravity, carbon sponging concrete, dimensions, string theory, and finding the dark particles were all brand spanking new to humans. Any industries that grew from those discoveries would also be brand-new. So, the risk to the family from the remaining intel was close to zero, but the benefits were huge. Jack felt like clicking his heels. *At last*, he thought jubilantly.

His mum and dad could now breathe and even afford a smile. And Jack too, could exhale fully and smile like he meant it, because his parents were finally safe. His fears and the gut-wrenching images of them being tortured and killed, could now stop.

Backing the government into a corner on UFOs might be a problem, though. They were trying to hide them, but he'd essentially, done the opposite. He had unceremoniously revealed them to the globe. *They're real and they're non-human*, he had yelled. Our threat to the government had to be clear and present, he thought. As long as we remained nameless, we *should* be fine, Jack thought, smiling nervously.

Government aside, the impact from the remaining intel was all positive in the short *and* long term. Jack was mightily reassured by it, but now he worried about the response from his own government. No-one was likely to come after them for the intel, but the US government, he wasn't so sure. They'd flown directly against them, by confirming UFOs as non-human.

Jack thought about it, and reckoned the visit had to be by an arm of the government at the Pentagon. The CIA, DSI, NSA or maybe Homeland. These departments had some sites on the internet surveilled 24/7. When they saw his intel, they hopped into action. Their fulltime mission was clear; delete anything with national security implications. And these departments believed ZPE was exactly that.

Jack believed that Lockwood Martin, one of the government's defence partners, already had ZPE pegged. Under a principal and agency agreement, they and other defence partners, received downed non-human space-craft from the US government. To attempt to reverse engineer their tech. ZPE-conversion was part of it. The government needed plausible deniability, and by off-loading UFOs, they had it.

Jack had heard that a four-star General from the US, who was trusted with the lives of thousands of Americans in Afghanistan, said our planet was being visited by 57 species of non-humans. *Earth – the pale blue dot*, was a planet among planets, that appealed to every intelligent species in possession of a large sectioned telescope. Everyone, inside the Galaxy, and out of it, that can visualise the blueness of the planet, and can detect the artificial satellites in orbit, and oxygen in the atmosphere, wants to visit it. *Period*.

Jack's mind went straight to SETI. What the hell were they doing? Jack wondered angrily. He felt like laughing in their face. They didn't need to look light-years beyond our planet for complex, intelligent life. Earth, itself, was a genuine alien thoroughfare. NHI were in SETIs *fucking* back-yard. Jack reckoned they could save a lot of money and time, by simply opening their eyes, and acknowledging the obvious. Currently, the Carl Sagan Centre looked like a training-centre for clowns. They were doing the great man, a gigantic disservice. For a man who championed open-mindedness, it truly was a travesty.

Jack knew SETI had it embarrassingly wrong, looking for distant, artificial EMAR discharges. Humanity and Earth weren't doing it. So why should anyone else? Most TV was streamed, so again, why shouldn't that be the norm? SETI had to look a lot closer to home. So, instead of becoming irrelevant, which it was on course to be, SETI needed to take the bull by the horns and admit that the obvious was true. They needed to ignore prejudices. Earth was a daffodil to the Universe.

Jack reckoned non-humans would have seen a huge number of artificial satellites in orbit, and realise a population of intelligent beings put them there.

A huge number would desperately want to visit our world, just like humans wanted to visit Disneyland. Jack reckoned you simply had to be honest with yourself. Who wouldn't want to visit a warm, blue planet, full of oxygen, that had its own indigenous population and protective magnetosphere? See where they're at. See what we can learn, maybe help them, if it's required.

Tech would be the only barrier. If you had the ability to get there, it was no surprise to Jack, that Earth was bumper-to-bumper with non-humans. Like honeybees to nectar. Earth was a massive, hugely attractive, daffodil.

Many non-human races could fold space into a bubble, and travel inside. Jack knew space could be shortened in one direction of travel and lengthened in the other. So, without mass restrictions, they could jump a light-year in a few minutes. Or, like the Pianif, turn space into a fabric, and have your own personal wormholes. In either case, travel over vast distances was easy and very, *very* quick.

So, they're here...or at least some of them are, Jack thought. And, if there's so many, Jack estimated, no wonder some of them are altruistic and benevolent, like the Pianif. There'd be a whole gamut of mind-sets, in Earth's atmosphere.

* * *

Jack uploaded the documents to *reddit.com* three days ago. There had so far been little response. Earth was seemingly *ho-hum* about it. Posts on Twitter or X were probably the best – but like all the others, they used the words *dubious* or *flimsy*. Jack read, in a broad-sheet newspaper, that the pages on *reddit* had been sent to MIT in Massachusetts for comment. Until they received word back, it looked like it was crickets.

'Jacky don't lose hope, yet. Remember what I said...patience is required. The general population won't know good formula from bad. Most people will assume it's a work of fiction. It has to reach somewhere that understands it for what it is...like MIT. Just wait Jacky.' John gestured to his son to pump the brakes and for God's sake, calm down.

* * *

The next day, four days since Jack had uploaded it, *all hell broke loose on Earth.*

The faculty at MIT made a grand statement, direct to the Whitehouse. They'd already spoken to the local mayor, Maura Healey. MIT said it was stunning intel, and that the voyage as described, was probably true.

They had perused the documents fully, and had two seminars about the contents, some with the full university, debating how philosophy will change, moving forward. It was obvious to them that the physics did not come from this planet. Some of it was new, and very different.

Having read the words, Jack's heart started thumping in his chest. *'This is more like it,'* he shouted, making sure he was alone first. He got on his knees and prayed it wouldn't stop. Momentum was everything, he knew. The time is *NOW. Please, please, PLEASE,* he screamed. The Pianif wanted humans to have the intel and put it to good use. Jack could feel Swann's heat to help humanity and Earth coursing through him like electricity, seeing glorious Pianif tech on our planet, and in the hands of his fellow homo sapiens. Jack made the sign of the cross and desperately hoped humanity saw the potential of what he'd so carefully uploaded. The shining image of Swann was front and centre. Jack desperately hoped humanity used her pages of intel and did them the justice they deserved.

A topic that received little credence, had delivered God's own work to Earth. Never again would the population of Earth question non-human UFOs as a legitimate field of study. With this intel, would come the firm understanding of non-humans in Earth's atmosphere. What was fringe, was now rigidly mainstream, and was accepted by most humans as fact.

X, Facebook, Tik-Tok, Snapchat and Pinterest were full to bursting with it. And the same with the legacy media. Broad-sheet newspapers carried the story on the front pages. Jack smiled ear-to-ear at his father without making a noise.

They were inside a newsagent in Tucson. Every paper they could see had their story splashed over the front pages, and asking, "Who Are They?" It was the same on TV. News telecasts were filled with it, and UFOs were treated similarly, with documentaries and feature films, that garnered huge ratings.

The front pages of the New York Times, the Washington Post, the Los Angeles Times, and the Chicago Tribune and others, were largely devoted to it. Thankfully, the media didn't know the identity of the two, who were whisked away from Earth, and ended up collecting the technical glory of the aliens.

The best part of it, the most satisfying for Jack, was that it was now globally accepted. Of course, the fact that MIT had provided its tick of approval didn't hurt. The worst part was they were searching for the two who had been the prime movers. No doubt the CIA, DSI, NSA or other covert government agencies, were also involved. We had broadcast the exact opposite of government policy on UFOs, so we expected to be the government's number-1 target.

Jack knew for certain a search was underway, and wondered nervously who, and mainly *how* they were looking for them? He was satisfied with the upload. That part had gone well. There was no way they could tie any of them to it. But the radiation stood on its own, as the biggest foible, the most easily leapt puddle, in this whole event.

If it was the CIA, or whomever does the looking in such cases, they'd be intimate with the relationship between UFOs and radiation. They'd soon realise, that's all they had, and really focus on it. *Then,* we might be in trouble, he thought. Jack had fingers on his chin, drew in a quick breath, and hoped their plan didn't go belly-up. Jack knew his mum wanted the intel from Pianif shredded. And her opinion, initially spurned, now seemed to carry water.

Unfortunately, certain things were against him from the start. His parents were so naïve and green to the ways of the world...and Jack knew it. He loved them both dearly, and desperately wanted to keep them safe, but sometimes...he wondered.

His folks once received a demand from the federal government to pay $10,000, or the internet would be cut off. When Jack finally got back from Wisconsin, his parents were essentially running around the house in panic. It was clearly a scammer's letter, so Jack screwed it up, and threw it in the bin.

Neither of his parents could believe he was being so flippant with an official letter. Once they realised it was a scam, they followed his advice on *everything*, like he was a God. Suddenly, Jack knew all. He was installed as the family's all-seeing and all-knowing eye.

That's what he was up against – their wide-eyed childishness. They should have known better. The way of the world was a mystery to them. He loved them dearly, so protecting them was his lot, he mused. They meant the world to him, so, if the government or anyone else wanted them, they'd have to come through him first. And he'd protect them like a wild animal.

Jack wondered if his entire family should just leave the country, while they still could.? When they finally caught up with them, and they would, the shit would truly hit the fan. Jack's biggest worry was being outed by the federal government, who would also, probably, in a few years, reveal that they had the secret to ZPE. Using Eminent Domain, the secret would be ceded to the ownership of the government. All the family would get was years in gaol on some trumped-up charge if they were lucky. If they weren't lucky, they'd be killed. Or spend decades hidden at Guantanamo Bay.

8

Future

"I don't think ants have the foggiest notion that humans exist." — Carl Sagan

It was six long months since Jack uploaded the Pianif intel. There wasn't even a whiff of accessing Zero Point Energy...yet. Whoever took it, kept it deeply hidden. It was *gone*, and Jack couldn't re-create it.

Jack knew ZPE was out there, most likely with the federal government. Jack reckoned the CIA had it and were still trying to decide what to do with it. Hopefully, Big-Oil were being warned of its impending release, but he wouldn't put his house on it.

With intel on preparing the new concrete, the pressure was off governments around the world. Carbon dioxide, the climate-poison produced by burning fossils for energy, would be absorbed and removed by the concrete. It was subject to many tensile tests, and it was even slightly superior to regular concrete. The report was very positive indeed.

It was scheduled to be laid in Wisconsin and Missouri in a few days, to re-surface ageing roads. If successful, which it was expected to be, it would be used in the other 48 states. And sold under license to the rest of the world. Climate-change was expected to be eliminated from Earth, according to the messaging of the Net Zero Coalition, an arm of the UN. They spoke to the public through news and adverts in social and legacy media. Its rollout in

Wisconsin and Missouri, was still big news. Because it meant the end of world threatening climate-change.

Fields of plants were being grown in Washington State and Oregon, grown from Jack's seeds, called Piafinum. They looked like fields of Sorghum plants, but these had been raised for a very different purpose. They were now being harvested by hand, having grown to maturity over the past six months. This allowed the first pouring of the concrete, some for further testing, and the rest earmarked for the two states of North America.

It was here that the US government seemed to have their cake and eat it too. The Department of Agriculture grew the seeds, Jack buried, to seedlings. And they were now ready to harvest. They would supply sterols to the new concrete. This would effectively do the government's bidding, to reverse climate-change.

Who needed ZPE, when government-controlled carbon concrete was available? Fossil fuels continued to be burnt. Trouble was the world would eventually have the same problem. And next time, Earth couldn't be saved the same way.

Jack wondered skeptically - would Earth enter a period of recycling, where roads and buildings are constantly demolished, and re-cast with new carbon concrete? All while the government hides its knowledge of ZPE? Jack shook his head indignantly and brought a shaky hand to his eyebrows. *Surely not*, he thought bitterly. He wiped sweat off his brow. This was becoming a logistical and strategic nightmare, to the point where he thought his head would explode from over-thinking.

Jack jerked his head back and felt a heavy feeling in his stomach, realising with a yelp that the intel, gave the US government license to keep the status quo of the world *intact*. The sudden realisation made his heartbeat like an iron-block against his ribs. Earth could keep chugging carbon dioxide into the atmosphere and removing it with the green concrete. All while the energy structure of the world stays exactly the same.

What happens when Earth runs out of fossil fuels? Oil and coal are finite resources and are almost tapped out. *What then?* Jack wondered heatedly. The government must know the writing is on the wall with fat black letters.

Jack felt like screaming, hysterically. Unbelievably, his actions had *encouraged* the government's piss-ant behaviour. And now, they could have their cake and eat it too.

In future, if we ever needed it, the government could unveil ZPE. *Wallah. Look what we've got?* Jack just hoped that the family's identity wasn't revealed along with it.

Jack firstly made sure his mum could hear him too. '*Dad,*' he waited until John looked at him. 'We have nothing to worry about, you know. The only threat was from Big Oil. But since ZPE isn't part of the equation.' Jack smiled deliberately and threw his arms in the air. 'The status quo will remain. Fossil fuels will continue to be burnt, in conjunction with the roll out of the new concrete. *So, we are all scot-free. Everyone in the family. How good is that mum...dad?*'

Jack forced a smile at both of them and intended to press it home. 'Whoever *they* are, have deleted the problem for us. What remains, is no threat to anyone, and certainly no threat to you or mum. If ZPE raises its head in the future, it will be the government's problem – not ours.' Jack had a relaxed posture and continued smiling. What he said was true, but if they were outed, he still feared the government. What he and his dad did went directly against their conceal-at-all-costs policy. Their reaction could be anything.

'But you and dad,' his mum said fearfully, 'they are still searching for you, right?' Irrespective, of what Jack said, she was still expecting a knock at the front door, anytime, day or night. Jack worried too, but he reckoned it was more of a grim reality. The government had so many resources, it was hard to believe that the CIA or FBI couldn't find someone, if they were really trying.

'They'll never find us,' Jack said calmly, and confidently, even though he thought being found was a fait accompli. 'I was ultra-careful in uploading it all.' Jack tried to be as commanding as he could, trying desperately to instil some belief in their safety.

'What about the radiation?' John croaked morosely, 'the government,' he pointed at them with a crooked finger, 'will know that we, *as in us*, were in close proximity to a UAP and likely, uploaded the intel on ZPE. So, we need to factor that in.' John exhaled sleepily.

Jack and John fully expected to be eventually found out. John could see how down Jack was getting. The fact that ionising radiation was such a definitive tell-sign, which is what Jack had said, pushed it front and centre in his mind. If Jack was worried about it, so was he.

***

Because of the stellar response from universities, of which, the US had some of the best, the US government organised meetings to thrash out the new intel. The government was told by their science advisors the intel was real and originally came from beyond the Earth. They reckoned there was little doubt about it.

But no-one made any disclosure of such to the public. The government continued their denials of anything related to aliens, or simply didn't make any comment.

The US government organised a series of meetings at the NASA-AMES Conference Centre at Moffat Field in California. Invited, were ten techs from Lockwood Martin, six from Northrop Grumman and five from Boeing, representing Defence Partners, and Aero-Space companies. Ten from NASA were there, and several from SpaceX and the other space venturers, including also ESA, JAXA and ISRO. Seniors from MIT, Stanford and Princeton Universities were also in residence.

Interestingly enough, Jack thought, the Department of Energy, was the facilitator of the meetings. That meant, they had to be intimate with the topic, which was interesting in itself.

There would be three meetings to start with, and probably more to follow. The Secretary of State, Bill Goodings, said as much on TV, and social media with posts. He said that they wouldn't stop until they were fully across the intel. To the benefit of all Mankind.

Watching sites like Youtube, or reading stories in the legacy media, it seemed that no-one had a decent answer to the ruse being perpetrated by the US government. Apart from the comment that, "it was clearly more of the same." The US government still wouldn't confirm that we weren't alone in the Universe, despite working on intel that they'd confirmed as being "from the stars."

Because of Jack's intel, and the long history of UFOs in America, the US government was receiving 5,000 letters a day, urging them to disclose the obvious. Many of the letters urged POTUS to start with Roswell, and work it forward, from there.

John and Jack both knew the US had access to downed non-human craft. The craft had crashed and been taken down forcibly. And landed, courtesy of the government's telepathic recruits. Then they were "handed" to their defence partners - to try and reverse engineer their tech and get them flying again. They were also sent there to give the government plausible deniability. To create some distance between them and the craft. They'd had some success with the tech, but certain devices on-board remained an abject mystery.

Anti-gravity and propulsion from Dark Energy were on offer to those who were successful. If their efforts were fruitful, they'd be superior to any nation on Earth – notably, China and Russia. And that was the US government's aim. To create air and sea superiority, over the main adversaries. The conspiracy to hide non-human craft in the US, was fundamentally a cold war with Russia and China.

Anti-gravity, FTL flight, Dark Energy and gravitational propulsion, Jack knew, would be game changers for the US military and NASA. Not only would they provide the USA with complete aerial and oceanic superiority. The intel could importantly, be weaponised. And NASA could go wherever the hell they wanted. Relying on Breakthrough, to get to Proxima b or wherever, was not necessary any longer. The Administrator of NASA said excitedly that they could now get to Proxima in an hour. And return to Earth, the same day, with *answers*.

Other countries were also interested, including companies and the government from China and Russia. But as *reddit.com* was an American website, the US made Eminent claim to it and sent them packing. The US invited who they wanted. And it didn't include them. They could organise their own meetings, they said.

9

Agents

**"The pale blue dot is the only home we've ever known."
— Carl Sagan**

Krissy heard the squelch of gravel as two Chevrolet Suburbans parked near the house. A quick look through the blinds told her all she needed to know. She felt sick and ran to the toilet as fast as she could expecting the worst. *They were here! Holy shit,* she thought morbidly, seeing bright lights and sparklers before her eyes. They'd been *found out* and were now at their whim.

In the newly arrived vehicles, were seven-armed government agents in black suits. There was a loud thump at the door, followed by someone calling out their names, one after the other. The sound that wafted into the house was ominous.

Krissy was back from the toilet, and stood anxiously near the blinds, that were partially open. She peeked nervously outside by crimping one of the blinds. At the sound of more thumping, she took a quick intake of breath, and snapped her head around to Jack. '*What do we do?*' She snapped like a gunshot. Krissy looked at her son with bulging eyes, and deep lines everywhere. Because she knew who it was, where they were from, and what they wanted. They were here with a warrant. To execute it. Jack had put the fear of God into them and, despite his efforts, she was still panic-stricken.

'Let them in of course.' Jack said calmly. He had put a fair bit of thought into this eventuality. He expected it. We were the #1 target in the USA. Jack knew that resources to find them would have been infinite. The Pentagon, CIA, FBI, DSI, Homeland, DoD; they would have worked together, using software, and hundreds of agents, to finally pin-point them.

Krissy walked toward the door, but John made it first, and opened it before Krissy could get there.

'Yes?' He said nervously. His heart was thumping in his mouth, enough to give him a jaw-ache. He knew Jack was terrified by these people, which was enough for him. John felt like running and hiding. There were enough agents at the door for a bloody soccer team.

'You're John, right? My name is Jeff Kreston, from the federal government. These are my colleagues. We...ah, have a few questions. May we come in?' Jeff looked directly at John, and nodded at him, hoping for cooperation.

John glanced nervously at Jack and thought...*options? Slim and none.*

'Of course.' John opened the door fully, and all the agents filed into the house, making the Baltic floor-boards creak with their weight.
Six of the agents squashed onto the sofa, as directed by John, while the one doing the talking, stayed standing, and bent over them. To do more talking, presumably.

'You have been difficult to find,' said the lead agent. Jack had already decided to be cooperative if they were found. He knew their identification was only a matter of time. The report by Dr Friedman to the CDC had fingered them, no doubt about it. Dr Freidman, in all his good intentions, set the stopwatch ticking. And now the government had us. Jack swallowed hard, trying to control the urge to retch. He knew he had to set the example. Stay calm, *relax.* Be like the government, and *deny, deny, deny.*

All the agents looked uneasy, crossing and uncrossing their arms, waiting for directions from Jeff, the lead agent. Jack reckoned he would be quick to pull out his gun. Jack's job was to give him no reason to do it.

'Er...what are you, er...here for?' Jack asked innocently, trying to ignore his racing heart. He didn't want to assume anything or give anything away. The query seemed to take the agent off-guard. It was a fair question, Jack thought. *Why the hell are you lot here?*

'Okay then,' the lead agent said. He looked confused to be asked that question so directly. 'We believe it was you, and your dad that were taken by the Pianif. And on your return, you uploaded the data to *reddit*.' Take that, lead agent thought, with a wry smile.

Jack stared at the agent boldly. 'What if it *was* us?' Jack piped confidently. He looked at the lead agent, straight in the eye, without giving an inch. He felt like admitting it, straight to his face and following up with, what are *you* going to do about it? Trouble with that approach was, he was afraid of the answer. High in his mind, was he and his dad's transgression of the *concealment-first* government policy.

Best not to rile them up, he decided. They knew for certain it was us, so he'd just leave it unsaid. Where the intel on ZPE had gone, as in who deleted it and who held it, was front and centre for him. He really wanted to throw it at him, pose it *angrily* to him like a fierce volley, but that would give the game away, lock, stock and barrel. Not yet, he reckoned.

The lead agent looked directly at Jack and spoke confidently. 'Our department monitors four thousand *high-risk* websites. A simple key-word search brought us to your upload, guys. No doubt, you were wondering how we located what you had uploaded.' Lead agent jutted his chin out and crossed his arms. 'Well, turns out, it wasn't difficult.' He said proudly.

'We knew it wouldn't be hard - with the resources you probably have.' Jack said honestly. 'Not that we're admitting anything.' It seemed to take the wind out of Jeff's sails. He visibly sagged.

Lead agent's smug smile disappeared. He realised he was only as good as his resources.

'Er...okay, we will now discuss Zero Point Energy.' The lead agent looked pointedly at Jack. 'It was our agents that deleted it,' he said. 'Defence partners almost know how to extract vacuum energy, from The Program. What we haven't got from non-human craft, your upload filled in nicely. Our techs at Lockwood's now have a full view of the Casimir Effect, and Harmonic Oscillators, as it pertains to ZPE.' The lead agent took a long and whistling breath, that seemed to emphasise how important that was.

'The main reason it was removed,' lead agent looked directly into Jack's eyes and smiled like a lunatic. 'Was, the National Security Act and the Inventions Secrecy Act.

Jack's eyes widened and then narrowed knowingly. Secrecy Act, he *knew*, was the main problem. Anything new and radical that works, the government takes as their own and cites bullshit laws to cover their arse. They love playing the hero. *It was us* - they yell.

'ZPE was covered by both of these,' Jeff said. 'It would transform the paradigm of Earth's energy network. ExxonMobil and Chevron and many other trillion-dollar companies would simply cease to exist, Jack. The macro-economics of the planet would spiral into oblivion. We have nearly two billion cars that *need* petrol.' Lead agent was getting worked up and had tears in his eyes. He knew exactly what it would mean. 'It would be the end, and a difficult beginning,' he said dramatically. 'Earth would be reborn as something entirely different.' His voice took on a frightening note.

'The remainder of your upload just scraped through.' He said ominously, looking straight at Jack. 'But anything to do with free energy, was in the same boat as Nicola Tesla, so it was deleted, and taken by the government, and scheduled for a later focus.' Jack raised his eyebrows and shook his head skeptically. He knew that Big-Oil was a protected species on Earth, because of what it did. Without them, governments and countries would crash and burn. *Yeah, yeah*, Jack thought tediously. He'd heard and read it all before.

'You're kidding right?' Jack said. 'I don't want to be the doubting Thomas, but the government will *never* decide to release it.' Jack tilted his head and paused. 'Especially *now* that they have the key to curing climate-change.'

'We have started negotiations with the big players in the oil and gas industry,' Jeff said. 'They have been given five years until Earth changes to a ZPE energy base. Five years to enjoy the profits, and get their houses in order.'

Jeff turned to look directly into Jack's eyes. 'There are 500 high-level humans, we have already placed in the Energy Transition Team (ETT) that work for the US federal government, out of the Pentagon. They're mainly concerned with ZPE supporting-infrastructure and believe in five years it can be landed safely. They all realise it is inevitable. If humanity and Earth want to survive, which they obviously do, then ZPE is non-negotiable. It's energy-dense, which is essential to our economy, and is the difference between dying as a species, or not.

'There is no way we can keep this hidden from the media, but we will all try, won't we?' Lead agent wanted the family's nods, which he got, effusively. His mum and dad were still terrified, with wide eyes. They both now expected to be shot as traitors, along with Jack. John and Krissy took shaky breaths, and listened to the lead agent closely, with twitching eyes, expecting him to pull out his gun at any moment.

'We would ask you not to discuss *any part of this*, with *anyone*.' His voice was low-pitched and cold. 'We know you have a sister in Canada and a niece in Spain. If you wish everyone to continue their good health, please *stay silent*. Best you now forget about your ET episode.' His voice had lost any sense of friendliness and lightness and now sounded harsh and threatening.

His ominous nod and set jaw made Jack's back hair stand to attention. He was a man *not* to cross. This guy and his cronies meant business. If we spoke further about this, it was goodnight to the family, including those in Canada and Spain. Jack's mum was sobbing with terror, and his dad wasn't far behind. There would be no second warnings - that was clear. John pushed a fist to his lips, to help choke it down. Lead agent was smiling at his colleagues; both Jack's parents sobbed in the background.

This was normal behaviour for them, Jack thought, intimidating elderly people, and making them sob with terror. Jack supposed national security work was like that. These thugs were perfect for it. He watched as they smiled playfully and winked at each other. He reckoned the family got off surprisingly lightly.

'We um...haven't and we won't ever mention it.' Jack promised him nervously, biting his tongue. John and Krissy nodded quickly and kept nodding. Their agreement was total.

Bastards, Jack thought maliciously. Each of them, but mainly the lead-agent, who continued to grin and wink at his friends. Even though he was relieved, their behaviour was abhorrent, akin to a group of nazis.

'Okay then, we have an agreement,' lead-agent said spitefully. With that, all the agents got up and filed to the doorway. Krissy let them out, so they could get in their cars, and be someone else's problem.

'Goodbye,' she said impatiently. *Good riddance*, Krissy really meant. The noise of their Pirelli tires on gravel was the finest symphony to her ears. Krissy watched them reverse to the road, and she waved them happily away.

They returned inside, and took a deep breath of relief, shocked it had gone so well, and they were still free to roam around. Krissy and John smiled uncertainly and nervously, stunned they weren't arrested, or worse. Jack had put the fear of God into them, but thankfully, the agents left without a whimper. They knew it was us, but strangely, no confession was required. Odd behaviour for a security-agency, Jack thought.

In an ominous tone, Jack said, 'rightly or wrongly, we have just been threatened by the CIA.' Jack looked directly at his parents and nodded. 'We need to take their visit seriously guys, or everything and everyone is lost. By that, I mean *everyone* we call family.' Jack sat down next to his mum, and picked up her hand and squeezed it, then returned it to her lap, hoping like hell that she took heed from his words.

'Make no mistake they are unyielding, and are empowered by the Whitehouse and the Senate. Murders have happened before, to cover the real nature of UFOs. And what we've brought to the table is much more than just that. Remember, the assassination of JFK? That's why we need to be ultra-careful.' Jack's voice reduced to a whisper. 'This area is deadly.'

'You mean *they*...shot him because of that?' Krissy asked, taking a deep rasping breath, with swollen, questioning eyes.

'The CIA did it, by all reports.' Jack said, 'to shut him up. He'd been warned apparently, but it didn't work...so *bang*.'

'So, we have to be wary guys and follow their directions. Or we could potentially suffer a similar fate. Just because we seemed to win this time, doesn't mean the government will always be so easy to get on with. In the future, they could return with machine guns, and turn the whole house, and us, into swiss cheese, or burn the house and us to the ground. Krissy was rigid, and listened to her son with wide, teary eyes.

'At the moment, UFOs seem less of a no-no, than at previous times.' Jack pondered the government's odd behaviour, and his eyes glazed over. Was that the government, finally yielding to overwhelming evidence, or did it just seem like that? 'The world must never know we were the ones. Even though the government assumed it was us, we never formally confessed. They made us swear to utter silence and total secrecy. The lead agent said they'd always keep our names out of it. It was all *very odd* indeed – there's clearly something we don't know about, because it doesn't make sense. And that's *not* how they roll.'

Jack and John fairly much knew how the CIA, the Pentagon, and similar intelligence and security agencies operated. It was their way or their way. Options were nil. The options they provided for regular citizens was comply or suffer. Jack understood perfectly what they meant. And what their veiled threat meant for the family.

Jack was stunned that they still had their freedom. Even with ZPE off the table, a non-human, *alien UFO*, was still fundamental to their story. In effect, the government had acknowledged it as real, a similar craft as seen at Roswell, USS Nimitz and O'Hare. To Jack, it didn't make sense. Was the US government's *conceal-first* policy on UFOs softening after nearly a century? It seemed too much to hope for.

***

Jack was over the moon with the way it turned out. His priority was always his dad and mum...*his family.* Somehow, which he still found difficult to believe, non-humans had cured his dad of, what on Earth, was a *terminal* disease.

So, non-humans essentially gave him a second shot at life. On Earth, the best he could hope for, was a drawn-out death. So, neither had too much to complain about.

Jack realised he should be thankful, they were chosen by the Pianif, that fateful day in June 2024. If they hadn't been, his dad would probably be dead, reposing at the local Tucson cemetery. Jack swallowed hard. The thought of his dad in a coffin was too much to bear.

10

Outcome

"In some respects, science has far surpassed religion in delivering awe." — Carl Sagan

The New York Times front page sat untidily on the kitchen table like a crumpled rag. X, Snapchat, Instagram and Tik-Tok were full of posts about non-humans. So were Youtube and Facebook. Every newspaper asked the same question in large, bold letters.

Who were the abducted duo, *who* uploaded the extraordinary non-human tech to *reddit*? The FBI, CIA, NSA and DoD were onto it, apparently. Jack was sick and tired of reading about it. Every source of media asked the same thing. *Who, why* and *where*? The government said names and addresses were confidential and covered by the privacy act. They couldn't release them even if they had them. It was up to the people themselves to come forward. Still, it was the first question asked. Secretary of State, Bill Goodings, was so sick of the question, he started each Press Briefing with the fact that they didn't know who it was and repeated it before questions were sought from the press. He made no reference to a meeting, or having any decent leads, or suspects.

Jack was bemused - something didn't add up. He could smell something off in the wind. They'd tracked us down, but there was zero disclosure. Jack was happy with that, but suspicious. Were they keeping us a secret, to be revealed when it most suits them? He hoped he was reading it wrong.

NASA-Ames had huge confidence in the intel, and invited the G7 to attend, with the view to showing them what it represented, and what it could potentially lead to. Venture capital from the world bank was on offer to vetted sources, to convert showhouses at various locations.

If successful, they would form part of a huge new industry. Many believed the demand on Earth would eventually be enormous. NASA believed many new industries, and new modes of transport would result from the information. NASA and SpaceX eyed the intel hungrily. Many more would follow.

'*Holy shit*,' Jack huffed, when he finally caught up with X. 'They've found two suspects, they say. Jack unzipped his jacket and shook his head, glancing sarcastically at John.

'Well, someone did pay us a visit. They were CIA out of the Pentagon, I reckon.' John said. 'Even though they didn't bother to say. We are free though, so caught or not caught...it probably doesn't matter. Odd though.' Jack scratched his chin.

'Still, we all need to keep a low profile,' Krissy said, ducking her head for effect.

'Too late for that mum. The government knows about us.' Jack brought a trembling hand to his forehead, wondering how the fuck their lives got so complicated. He gawked at his dad and knew the answer. Still, it was a lot better than he anticipated, which in itself was odd.

As far as his mum knew, Jack thought amusingly, the government were tight-lipped about everything, especially the CIA. What a load of unmitigated bollocks, Jack thought sourly. They'd tell anybody, *anything*, if it was to their advantage.

'Mum, the government, in our case, the CIA, does what's good for the CIA. Giving some misleading crumbs to the media is all part of it. Our details should remain hidden. They don't want us located any more than we do. So, we should be okay, for now.' For the first time in yonks, Jack felt safe. He wasn't sure, but the attitude of the government seemed to have changed a bit.

John glanced at his wife and saw her face contorted with shock and terror. He grabbed Krissy's trembling hands and looked straight into her swollen eyes. His expression became a dazzling smile. 'It will be fine, love. It's all taken care of.'

With that, John pushed her back gently on the sofa, so the back of her head rested on it. 'Time for shut-eye, love.'
Jack peered at his dad and smiled happily, knowing from his own experience, what a beautiful man he was.

11

More Agents

"Every saint and sinner in the history of our species lived there on a mote of dust suspended in a sunbeam."
— Carl Sagan

Sitting at the kitchen table, Krissy heard the squelch of gravel as another car approached the house, coming quicky up the driveway. Looking through the blinds, Krissy confirmed nervously, that it was a black van that contained two men only. She was confused; they'd already been here. And seemed satisfied when they left. But they were back. With a dry mouth and butterflies in her stomach, Krissy felt like running. What in God's name do they want now? She wondered anxiously.

They were dressed in pressed suits and wore dark glasses. Only two this time. Jack wondered what that meant. To be back so quickly, was probably not good news.

Jack and John were waiting by the door. They too heard the approaching car and initially ran to look out the front window. They knew who it was, without Krissy's help. Jack wasn't surprised they'd returned. He *expected* it. If they'd come once, they'd come again. That's how they rolled. But so soon after the first visit, he couldn't explain that.

His parents didn't deserve to be threatened and pressured by the CIA. While he answered the door, they sat like saints on their chairs in the living room. Did they now want to press charges...or worse? Jack counted to ten and tried to stop guessing.

'I'm Peter,' the first one said, smiling broadly, while removing his sunglasses, 'and that's Chad. We're from the government, and we need to come in and speak to you.' His voice was confident and business-like.

'Sure,' Jack welcomed them in and directed them to the sofa in the living room.

'Back again?' Jack said casually. His heart was in his mouth. The agents might have seemed happy, but Jack doubted that's where they were at. These were different agents than before. Jack didn't know why that would be. But it worried him.

'We are here for a specific reason.' Peter paused and looked at the family photo on the wall. Just when the silence was becoming uncomfortable, he continued. 'The Dept. of Justice has a computer system called RAIDs,' he said, 'which analyses evidence for us. It has come up with something, we found interesting.' Peter glanced at Chad, then grinned disarmingly at Jack.

'It told us that you and your dad,' He glanced at John, 'are 78% likely to be the ones who uploaded the information onto reddit from the non-humans.'

'Hardly quantitative,' Jack said...'but, er...you're aware we didn't resist the charges, the first time, right?'

'Er...we've never been here, so, no.' He was clearly bewildered, and glanced at his partner, to share an eye-popping glance.

'Hang on,' Jack said cautiously. 'So, are you saying this hasn't been followed up before?'

'That is exactly what I'm saying. There has been no involvement from anyone in the government. Nor Homeland the FBI, or DoD...*nothing*. There is just clean air in our database. We are the first to use it.' Peter glanced at Chad and frowned, as if to say, *huh*? 'These other agents, did they say where they were from?'

'They suggested they were from CIA.' Jack said uncertainly, looking sternly at Peter, as if to say, how do you like them apples.

'Um, er...that's not possible,' he glanced vacantly at Chad who now looked as lost as Peter. There is nothing in our database, in fact, the file hasn't been touched since it was opened back on the 4th.'

'So, we were visited by ghosts?' Jack said, trying to keep the sarcasm out of his voice.

'No, of course not. I cannot explain who those other agents were, which is disappointing for you, I know, but you said you didn't resist their statements? Would you repeat that to me? As in a confession.'

The word bit hard. Jack glanced knowingly at his parents. 'Depends on what would then be forthcoming for my parents. I can take it, but they are on the wrong side of sixty and deserve some respect. These people don't deserve your ire.' His voice was bleak and shaking with despair and bewilderment. Jack glanced at his parents and teared up. They looked so innocent, surrounded by clouds of after-shave and the CIA in black suits, who were quiet, but breathed fire.

'*Oh Jacky,* his mum sobbed. It'll be okay...like last time. His dad dissolved into tears. The entire family had tears pouring down their face. None of them had a clue. In the back of Jack's mind, was the family's transgression of the government's deny, deny, deny "policy" on UFOs. How these agents related to that, he didn't know.

They were confused and frightened by these agents who knew *nothing* of the earlier visit. John and Krissy were terrified of Jack's warning coming true. Being arrested and handcuffed, and hauled off to Guantanamo seemed a real possibility, because this was the *real* CIA, apparently.

'You know,' Peter said, concerned by their emotional reaction, 'you have nothing to fear. None of you. The section on ZPE was removed under the Secrecy Act. The rest of the intel is just new tech that the planet didn't have before. No current industries were overly affected. Except rocketry, and the government will help them out.' He continued, 'We understand the issues around oil and coal – but they don't apply to the rest of it. So, you're remaining anonymous for no reason.' Peter smiled at them uncertainly. He thought it was them, but he wasn't 100% sure.

John's head came up to its full height, and he stared at his son, befuddled, not sure how to treat the new info. What the agent said made sense to his ear. He wiped the tears from his eyes.

Jack said upbeat, looking straight at Peter, 'hypothetically, what would happen to my folks, if you decided it was definitely me and John?

'Well, you haven't broken any laws...so, *nothing*. It would allow us to close our file. That's all.'

'And the fact that it confirms UFOs, and their alien nature? Jack held his breath. This was a big one.

'Doesn't matter. It is what it is.' Peter said decisively. 'As long as it is *never* mentioned again.' His voice was sharp, and firm.

'These people here wouldn't be connected to the ZPE data?' Jack asked, his eyes gaping. 'I, uh...assume it will be released eventually.'

'Not at all,' Peter said calmly, looking at John and Krissy. 'ZPE will be released in stages, quicker than you think. Where it came from, won't be discussed – *ever*, but people might put two and two together.'

Jack thought about it and glanced at his dad hopefully. His mum as well. The decision he made couldn't compromise their safety. Not at their age, or any age really. What the agents said, put his mind at ease, but could they be believed? The government had a penchant for lying, especially about UFOs.

He assumed this was the real deal now. Which meant their intel about ZPE wasn't uploaded in vain, it would be implemented later. But...who in God's name were the previous agents? Were they charlatans, or the real CIA, who forgot to update their own database? There was a car full of them for Christ's sakes.

Over the years, these government types had done a lot wrong. The US government had treated the public of America like pre-schoolers. Jack was more confused now, than before. He didn't know who to believe, but this current lot of agents seemed legit, so he'd go with them. The previous lot may have been from ARRO. The Pentagon's UFO people. He'd have to go with his gut because he had nothing else.

This couldn't be decided by his gut. Mum and dad needed to take charge of their own affairs. Acknowledging their guilt was not his job. No way he could plead guilty to these people, on behalf of his parents.

'Can we have a minute to talk amongst ourselves?' Jack asked Peter, who seemed like a reasonable person.

'Of course,' he replied, and the agents retreated to the lounge room, and stood next to the oil heater, and continued to talk quietly, agent to agent.

The three of them sat at the kitchen table and gazed at each other. His mum and dad were still upset, but they needed to make a decision, right now.

'What do you reckon guys?' Jack whispered. This, *right here*, is mega-important. His parents had tear-filled eyes and had no idea what to do. They continued to stare at him blankly, expecting him to take the reins - and make the decision. They were far better suited at a farmers' market, looking at fruit and veg, than here.

'We'll go with you Jacky, won't we love?' John looked passionately at his wife and son, and nodded nervously. 'What you said, made good sense, to us Jacky.' Jack rolled his eyes skeptically and was lost for words. His dad didn't have a cynical bone in his body. Sometimes, that worked against him.

'I don't trust him dad.' Jack eventually said. The government is liable for all sorts of underhand bullshit. They deny things that are in your face. Anyway, it's up to you guys. Admit it or don't. Totally *your* decision.' Jack wished they were the suspicious and distrustful type, like him, but they weren't. To them, the government was always right, and always to be trusted. They were so naïve; two leftovers from a simpler time.

Jack scratched his chin and felt like pulling his hair out. He found their behaviour toward the agents and the government, exasperating. Jack was almost the opposite – he trusted them about as far as he could kick them. Their track record in keeping the public in the loop was terrible.

John nodded at Krissy, and whispered to Jack. 'I want to admit I was one of the two, who were taken by the Pianif.'

Jack looked at both of them sternly – there was no point arguing, he could see that. 'Okay, if that's your final decision, I'll call them back over.' Jack expected it, so, it was hardly a surprise. Jack called to them to rejoin the group.

Peter and Chad walked slowly and curiously back to the rectangular table and sat down, looking directly at Jack and waited with wide, expectant eyes.

Jack eyed Peter grimly and nodded. 'It was us that uploaded the intel.' Jack said dramatically. There, he thought, *done.*

'We thought as much.' Peter started rummaging around in his briefcase, looking for something.

'There is one thing I didn't upload, that you might find interesting.' Jack said. 'In fact, the whole planet might find it, uh...intriguing. I didn't mention it, so we would remain anonymous. That probably doesn't matter so much now.' Jack took a few steps toward Peter, more confident now, and spoke in a voice that reflected it.

'The Pianif cured my dad of Stage 4 cancer.' Jack said loudly and proudly.

Peter's mouth literally fell open. '*Whoa*,' Peter blurted suddenly, and Chad gasped in sheer amazement. They knew how huge it was. They knew humans could only dream of it. 'On Earth, he would have died.' Thousands of medical teams on Earth researched it. Some could slow it, but *none* could cure it, lock, stock and barrel, like the Pianif. This was the stuff of the Gods.

Jack let them recover from that little pearl, and proceeded, when it was quieter, and their exhortations had finished. 'Dad was initially in surprise remission from multiple tumours in his stomach and kidneys when we went on the fateful mission to the desert. We saw a shiny object in the sky were teleported onto an alien craft. But the cancer came back mid-flight, and my dad was suffering from severe pain in his abdomen and back, to the point where he basically couldn't move.'

'The Pianif were taking us to meet their Ruling Council.' Jack said. 'But to do that effectively, they either had to take us home, or treat him for the pain. Turned out they chose to do the latter. The Pianif refused to take us home, so they *had* to treat him...to allow the meeting to proceed. An event they held highly, in great esteem and the main reason for their trip to Earth, apparently. They needed to harvest specimens of humanity to satisfy their Council. Hence, me and dad were easy to get in the abandoned area of the old Yuma mine ruins..

Jack was sweating and breathing loudly, as he recounted their interactions with the Pianif. He reiterated looking at his dad, on the way to their planet. The yellowness, loose skin under his eyes, and the sheer agony, that hit Jack like a Mack truck. He realised his number was almost up...which would leave *him alone*.

He had to swallow down tears, because he remembered how deathly distressed, he was. He was certain that his dad was going to die among the stars. Jack recalled trying to hide his concern, not wanting his dad to know how truly terrified he was. He was trying to think of a way to break it to his mum. He would never, *ever*, forget how hopeless and desperate he felt. Everywhere he looked was the vacancy and blankness of the Pianif and their black, soulless eyes. Any real help for his dad was light years away.

The Pianif's ability to deal with genetic disease like cancer, was a total shock to Jack, and subsequently, to both the agents in front of him. Jack thought, at best, they may be able to irradiate him. Curing him, didn't enter his mind, until it happened. Jack and his dad were floored, pure and simple.

'A great story...is it ours to disseminate?'

'Of course,' Jack said. 'We don't want to hide it,' he said. Then, he thought, good a time as any. 'Er...what happened to the pages that were uploaded?' Jack looked straight at Peter.

He said, 'NASAs got their part, a bit went to MIT and Stanford and the rest went to our defence partners, mainly Lockwood Martin and Northrop Grumman. They are all very excited indeed. They realise where the information came from, and they were, uh...jubilant.'

'Lockwood's said, it was nice to get something from non-humans they could sort of understand. Headway on the craft they inherited from the US government was next to impossible because the craft and all the tech seemed to be bonded at the atomic level. And elements used were all permanently stable, and well beyond the human periodic table. Any progress demanded a solution to those pickles first. So, the intel from Pianif was a blessing.'

Chad spoke for the first time. He grabbed onto Peter's shoulder, and stood up, looking animated. He peered straight at Jack curiously and said, 'POTUS will be very interested in the cancer story. *Very interested indeed.*'

12

Disclosure

**"We are ready at last to set sail for the stars."
— Carl Sagan**

Jack wondered what Chad meant by POTUS being *"very interested"* in the cancer story. He said it with great emphasis and enthusiasm, suggesting that the US President thought it would capture the imagination of the globe. Jack reckoned he was spot on. Because humans, despite years of expensive research, could do little with cancer. Chemotherapy and radiation remained the prime responses.

Humans had a knock-the-doors-down approach to cancer, that *might* result in remission. The cancer cells remained but were inactive. That is the high point for humanity. The Pianif truly understood the disease, and could cure it, with the snap of their fingers. Cancer cells were removed entirely, so the risk of it coming back was nil.

Humans needed the Pianif technology. Fifty million people worldwide had cancer on Earth. Ten million people die from it every year. Marriages are destroyed; families demolished and lives ruined. All because we don't have the technology to be like the Pianif. Incredibly, cancer to them was not a serious disease.

Humanity would soon know about the magical abilities of the Pianif. Maybe humanity should go to Swann, cap in hand, and ask her for it? They are a very reasonable race. Perhaps there is something we can do for them? Jack wondered if human pride, or ego would get in the way. *Quid pro quo* might work. Humans can't get there, anyway. But with the new tech, we probably could. Surely this is something to think about seriously. This would be a good use of space travel. Perhaps to test out the newly acquired tech?

A hundred million humans hoped Mankind would at least try. The cat was out of the bag now. People would soon know that cancer sufferers died unnecessarily. Jack reckoned there would be a global outcry, that could push humanity to their distant doorstep. Fingers crossed.

***

The Press Secretary for the US told the media that POTUS would arrive in the James Brady room at 3PM to make a major announcement that was "globally critical". The 49 seats in the room were quickly reserved by the media. There were guesses, inferences, speculations and predictions – but none of them were right. In fact, none were even close. This was a world-shaking announcement about something that had been hidden for a long time. It turned out that recent events were a perfect lead-in, and in fact had been the catalyst for it. The US government had decided to change its behaviour significantly.

POTUS arrived, with the Secretary of Defence, and the big wigs from the CIA and the Joint Chiefs by his side. The Secret Service maintained close contact and high focus.

POTUS had always believed in the reality of UFOs, as being an off-planet, non-human, high-intelligence. Mainly because POTUS had seen one. Near Fort Worth at night, POTUS and the father, saw three lights in the sky that did things no ordinary aircraft could do. The lights above them displayed the "five observables" and zipped and zapped all over the sky, before seemingly landing somewhere in the distance. It was actually "six observables" because they could do Mach speed, and instant velocity, submerged in the ocean if required.

Dad, and today's POTUS, then in Congress, winged it in their Chevy, wondering what the hell the object was? After the event, POTUS was thunderstruck, and realised that UFOs, replete with extra-terrestrials, were ridgy-didge, although it was never mentioned. They tried to find the landing spot but couldn't.

When POTUS was elected, one of the first tasks was to ask a friend in the East Wing what America knew about UFOs. The friend had worked for a director of the CIA in the Pentagon, and said he'd do some digging and come back.

Not only didn't he get back, he disappeared entirely. POTUS meant to follow him up – but the pressure of work in the first term had, so far, prevented it. POTUS rang him internally, and was told he no longer worked in the Whitehouse or for the government. The President was stumped. There was something very nasty going on, that was activated by simply trying to access information on UFOs. Paul wouldn't leave the CIA without a phone call. Something illegal and dark had happened to him. Ringing him on his home phone didn't shed any light. Several messages left on his answering machine, remained unreturned.

POTUS hadn't and wouldn't say anything to anyone, about the one that was seen, or that she was interested in them. What happened to Paul taught her a good lesson. Searching for information on UFOs was a death-trap.

The CIA, DoD and many of the Joint Chiefs were lost for words. They couldn't believe a President was being so cavalier with the truth. How dare you tell the truth. All of them advised POTUS emphatically and repeatedly against it, citing Defense Policy, and Article 1, Section 8 of the American Constitution. '*Don't do it*,' was the panicked advice. 'You won't live to regret it,' they warned. 'Remember JFK,' they yelled passionately. There were similarly ominous and direct warnings, but she refused to back down. *The time had come.* Inaction and subterfuge had gone on too long. Still, the robust advice, took on the tone of a shrill warning.

'*Public interest disclosure*,' POTUS fired back on more than one occasion. She was determined the official denials would end, and she wouldn't be put off by officials or even friends, citing bullshit laws. The CIA and the DoD wanted to meet, but so far, she'd managed to evade them. The Founding Fathers would approve of her actions. And they were the boss.

POTUS was aware of JFK, when disclosure came close, so extreme care had to be front and centre. The story of Jack and John Stevens was a perfect lead into disclosure. You can't acknowledge on the one hand and cover-up with the other. You'd look silly, and that's one thing she wasn't. She was a proud leader. And the American people would be finally respected with the truth, under her administration.

The cancer story was invaluable and would help POTUS sell the whole thing to a planet, where countless people were literally craving disclosure. Many knew that UFOs were real, and were explicitly non-human, but just as many thought they were a drug-induced hallucination or misdiagnosed drones. She would need a hook, like the cancer-story, to force, if necessary, acceptance. *We are not alone* - she thought to herself. Humanity is only *one* of the many intelligent species. Time for *everyone* to know, she reckoned.

There was so much disinformation and flat out lies on the topic – POTUS had, heard more than enough. A lot of people in America and around the world had similarly had their fill of official denials. *Fuck 'em*, she reckoned when she thought of the CIA, DoD, NSA, ARRO and the Pentagon. Their arrogance and criminality were too much. As President, she alone, would decide when it was time. And it was NOW.

***

POTUS stood tall behind the podium and read from the teleprompter and made the pronouncement to a room full of wide and teary eyes. Many thought it was time to raise the curtain. Official denials were yesterday. Today, the Sun rises on a brand-new world.

Among the players in residence were the NY Times, CBS, MSNBC, FOX, CNN and NBC. Government employees, senators and reporters were five-deep near the walls. No-one wanted to miss this once-in-history announcement. Most knew it was coming, but didn't think it'd ever get here. Jack reckoned it was like fusion energy. On the horizon, almost here...but not quite. Today, non-human UFOs would become *fact*. The days of naysaying and storytelling were over.

The information they all heard would fill the media for months, in all its guises. Everyone, the world over, wanted to hear the details of the President's talk.

Jack was there, standing near a wall, with his dad in front of him, and fenced in by a pack of others. John was gawking curiously at the media that were there, some of whom, from MSNBC, he recognised. Jack knew exactly what POTUS was going to reveal. Their presence wouldn't have been demanded, otherwise.

They had received an invitation to today's conference, last week. And travelled to the Whitehouse in a beautiful, shiny, chauffeured black limousine. These press conferences were normally off-limits to the public – but Jack and his dad were more than that. Jack and John were anonymous in the room, but were heroes in the eyes of many officials, who knew exactly who they were.

The invitation, addressed to them personally, was signed by POTUS herself, and Jack would keep that always. He looked at her and saw how at home she looked behind the podium. *It's about time*, he thought jubilantly. She lost four years ago, but thank God, not this time. *What a rock star.*

Tomorrow, POTUS would address the American public itself, by fronting TV stations, NBC, CBS, FOX and ABC. She would tell them exactly what Jack had imparted, plus a lot more. So, a huge slice of the American public would know *the truth*. And it would be picked up by the media, both social and legacy, globally from Russia to China to Fiji to Africa.

It turned out that the US government had kept a huge secret from its people. *Humanity wasn't alone in the Universe.* The cloak and dagger cover-up was for covert reasons, Jack knew, and it covered the past century. So, their adversaries didn't know they had numerous UFOs and were trying to reverse-engineer them and the tech they held. The winner would have aerial and ocean supremacy over every country on Earth. Apart from it being highly illegal, one couldn't blame the US from going hell bent for leather, to be the first.

Jack and John were absolutely sure. They'd rather live in a world where America was in charge of the skies and the seas. He thought of Earth, where an oligarch was in charge, and Jack felt like dry retching. *No way*, he pleaded. Russia or China owning the skies was a bleak prospect, he didn't want to live through. Because, if they owned the sea and the sky, they'd own the *world*. Including where you lived.

POTUS would take no questions from the media, so more accusations of a coverup, would not be her's to answer. Not yet anyway. POTUS knew parts of the Pentagon and the CIA, amongst others, had a lot to answer for. POTUS was also aware that President Eisenhower had come close to non-humans at the Edwards Airforce Base in New Mexico early in 1954. To see if a conversation was possible, which it wasn't. She'd seen the documents. But she kept that little pearl to herself, because it involved a lot of references to telepathy, which no-one was ready for, *yet*. The population of Earth regarded that as science fiction. *Soon*, she thought firmly.

POTUS disclosed nearly everything. She acknowledged that the USA were competing with Russia and China. The winner would rule the world, she said, knowing that would earn her some brownie points at home.

POTUS started in the 1940s with the Foo Fighters, then Roswell, which was real, the 1980s with Rendlesham Forest in England, Varginha, Brazil in 1996, to the more recent Tic-Tac and the Go-Fast objects. They were up there, right now. 'Earth, with its colour and oxygen, is a non-human drawcard, that attracts them like honeybees to a Sunflower,' POTUS said, smiling proudly. Like only she could.

'The US had hold of UFOs, that crashed and, in some cases, had been forced down with microwave weapons. They had formal programs, with ready and able retrieval choppers. Recovered craft were stored with defence partners, she said. And underground at Area-51, and various air-force bases. The US have been trying to reverse-engineer them since 1930, she said. 'To see how they work.'

'But so far,' POTUS said, 'we er...aren't where we want to be.' She laid out Jack's and his dad's case in detail, and emphasised the cancer part and described how truly seminal it was, because it showed that the disease *can* be beaten. John Stevens was humanity's first example, she said quite emotionally. POTUS swallowed down a sob and with teary eyes, she acknowledged her mum. She died of cancer, and POTUS wondered *why*? She confirmed that some humans had incredible abilities and could psychically interact with non-human craft. The crowd made a *woo* sound at this, and a few laughed skeptically. POTUS smiled, and said that she didn't initially believe it. 'But incredibly, it is true. Teams of humans under the guidance of a Pentagon-based department, call silently to NHI, to bring them close. Truly stunning, and yes, unbelievable...but it's a fact.' There was a raucous round of applause that went on for minutes, after she stepped away from the podium. POTUS smiled through a wave of tears.

John, Jack and Krissy watched it again on TV, in their lounge-room. The cancer-part sounded drop-dead amazing. Jack revelled in his dad's tanned, brown complexion. There was no writhing in pain, or an agonized face. All that was thankfully behind them, courtesy of the Pianif. Jack two-finger saluted them in his mind.

Yes, they were abducted against their will, but without their tech, his dad would be dead. Simple as that. On Earth, there was no coming back from the aggressive cancer that he had. It was a death sentence, and they both knew it. Everyone on Earth, *the entire population*, now knew it.

13

Exposed

"For me, it is far better to grasp the Universe as it really is than to persist in delusion." — Carl Sagan

'Nuh-uh, no way, no chance...absolutely not,' Jack blurted firmly, when confronted by the Secretary of State, Bill Goodings.

The Whitehouse wanted Jack to own up to it, to agree to expose their identity to the public. To disclose to the people of Earth, that they were the ones who were taken, and returned with the intel from Pianif.

Bill made claim that they now had *nothing* to worry about. It would simply be rainbows and teddy bears. And white fluffy clouds. ZPE would no longer pose a risk to the family, apparently. They could admit to it, and frolic on the front lawn, without a care in the world. Why? Because the government said so! Oh, the glory.

The release of ZPE would solely be owned by the government...apparently. From information and data, the government gleaned from UFOs. From reverse engineering their tech. There would be absolutely no reference to the Stevens family, Bill said. Poor old Bill would struggle to sell heaters to the Eskimos. Ire from Big-Oil would be solely directed toward the US government, he said. Jack didn't believe him and was quite convinced there would be blowback...*somewhere.* Bill was as convincing as Ruby Rose in Batwoman.

Jack reckoned the government had proven that they can't keep a secret. The President had sent Bill to get it stitched up, but he was having predictable difficulties. Jack was like a brick wall and trusted the government like he would a weather forecast. Bill scraped and almost begged, but Jack was having none of it. Bill was up against his parents... a losing battle.

The Secretary of State thought we'd be pushovers, low hanging fruit, *easy-peasy*, Jack reckoned. Drive to the doorstep in your shiny black government limo. Then come inside flashing your expensive Fioravanti suit and expecting us to melt like butter in your presence. Jack simply refused to cooperate with him, and gave him a rundown of his government's failures, starting with WMD in Iraq. He sent him packing, back to The Whitehouse, with his tail entrenched between his legs.

A week later he received a specially delivered letter from POTUS herself. It asked him to present at the Whitehouse, Tuesday next, for a meeting with her, in the Oval Office at 2pm. Jack was stoked, but he knew what it was about.

Bill Goodings had been unsuccessful, now it was her turn to have a go. John didn't want to go. For him, it was too overwhelming to front up at The Whitehouse in front of the President. This was way above him, he said. Jacky by himself would represent his dad and him and make the final decision. John had already spoken to Jack and given him his opinion.

She said the same things that Bill said, but it was harder to bat them away. POTUS was the leader of the free world, and Jack was a fan of her politics. One thing had to be kept front of mind for Jack. At the forefront of his thinking. Administrations change, and so do attitudes, policy and people. What is said by POTUS now, might be changed by future administrations.

Jack ended up saying yes to POTUS. He couldn't bring himself to do anything else. She was so persuasive, even without opening her mouth. The Oval Office made a good argument, before he stepped foot there.

As soon as he said yes, the old black and white photo that hung above the front door on a nail was all he could see. It was his mum and dad in front of the house, smiling for the camera. Country innocence and nativity was suffocating him. But everything POTUS said made perfect sense. And his dad wanted him to say yes, too. The Whitehouse was no place to say no to.

ZPE would be released in five years, and he agreed, she was very likely to win a second term. Meaning she would be in control when it was given the go-ahead.

Even before this event, he was deeply impressed by the current POTUS. Plus, disclosure of UFOs had just happened – on her watch. Co-operation with her came naturally. Like bread and butter.

POTUS told Jack that he and John would be interviewed by CNN on Friday, where he could spill the beans, and confirm to the world they were the ones who were *taken*. She confirmed again there would be no blowback. He begged to differ, but thought, what the hell?

She told him to expect popularity with news carriers and current affairs programs. Companies like ABC, NBC, and CBS and others will forge a path to your door, she said. And overseas companies, you've never heard of, will make contact. POTUS offered them both roles in the West Wing of the Whitehouse. *Non-human Advisors* to the President, on very healthy wages. Jack's eyes nearly bugged out of his head when she said that. Jack was stunned. He nervously said he'd have to defer to his dad, and was deeply unsure of his capacity, given that he'd recently been so sick. POTUS could see Jack was concerned and assured him the role wouldn't be demanding. 'It's more of a *thankyou*, Jack.' POTUS said warmly.

'It's not that, we live in Arizona is all. It's a long, *long* commute.'

POTUS looked at Jack knowingly. 'We have a property in Potomac you might like. Only a 20-minute drive to The Whitehouse, Jack.' POTUS' eyes were soft and her smile was wide and expectant. 'If you like it, it's yours. With what you brought to Earth Jack, it's the least we can do for you.'

'You mean...okay ... *okay*.' Jack teared up when he realised the magnitude of this gift. 'Thankyou madam President. I'll get Kris to have a look. Jack pressed fingers to smiling lips. He really couldn't believe any of it. He entered the Oval Office, as nervous as a kitten. This was the very last thing he expected. A gift from POTUS for services rendered to Earth.

POTUS rose from the Resolute desk and walked silently to her cabinet by the wall.

'*And that's not all*, Jack,' she purred. 'There is for you and one for your dad too, take it with you.' POTUS gestured Jack to approach. The Presidential Medal of Freedom, the highest civilian honour. Congratulations Jack, and *thankyou* to you both. She pinned the medal to his shirt. POTUS also handed one to him, 'please give this to your dad. Give him a kiss for me.'

'Thankyou madam President. I w-will.' Jack was overwhelmed and returned to his seat on shaking legs and gratefully sat down.

14

Non-human

"For small creatures, such as we, the vastness is bearable only through love." — Carl Sagan

The Hubble and James Webb telescopes, by using spectrographs, have deciphered the atmosphere of exo-planets that are light years away from Earth.

Similarly, non-humans have known that Earth contains oxygen for millennia. Their sectioned mirrors are much larger than the JWST. They know Earth is blue, has 40% land, and is oxygen-rich. That was sufficient to prioritise our planet for scrutiny and analysis. Earth was a planet, that non-humans *had* to visit.

When John went to bed, he did it pain-free. He hadn't done that in years. By the hand of Pianif technology, and his son, he had somehow transgressed the odds, which were close to 0% of him surviving a year. Without Pianif technology he would've died aboard the Pianif craft. But now, incredibly, he stood in Arizona, in the pink of health. He thanked God, because he was essentially, back from the dead.

Jack watched him devour his vegetarian ravioli with gusto. It was his favourite, ricotta and spinach, and now he could eat it and savour the experience. It beat the hell out of instant noodles. Now, Cancer and radiation, no longer clouded his skin.

The paleness and yellowness were yesterday's colours. Jack walked up to his dad, with a boyish grin, and grabbed his dad's hand. Jack looked at his mum and dad lovingly. '*Somehow guys...we made it.*'

'Thanks to you, Jacky, yes...we did.' His dad's voice trailed off. 'Y'know, if you hadn't asked Pietr firmly, to look after me before we met their Ruling Council, *I'd be dead.*' John stood up and hugged his son tightly. His mum looked on with teary eyes as she watched them embrace. She'd never seen them closer. She could see that the forced trip to another planet had bonded them closer together like steel blocks and supa-glue.

It was dark and the whole family were standing together in the backyard, hanging onto each other. S*omehow,* they'd managed to come through, not only alive, but *even better* than they were before.

Millions of others, the world over, similarly afflicted as John, had suffered, then died. But *he* lived on, courtesy of the Pianif, and their extraordinary skill, and knowledge of the natural world.

Jack inclined his neck and lost himself in the wisps of the Milky Way Galaxy. He gazed at the Galactic centre and smiled widely. He recovered his focus, and looked back at John, and nodded and kept smiling, knowing John was thinking about. *The Pianif.*

Teegarden's star was in the Aries constellation. Jack knew broadly where it was, but it was too dim to see with the naked eye. He looked slightly north of straight up, but there was only bright stuff to see.

That's when it truly dawned on him. Like the birth of a child. The hair stood up on his neck, and his heart pounded in his chest like a jackhammer. Jack shuddered as he drew in a quick breath.

It was Incredible, but he and his dad had visited *another Goddamn planet*. The words sounded ridiculous. The concept a mind-boggler. What they'd done seemed a lifetime ago. The feeling of awe nearly pushed him to the ground. Jack gazed at the stars, and then he realised with breathlessness, disbelief and incredulity, that he'd rubbed shoulders with the rarest resource in the cosmos.

Jack looked his dad up and down and drank in his patent good health. He watched him smile and hug his wife and pondered all they'd achieved and avoided in the last few weeks. Jack felt full body tingles, like he'd fallen into a bed of cacti. He was contemplating and watching his dad, who would be *dead*, if left to his own devices on Earth.

Inconceivably, his dad was cured of "terminal" cancer, and Earth was changing and updating for the better *right now*, because of the intel they'd collected.

Jack was enormously proud of his dad, and smiled ear to ear. They had brought alien technology to Earth and it would reshape Earth as a cleaner, healthier and safer planet.

Imagine giving Chevron or British Petroleum *the news* that their energy reign over the planet was nearly over. Their reaction would initially be disbelief, followed by deep, dark horror, and later, acceptance, when they realised it was over for real. Their annual billion-dollar profits were at an end. And there wasn't a thing they could do about it. Their product simply wasn't up to scratch. It had been superseded by something a lot better.

Big-Oil left in control of energy would almost certainly have turned Earth into Venus.

Jack watched his parents' interaction with delight. They were relaxed and loving. Krissy was singing Golden Brown to anyone who cared to listen:

> Never-a-frown-with-golden-brown,
> every time-just-like-the-last,
> never-a-frown-with-golden-brown♪

Normally, she'd sing to her cows, during milking, but with them gone, anyone could be the target. John was making drum noises with his mouth, while Krissy sang.

Now that people on Earth knew about these '*others,*' the human population would hopefully, mature overnight. Everyone now knew that humanity as a species, was not alone in the Universe. Jack's hope was that the notion of country as a home would gradually be replaced by '*Earth*' being home.

Jack sadly knew that pure benevolence probably didn't exist in the Universe. From his discussions with Swann and her disciples in the Ruling Council, Jack was sure *quid pro quo* came along with the intel, and one day the Pianif would come our way to collect.

THE END

ABOUT THE AUTHOR:

Scott Bywater lives in Adelaide near the southern coast of Australia with his wife Mary and two kids, Josh and Alysha. Scott has an Honours Degree in Geomorphology from Flinders University, and an obsession with anything astrophysical. While at University, he published three mineralogical papers in the Mineralogical Record out of Tucson, Arizona. To help facilitate writing on the subject he taught himself the finer details of quantum field theory, General Relativity, and in particular, String Theory and anthropic cosmology. Scott believes that anyone who has looked up at the night sky and wondered why, or contemplated some of the deeper reasons for their existence, will derive much pleasure from this book.